THE CRONE WARS

BECOMING CRONE

LYDIA M. HAWKE

**Published by Michem Publishing,
Canada**

BECOMING CRONE
June 2021

Cover design by Deranged Doctor Design
Interior design by authorTree

ISBN: 978-1-989457-08-05

MICHEM PUBLISHING

To the crones of the world...
may you embrace your wisdom and power

Acknowledgements

It takes a village to raise a child, it's said, and I think the same is true about writing a book. Because as solitary a pursuit as it seems at times, you really can't do it without the help of others —a lot of others. This is where I get to thank the people in *my* village.

First, my husband, Pat, whose love and unflagging support has carried me through so many crises of confidence, I've lost count. He has listened to me weep and wail and gnash my teeth when book-things don't cooperate; stayed out of my way when they do; and willingly shouldered the brunt of household chores (and eaten a lot of takeout and leftovers!) when deadlines loom. My world is infinitely brighter for having him in it.

Second, my daughters, Chloe, Emilie, and Mikhaila, for inspiring me to lead by example...and for leading me with the examples they themselves have set. My world is infinitely brighter for having them and their families in it, too.

Third, my tribe: Ardelle Bernardo, Marie Bilodeau, Maureen Daly, Claire Faguy (who graciously let me use her name for my heroine), Doris Nabert, Laura Paquet, Nadine Proulx, and the many, many other women who have passed through and touched my life. I would not be who or where I am without their strength and perseverance to inspire me, and their love and laughter to carry me through. Each of them has helped shape the characters in this story.

Thanks also to Luke Marty of Your Beta Reader for his insightful comments and suggestions for improving the story, and to my editors, Laura Paquet and Jess Torrance, for their sharp eyes and attention to detail. My words shine brighter because of these people, and they—the words, not the people— are a lot more readable, too.

A grateful mention, too, to my designer, Deranged Doctor Design, who captured Claire in such a spectacular cover. I smile every time I see it.

And finally, to you, dear reader, for picking up this book and letting me introduce you to my Crones. I hope you enjoy!

CHAPTER 1

I NOTICED THE FIRST CROW WHEN I OPENED THE FRONT door for the cat on the morning of my sixtieth birthday. It—the crow, not the cat—sat silently on the bottom branch of the maple that shaded the porch, rather than high up where crows usually hung out.

And it gave every impression of watching me with an intensity that made me pause and blink, twice, before closing the door.

By noon, one crow had become fifty.

"You know that's weird, right?" My next-door neighbor waved at the tree as I let her in. It was dotted with silent, black-feathered bodies.

"I mean, I wouldn't think so if they were at Jeanne's place," Edie James—short for Edith, but not if you cared to continue breathing—continued, "but here? Weird." She shoved a bouquet of flowers and a muslin bag tied with twine at me. "Happy birthday. It's a bath sachet to help you relax. I figured you'd need it after the party."

"Thank you." I leaned in for a cheek buss and a hug, choosing to ignore her jab at our across-the-street neighbor. Edie and Jeanne and I had known one another for thirty years, ever since we'd all moved into what had been a brand-new development at the time, and the two of them were frequently at odds with one another. I'd hoped they'd settle their latest spat before today's party, but according to Jeanne, Edie had stepped too far over the line this time when she'd voiced her opinions of Jeanne's husband.

I secretly agreed with much of what Edie had said about Gilbert—specifically with regard to the way he spoke to Jeanne. The man had always been a self-important, obnoxious prick, in

1

my opinion, but he was still Jeanne's husband, and on the few occasions I'd expressed concern to her, I'd done so carefully. Respectfully. In part because I could sympathize with her staying married to a man who was less than respectful himself.

Edie, on the other hand, could be...

Well, let's just say *blunt* would be the understatement of the century.

I gave the crows in the tree a final glance, then closed the door and followed Edie down the hall to my kitchen. She stood with fists on hips, surveying the disaster I'd created. She looked over her shoulder at me and raised an eyebrow.

"*What* time is the party?"

I sighed. "In an hour."

"And you needed to clean out the fridge now because...?"

I sighed again. "Natalie needs space for the cake."

"Then Natalie and Paul should have hosted the party at their place." Edie sniffed, peering at me over the tops of her old-fashioned bifocals, her brown eyes daring me to disagree.

I didn't. To be honest, I'd thought at the time my daughter-in-law informed me of the plan that it was rather presumptuous of her to expect me to host my own party, but I hadn't had the heart to say anything. I knew the party idea had originated with my son, who assumed Natalie would see to the details, just as I had seen to the details of his father's many ideas over the years.

I loved my son dearly, and I knew he loved me, but I had failed him miserably in that respect, and now poor Natalie had to deal with my mistakes. I'd tried to talk to her about it once, about how she should stand up for herself as I'd failed to do, but she'd laughed it off with an indulgent, "Oh, Maman, you worry too much!"

Maman. She'd called me that since the day Paul introduced her as his fiancée, swearing up, down and sideways that she would look after me as she would have cared for her own mother, who had died too young. I didn't care for the name any more than I cared for the way she hovered over me and sent me endless articles about age-related illnesses, but it seemed to make her happy, so I didn't object.

I never objected. Sometimes I mumbled under my breath and/or harbored secret resentments, but usually I just adjusted my plans and rearranged my life to accommodate what others needed. It was easier that way. More peaceful. Expected.

And it was how I'd always done it.

I watched Edie roll up the sleeves of her bright pink floral blouse, worn with equally pink slacks. She'd made an effort to match for a change, and her gray hair was pulled back in a tidier-than-normal ponytail. I knew it was for my birthday. For me. I opened my mouth to compliment her, but she cut me off.

"Right," she said, with the brisk authority of the high-school principal she'd been for twenty-five years before retirement. "We have ten minutes to clear this up, and then *you* need to go put on your party clothes."

I glanced down at my slacks and t-shirt, both beige. I'd made an effort to match today, too. "But I thought—"

"That you could blend in with your walls so no one would see you?"

Like I said. Blunt.

"Ouch."

She shrugged. "You dress like that for a party, you get what's coming. Now, what is all this?" She waved a hand at the bottles and jars and packages covering the table. "Any of it still good?"

I bit my bottom lip and wrinkled my nose. "Ish?"

"What kind of answer is 'ish'?"

"The kind I give when I don't want to waste something."

"But?"

"But..." I trailed off, not wanting to admit that all the food items on the table had been bought when Jeff was still here, and I was still hanging onto them a year after he'd left.

Not because I harbored any secret hopes that he'd return, mind you. I didn't think I wanted him back, but neither had I ever quite reconciled myself to him being gone. To being alone in the house we'd bought together and had planned on growing old in, together.

And I certainly hadn't reconciled myself to starting over on my own at the age of sixty.

Sixty.

How on earth had I arrived at that number in my life?

"I see," said Edie, and I knew she did, because she was as perceptive as she was blunt. Another holdover from her high-school principal days. She picked up a jar of pickled eggs. "Do you even like any of this?"

"Honestly? No. But—"

"But nothing." She swept up an armload of jars from the tabletop. "Never mind helping. Leave this to me. You put your flowers in water before they go any limper than they already are, and then change. And I expect color from you, woman. C.O.L.O.R. You're sixty, not dead."

She turned her back on me, shoved Merlin's food dish out of the way with a sandaled toe, and set everything on the counter by the sink. The sound of running water and the clank of glass as she emptied and rinsed jars drowned out any objection I might have made. If I'd wanted to make an objection. Which I wasn't sure I did. Even if I felt I should.

I stood there waffling until Edie leveled a glare at me over her shoulder and raised her voice over the commotion. "You're still here, Claire Emerson. *Why* are you still here?"

It was no wonder the town's kids had been so respectful of her during their school years.

BY THE TIME I RETURNED TO THE KITCHEN TWENTY minutes later, my friend had worked a minor miracle. The table was clear, the counters and sink clean, and the fridge interior wiped down. Lips pursed, Edie dried her hands on a tea towel and studied me.

Following her request for color, I'd pulled out the only thing in my closet that wasn't gray, beige, or black—a sleeveless, purple floral maxi dress I'd had for at least ten years. Or maybe twenty. I didn't remember the last time I'd worn it, probably because it pulled so much across my boobs and stomach. And because of the upper arm flap I had going on these days. Fortunately, a light cardigan camouflaged the latter, the dress was long enough that it didn't matter that I hadn't shaved my legs, and if I kept my belly sucked in enough...

"Maybe do up the buttons on the cardigan?" Edie suggested.

That bad? I looked down at the dress buttons straining across my girls and groaned. "Or I could just change back into my pants?" I asked hopefully.

The front doorbell rang, the door opened, and a child's excited voice shouted, "Grandma! We're here! And we have a cake and presents and Mommy invited a man for you to meet! His name is Dave and he's bald but Mommy says that doesn't matter. *Does* it matter, Grandma?"

Edie folded over in a bray of laughter, and I sent her a filthy look before I headed down the hall, trying to paste a semblance of a smile on my face as I fumbled with cardigan buttons. I had most of them secured when a small body launched itself at me and wrapped arms around my waist. Beneath the cardigan, a dress button gave way. Crap.

"You look so pretty, Grandma! You're wearing a dress and everything!" Braden exclaimed. Since he'd reached five years old, pretty much everything that came out of my grandson's mouth was an exclamation.

A genuine smile replaced the pasted-on one, and I returned his squeeze. "Thank you, Braden."

He pushed away from me. "Is Merlin here? Can I see him? Is he upstairs?"

Either an exclamation or a question, I amended.

"He's probably on my bed." Or more likely hiding under it. Merlin, a rescue cat I'd brought home after Jeff left, was about as much a fan of parties and people as I was. "You can go look, if you'd like."

Braden thundered up the stairs, and my son's embrace replaced his.

"Happy birthday, Mom," Paul said. "You look lovely."

"Liar. I look like an overstuffed sausage in this thing. But thank you for being nice." I stood on tiptoe to kiss my six-foot-two son's cheek. He hadn't gotten his height from me. Then I pulled back and narrowed my eyes. "Please tell me Natalie didn't really bring a stranger to my birthday party."

Another, I might have added, because Natalie meant well, but bald-headed Dave was the third 'friend' in as many months.

Paul waved away my question. "Oh, Mom. You know she's just worried about you. Dave's a nice guy. He did some work for us at the house—he's a plumber. You should give him a chance. Natalie's right about you not getting any younger, you know. You need to move on."

I felt a flush rise in my cheeks. I wanted to take a deep breath and tell my darling son where to get off, but I was afraid of popping another dress button.

Plus, old nonconfrontational habits die hard.

"Maman!" a cheery, feminine voice preceded its equally cheery owner. "Happy, happy birthday! You look..."

The voice trailed off, and I met the horror in my daughter-in-law's gaze across the ribbon-tied cake box in her hands. She blinked and snapped her mouth closed. If Natalie was anything, it was unsinkable—she had to be, married to Paul—and she recovered with remarkable aplomb to finish with, "Cheerful."

Her face brightened with triumph at having found a solution to her compliment dilemma. "I hope you don't mind, but we invited a friend of ours to come with us. Maman, this is Dave—uh—"

Friend, my patootie.

A beefy, florid man—as bald as Braden had said—stepped

into the front entry from the porch and held out a hand. "Meyers," he supplied. "Dave Meyers."

His handshake was clammy and flaccid, and I suppressed a shudder as I let go with more haste than was polite. Not that it mattered, given his fading smile as his gaze swept over my over-stuffed-sausage length and returned to rest on the gray braid laying over my shoulder. I found myself wishing one of the crows—I could still see them sitting in the tree by the porch—had dumped on him as he walked up the stairs. Then I berated myself for being unkind. Then I was annoyed all over again with Natalie for putting me in this situation in the first place and Paul for letting her. No matter how well-meaning.

More footsteps on the porch outside saved me from having to decide which feeling should take precedence. I shuffled sideways past Dave's belly.

"Jeanne! I'm so glad you could make it!"

My neighbor looked taken aback by my unusual enthusiasm, as well she might, because despite having lived across from one another as long as we had, we had never been all that close. Friendly, yes. Neighborly, absolutely. Jeff had given her and her husband a key to our house for house-sitting, and we had one for theirs; Jeff had invited them over for backyard barbecues every summer, and they had reciprocated; Jeff had dispensed construction advice when she and Gilbert had renovated their kitchen, and—

And with Jeff gone, I'd found little more than habit to connect us anymore. Which was how I'd ended up inviting her and her husband to the party.

But Jeanne returned my hug without comment, gave me the customary French-Canadian kiss on both cheeks, and wished me a happy birthday as she released me. Over her shoulder, I saw her husband, Gilbert, climbing the stairs with a large, ceramic garden gnome in his arms.

Another one.

I twisted my grimace into a smile. Jeff had admired Jeanne's collection of the creatures when we first moved into the house and introduced ourselves, and I'd made the mistake of agreeing with him because it seemed the polite thing to do. Now my own collection rivaled hers because I'd received one from her for my birthday every year since. As had pretty much everyone on the street, given her seeming determination to populate the entire neighborhood with the things.

"How lovely!" I said, despite the fact I'd run out of trees and corners in which to hide the detested things. It was a wonder they didn't haunt my dreams. And Jeff, darn him, had refused to take any of them when he'd left. It turned out he'd only been trying to get on Jeanne's good side so she'd be friends with me because he thought she'd be a better influence on me than the loud, aggressive woman next door.

Ah, Jeff. The more I thought about it, the less I missed him after all.

Gilbert crowded into the hall with the gnome, and I closed the door on the crows—odd how no one had commented on them—and pushed my ex from my mind. It was time to summon every gracious-hostess skill I possessed, see to the guests I didn't want, open the gifts I hadn't asked for, eat the cake I didn't need, and survive the afternoon.

Another button gave way beneath the cardigan.

All, preferably, without flashing my guests.

CHAPTER 2

SIXTY, I THOUGHT, WISHING I COULD WITHDRAW FROM THE party and disappear into the wingback chair in which I sat. I'd barely noticed thirty, forty had passed in a blur, fifty had felt like just another day, but sixty?

Sixty was hard.

Sixty came with reading glasses, hips that stiffened when I sat too long, fifteen extra pounds (which explained the popped dress buttons and too-tight bra), various minor injuries incurred while sleeping, and perpetually misplaced keys.

Heck, it had even come with a return of the hot flashes I thought I'd left behind. Like the one washing over me now, a slow, intense heat starting in my chest and radiating outward. I dug my fingers into the chair arms and tried to focus on the conversation around me instead of ripping off my clothes.

Braden chose that exact moment to pause mid-sentence and stare at me.

"Are you okay, Grandma? You're all red."

Thank you so much, grandson of mine.

All eyes in the room turned to me. The heat in my core increased. Edie's gaze narrowed.

"Hot flash," she announced.

Natalie's friend Dave stared longingly at the front door. Perhaps we had something in common after all.

"I thought you were past those," Jeanne said.

"They can hit anytime." Edie looked down her nose at Jeanne. "You're a nurse. You should know that. And they can stop and start up again, too."

"Of course I know that," Jeanne snapped. "It was just an observation."

Gilbert and Dave both sighed.

"I'm fine," I said, glaring at the women. "I'm just a bit warm."

"I'll get you more iced tea," Paul said. I suspected the offer came from a wish to escape rather than from any sense of compassion, but I appreciated the distraction nonetheless.

"And maybe the cake, too?" Natalie suggested. "I'll help."

I nodded with rather more enthusiasm than was polite. "Great idea," I said. Because cake meant gifts, and then everyone would go home, right?

"Is it time for presents yet?" Braden demanded. Without waiting for an answer, he dumped a package onto my lap, its bow hanging askew and several layers of tape holding unicorn-and-rainbow-decorated paper in place. "Open this one first. It's from me. I wrapped it myself."

"And a very good job you did." I folded my grandson close, breathing in his scent—a mixture of soap from the bath he'd had before coming and the lawn he'd rolled around on after Merlin had tired of his attention. Braden tolerated the embrace for roughly one-point-five seconds before wriggling free and pushing the gift into my hands.

"I found it at Mr. Arch—Arch—" He gave up struggling with the name and pointed instead to Gilbert. "His store. He said he gave me a good deal."

Gilbert, who liked to call himself a collector, owned a store on the outskirts of town called Archambault's Antiques. Archambault's Junk Shop would have been more accurate. The place was little more than a rundown shed, filled to the rafters with useless (and often broken) bits and pieces. It lost far more money than it made, in part because it was filled with rubbish, but mostly because Gilbert was always buying another estate lot in the hope of one day finding that one treasure that would make him rich.

His lack of interest in generating an income was the main reason Jeanne still worked as an emergency room nurse at the age of sixty-three—and the main bone of contention between them.

Jeanne, unfortunately, had bought into the "til death do us part' idea lock, stock, and barrel, even though they seemed to be in a perpetual state of conflict these days.

Which was probably what Edie had spouted off about in *her* last set-to with Jeanne. As if to confirm my hypothesis, the two women exchanged a cold look, and Gilbert scowled. I headed off any possible flare-up by turning Braden's package over in my hands, making a show of admiring the gaudy paper and bright pink bow.

"Are you sure you wrapped this all by yourself?" I asked, pretending awe. "You did *such* a good job."

Braden beamed. Dave and Gilbert both glanced again at the front door. Paul re-entered the room with an iced tea in one hand and a stack of plates and napkins in the other. He set the tea on the end table beside me and the plates on the coffee table with the cake Natalie had carried in moments earlier. While they began setting fire to the candles covering the cake top (it was a two-person job), I searched for a corner of Braden's gift not buried under layers of tape. I peeled back the unicorn paper to reveal a tissue-wrapped lump within.

"Careful!" Braden warned, hovering at my elbow. "It's fragile."

"Promise," I said, craning my neck to see around the blond head that had come between me and the gift. I unfurled the tissue paper, and a heavy pendant dropped into my hand. "Oh, Braden—it's lovely!"

An ornate silver frame encased a round glass center, flat on the back and convex on the front, and a small crystal was set below a clasp attached to a long, matching chain. I wasn't much for jewelry, but this was a stunning piece.

Braden grabbed the pendant from me and held it up to my eye. "Look! It's a magnifying glass. It makes things bigger, so you don't need your glasses to read your book or do your embroidery."

"Why, so it does," I agreed. I cupped his hand and moved it and the pendant to a safer distance from my eyeball. That it would be impossible to embroider and hold the pendant at the same time had no bearing on the thoughtfulness behind my grandson's gift, and my heart swelled with love for him. "It's a wonderful present, sweetheart. The best one ever."

It was also hands-down better than the gnome Jeanne and Gilbert had given me, or the gift certificate for Aquafit classes Natalie had presented me with—in private, thankfully. The gnome I could understand because it was my own fault for not saying something over the years. But Aquafit? So I could take better care of myself because my daughter-in-law worried about me now that I was *"you know, getting on in years?"*

Gah.

Even if she did have a point.

Sixty.

My God, how had that even happened? How had I lived an entire lifetime already, when it felt as if I should just be starting out? How could I be here, in this town, this house, this moment, and not remember so much of the journey? So many days blurring into weeks and months and years that had run together and slipped past, and now—

"Happy birthday to you! Happy birthday to you!"

The chorus of voices jolted me back to my guests and the alarming wall of flames coming toward me in Natalie's hands. I uncurled my fingers from around the pendant and sat up straight, forcing myself to smile at the people who had come together to celebrate me.

All except Gilbert, perhaps, who was neither singing nor celebrating, but staring at the pendant in my hand. My hand tightened reflexively on it, then I looped the chain over my head and slipped the pendant inside the neck of my cardigan. It nestled into the gap of the dress beneath, cool against my skin. Cool and safe and...tingling?

That was weird.

"Happy birthday, dear Clai-aire," the voices crescendoed. "Happy birthday to you!"

I leaned forward, took a deep breath, and with Braden's enthusiastic help, blew out the sheet of flames. I sat back again amid the chatter and Braden's cheers, my attention going back to the pendant. Not tingling, exactly. More like...buzzing. Like something electrical.

Really weird.

My gaze strayed over the assembly and paused again on Gilbert, who watched me with a curious look of indecision. I raised an eyebrow, and he jerked his head in a way that said, *"I want to talk."* I raised my eyebrow higher. He had to be kidding. I had never pretended to like Gilbert, nor he me, and now he wanted a conversation with me? On purpose? Not.

I turned my face away, and he took a half step toward me, but Paul intercepted him with a plate of cake, Jeanne murmured something in his ear, and I was saved. My shoulders relaxed.

"Are you all right?" Natalie held out a plate of cake to me, a fork standing upright in it. "Is it too much for you? The party, I mean? I tried to tell Paul it would tire you out."

Too much everything was more like it. Too much party, too many people. Far too much sixty. Between my breasts, the pendant's buzz had changed to a faint throb, like a pulse. Almost like it was—what, trying to get my attention?

Great, now my imagination was working overtime. Was that a thing at sixty, too?

I took the plate from my daughter-in-law. "I'm fine, thanks. It's a lovely party. Really."

"I'll herd everyone out as soon as the cake is done," she promised. "You probably had plans of your own with your friends today."

I opened my mouth to tell her it was a little late to be thinking of that now, but my churlishness would have served no purpose other than to hurt her, and so I smiled. I smiled, and I patted her arm, and I thanked her again. Then, as she turned away to speak with Edie, I heaved a sigh and nudged the slice of cake around the plate, leaving a smear of vanilla icing and a trail of crumbs in its wake.

Sixty.

How?

GILBERT DIDN'T GIVE UP, AND WHEN I WENT IN SEARCH OF something for the headache thudding at my temples, he followed me into the kitchen. He hesitated in the doorway, shifting from one foot to the other and back again, his hands clasped behind his back.

"Yes?" I asked. I didn't bother with pleasantries. First, because headache; second, because Gilbert. While I might be more circumspect than Edie where he was concerned, I was pretty sure my lack of use for him ran just as deep.

"The pendant..." He stopped and cleared his throat. "I'd like to buy it back."

Glass of water halfway to my mouth, I raised an eyebrow and said around the pill sitting on my tongue, "Ethcuzthe me?"

Gilbert switched to rocking back and forth on his heels. "I—ah—made a mistake. I didn't mean to sell it."

The painkiller's bitterness coated my tongue, and I took a hasty sip of water and swallowed it. Shuddering, I set the glass in the sink. "Let me guess. You found out it was worth more than you thought, didn't you?"

Gilbert's gaze slid away. "It's not like that. I've had an inquiry...the piece came in with an estate lot, and one of the heirs wants it back. It belonged to his—her—to someone special."

Sure it did.

I hesitated. If it had been anyone other than Gilbert, I might have been more cooperative. However, this was the man who didn't just let his wife do everything for him while also working to support him, but expected it. Who hadn't raised a finger to help a single person on the street in all the years I'd lived here. And who hid behind the curtains whenever the neighborhood kids were fundraising for something.

He was a miserable, selfish little man, and after thirty years of brushing off or ignoring his behavior, I wasn't in the least inclined to help him out. Especially when instinct told me he was lying, too.

"I tell you what," I said. "Why don't you tell me how much they offered you, and I'll see what I can do?"

The heel-to-toe rocking sped up. He shook his head. "No. Thank you, but no. I need—I promised—I feel obligated to return it to its owner. It seems the right thing to do."

Said the man who'd never felt obligated to do the right thing in his life.

"I'll trade you for something else in the shop," he continued. "Anything you want. I have a full set of bone china you might like. Or a pair of crystal candlesticks. And there's all kinds of other jewelry you can choose from, if you still want a necklace."

Again, if it had been anyone but Gilbert, or if Gilbert had been someone other than the man he was, or if I'd believed him even a little...

"I'm sorry," I said, "but you saw how happy Braden was when he gave it to me. He'd be devastated."

"Tell him you lost it," he snapped. "He's just a kid, for chrissake."

I drew myself up to my full height, a good head above him. "I said no."

"Oh, for—" he snapped his mouth shut and made a visible effort to control himself. He raked a hand over a thinning comb-over. "Just think about it, all right? I'm sure I can find something like it in the store. The kid will never even know."

"Everything okay in here?" Natalie asked, coming into the kitchen behind him.

Gilbert's expression cleared, becoming benign. "It's fine," he said. "I was just wishing your mother-in-law a happy birthday before I leave. I need to get back to the shop."

Natalie frowned, her gaze on me. Probably because I looked as angry as I felt. "Maman?"

I unclenched my fists and flexed my hands, coaxing my blood pressure down. Conflict wasn't my strong point at the best of times, and I couldn't bring myself to ruin the party Natalie had gone to such trouble to plan for me. Even if most of the trouble *had* been mine.

"Thank you, Gilbert." I forced another of my smiles. "It was nice of you to come." And then, because I wasn't entirely above stirring the pot, I put a hand over the pendant laying beneath my cardigan and added, "And thank you for being so sweet to Braden. I love the pendant you sold him."

Gilbert's lips stretched in an answering pretense at a smile. "It was my pleasure." He turned and edged past Natalie, shooting me a last, narrow look over his shoulder as he left the kitchen.

"He's such a..." Natalie stared after him.

"Little man?" I suggested.

"Yes. Exactly. I don't know how his wife puts up with him." She pulled a face, then her trademark cheeriness resurfaced. "Anyway. I came to tell you that we're heading out. Braden is pretty wired, and I want to go before—"

A crash sounded from the living room, followed by Paul's raised voice. "Braden Patrick Emerson!"

Natalie sighed. "Too late. I hate to leave you with the clean-up, but—"

"Go," I said. "I can manage."

16

CHAPTER 3

EDIE STAYED TO HELP CLEAN UP AFTER THE OTHERS LEFT. Jeanne offered to remain, too, but after my encounter with Gilbert, I didn't have the patience to deal with her and Edie sniping at one another—and I much preferred Edie's company. Sixty, it seemed, came with stronger opinions about who I wanted to spend time with, too.

As much as I loved Edie, part of me would have actually preferred to be alone, but a greater part appreciated the help with tidying away wrapping paper, dishes, and cake remains. And with removing vanilla icing and ceramic slivers from between the crevices in the wood floor after it turned out the crash I'd heard from the kitchen had been Braden knocking my newest gnome onto the cake, sending both to the floor.

I insisted on cleaning the floor myself while the now half-headless gnome looked on. It seemed the right thing to do, given that it required hands-and-knees work and Edie was ten years older than me, although my knees would have argued that last point.

"You missed a spot," she said helpfully.

"Where?"

"There." She poked a sandaled toe at a spot on the floor.

I had to squint to see an almost invisible speck. "Seriously?" I muttered.

"You'll thank me when you don't have a trail of ants making their way in here overnight." She turned away to gather napkins and stack plates while I scrubbed at the floorboards with an old toothbrush.

"Yeah, yeah." The toothbrush slipped, and I skinned my knuckles along the floor. "Cheesy rice on a cracker!"

The remains of a slice of cake landed on the floor with a little

squelchy noise. Sucking on my bruised knuckles, I scowled up at
Edie, expecting an apology. Instead, I found her glaring at me
over her bifocals. A second plate in her hand was almost on end,
and another glob of cake threatened to follow the first.

I popped my knuckles out of my mouth and leveled the
plate. "Edie!"

"*That*," she announced, ignoring me, "is the sum of what's
wrong with you."

"What does cake goop on my floor have to do with what's
wrong with me?" I pried the plate from her fingers and set it on
the table, then snagged a napkin and scooped up the new mess.
Her words registered, and I looked up again, brushing away a
stray hair tickling my forehead. "Wait. What do you mean,
wrong with me?"

"Swear for me."

"I beg your pardon?"

"Swear. You know." My friend planted hands on hips and
scowled down at me. "Curse. Worst thing you can think of,
right now."

"I—"

"Ha! I knew it. You can't, can you?"

I scowled back. "I have nothing to swear about."

Edie squinted at me, her mouth puckered as if she'd just
eaten a lemon. Then, before I could stop her, she dived for the
coffee table, picked up two plates, and shook their gooey
remains—mostly icing—onto the floor. The half-headless gnome
half-grinned down at the mess.

"Edith James!" I winced at the sound of her full name
coming out of my mouth. I would pay for that later, but I didn't
care. Not with more vanilla icing and pink sugar rosebuds deco-
rating my oak hardwood on purpose. "What's gotten into you?"
I demanded. "Cheesy—"

"*Jesus*, Claire," she interrupted. "It's Jesus, not *cheesy*. Jesus
Christ on a cracker. Say it."

I wanted to. I was mad enough to. I even tried. I opened my

mouth and everything. But it was no good. The words stuck in my throat, refusing to be uttered.

I looked up at Edie, at the pity in her eyes.

"You can't, can you?" she asked. "You can't swear, because Jeff didn't like it when you did."

"He said—" I cleared my throat. "He said it wasn't ladylike. And he was right." Oh my God, had I really just said that? In such a prim voice? To my best friend, who happened to swear like a sailor?

"Bullshit. But at least he didn't tell you you'd go to hell for it the way Jeanne tells me. I suppose that's something." Edie nodded at me. She was on a roll now. "That dress. I remember you wearing it to the end-of-year assembly once. Why haven't I seen it since?"

I opened my mouth to tell her about the gaping buttons beneath my cardigan, but then I remembered. I remembered the night Edie spoke of, and the fight I'd had with Jeff before we left the house. I remembered the real reason I'd never worn the dress again, the reason I'd stuck to colors that made me blend in with the walls instead.

It was because Jeff thought bright colors were too bold. He hadn't liked when I called attention to myself.

Slow understanding and hot shame unfurled together in me, side by side. I thought about Jeff's preferred foods still in the refrigerator, long past their stale dates. Jeff's closet sitting empty in the master bedroom, even though my much smaller one was overflowing. The collection of garden gnomes I detested and he'd refused to take with him. I took a long, deep breath. It caught in the back of my throat like shards of glass, and suddenly, I, too, knew what was wrong with me. Why my friend looked at me with so much sadness in her expression that *I* wanted to cry.

I was a mess. A total, complete mess, still living my life for someone who wasn't even here anymore.

And I was sixty.

"FUCK," SAID EDIE FOR THE HUNDREDTH TIME AS SHE headed out my front door half an hour later. She nudged me in the ribs, also for the hundredth time. "Go on. You can do it."

I rolled my eyes. "I'm not saying it, Edie."

"You have to start somewhere. You've been holding onto too many fucks for too many years, Claire. It's time to divest yourself of them."

I held back a snort of laughter that would have only encouraged her.

"It's time to divest myself of my clothes and have that bubble bath I've wanted all day," I corrected, shoving her across the threshold.

"Use the sachet I gave you," she ordered.

"I will," I said. And I would, because Edie's herbal skills were almost magical, and my body was already anticipating the sachet's relaxing effects. But I was still adding bubbles. "Thank you again. For everything."

"You're welcome for everything."

Her gaze followed mine to the maple tree where a single crow remained, sitting on the same branch the first had occupied this morning. A black shadow among darkened leaves, the porch light's reflection glinted in the eye it turned to me. I shivered.

Edie grunted. "My grandmother would have said it was an omen."

"Of what?"

"Beats me." She shrugged. "I never put much stock in her nonsense. But if I did, I'd say it was an omen, too. It probably means you're going to say fuck." She headed across the porch to the stairs, pausing at the top to look over her shoulder and fire a parting shot. "You know I'll win."

I didn't doubt it for an instant. Maybe not by getting me to use the f-word, but when it came to getting me to *loosen up*, as she put it, Edie would absolutely win. It just didn't have to happen all at once. Or tonight. "Watch your step going home."

"Fuck," she replied cheerfully. She waved a hand in the air over her head as she opened the gate's latch and stepped out onto the sidewalk. "Fuck, fuck, fuckity-fuck!"

"Goodnight, Edie," I called after her.

"Fuck, Claire!" she hollered back. Down the block, a dog barked, and across the street, Jeanne's front window banged closed. Edie cackled, knowing how much Jeanne objected to her language. She sauntered to the middle of the street and hurled her repertoire of French-Canadian obscenities in the other woman's direction. "And *tabarnak*, *esti*, and *calice* to you, too, Jeanne!"

Oh, for the love of—

Not waiting to see if Jeanne took the bait, or what would happen if she did, I closed the door, turned out the porch light, and headed upstairs past the creepily half-grinning gnome Edie had moved to the living room doorway.

I'd had quite enough sixtieth birthday for one day.

CHAPTER 4

"MENOPAUSE SUCKS," I TOLD MY EARLY-MORNING reflection in the bathroom mirror. It had been another sleepless night, thanks to hormones that had abandoned any semblance of order years ago, and the day stretching ahead of me looked even longer than normal.

I opened the cabinet and took out my toothbrush and toothpaste, wishing I'd left the party cleanup for this morning, just to give me something to do. A reason for not crawling back into bed and pulling the covers up over my head. I squeezed toothpaste onto the brush head, stuck the brush into my mouth, and recapped the tube. Then I studied myself while I scrubbed.

"Why?" I mumbled around the brush and foam. Why was this birthday hitting so hard? I didn't *look* any older than I had over the last few weeks. I still had the same lines around my eyes and the slight sag along my jawline that I'd been seeing for years now, and the same long gray hair falling past my shoulders that I'd had most of my life.

Well, except for the gray part.

I spat into the sink and started on the bottom row of teeth. My reflection scowled at me. I hadn't had an issue with any of the 'problem' birthday milestones—thirty and forty had passed in a blur of busyness, and I'd quite enjoyed reaching what I liked to optimistically refer to as the halfway point of my life at fifty. So why get so hung up on sixty? I still had years and years ahead of me. Good years. Productive years.

Assuming my health held, of course...and that I retained my mobility...and that I didn't fade away from boredom or loneliness...

My reflection and I blinked back a sudden welling of tears. I scowled. Now I was being maudlin, not to mention ridiculous. Turning sixty and getting a divorce did *not* mean my life was over—no matter how much my daughter-in-law's sympathetic murmurings suggested otherwise. I spat into the sink again, rinsed my mouth, and straightened.

Edie was right about that much. Enough feeling sorry for myself, and not just today. Jeff had been gone for more than a year now, he'd remarried, and the baby he'd had with Julia— they'd named her Josephine—was six months old. It was high time I moved on with life, too.

Somehow.

By doing something.

"Fuck," Edie's voice said in my head.

"Coffee," I countered with a sigh. "We'll start with coffee."

I turned and hobbled out of the bathroom on an ankle that twinged with every step because I'd slept on it wrong, or some other such lack of reason. It was irritating, but I knew from experience that it would straighten itself out eventually. Also for no good reason.

One more perk of getting old.

Downstairs, I went through the usual morning motions like a well-rehearsed ballet. I picked up the newspaper from the front porch (one crow, darn its feathered carcass, was still in the tree), wished Merlin a good morning as he streaked past me toward the kitchen, glanced around and mentally cataloged the yard chores piling up, closed the door on those chores, and followed in the wake of my orange cat.

In the kitchen, I scooped canned food into Merlin's dish, switched on the coffee pot, popped two slices of whole-grain bread into the toaster, pulled out a chair from the table, and reached for the reading glasses I kept on the stack of placemats in the center of the table.

The morning ballet skidded to a halt.

My gaze followed my reach. The placemats sat where they

should, with the flowers Edie had given me in a vase on top of them. But there were no glasses.

I frowned. How odd. They'd lived in the same place for the past eight years, ever since I started needing them and had bought a multi-pack at the local pharmacy. Four pairs. One for the kitchen table where I read the morning paper—Jeff had used a tablet device for his news, but I preferred the feel of paper in my hands; one for the little table beside my chair in the living room where I did my cross-stitch; one for the bedside table for reading before I turned out the light; and one for the table on the porch in summer, in case I decided to read or embroider outside.

Eight years, and not once had any of the pairs gone missing. I lifted the newspaper and shifted aside the vase of bright yellow rudbeckia.

Nothing. Where in the world...?

Then I remembered Natalie's takeover of the kitchen for yesterday's party and sighed. Of course. I looked over at Merlin, chowing down on his breakfast.

"You didn't happen to see where she put them, did you?" I asked the cat.

Round orange eyes, an exact match to his fur, regarded me for a nanosecond before he returned his attention to his dish. I sighed. Even if the cat could have answered, it would have been in the negative, because he'd hidden upstairs in my room for the entire time.

I returned the flowers to the table center. The glasses would turn up eventually, and I could use one of the other pairs in the meantime. The toaster popped, and on an ankle that was, as expected, fine again, I went to the counter and scraped a thin coating of butter onto the lightly browned bread. Merlin leapt up beside me, and I pursed my lips, looking sideways at him. "You know perfectly well you're not allowed up here."

The cat *mrrowed* a response and head-butted my shoulder. I smiled and gave him a scritch under the chin and then, purely out of defiance toward the man who no longer ruled my life, let the cat sit and watch while I finished buttering the toast.

The phone on the wall beside the back door rang as I took my first bite. I chewed, swallowed, and answered on the third ring. To my relief, it was Paul and not Natalie, who would have already tried calling me on the cell phone she insisted I carry for safety reasons at my age and would launch into a lecture because I hadn't answered on that.

I didn't like cell phones any more than I did tablets, however, and I could never seem to find the thing, let alone keep it charged.

"Hey, Mom," my son's deep voice was raised over the sound of a vehicle's engine. "I wanted to let you know I have your reading glasses with me. Apparently Braden decided you didn't need them anymore because he gave you that magnifying pendant yesterday. He put them in Natalie's handbag so we could donate them to Goodwill."

I couldn't help but laugh. "Well, you have to admire his logic, I suppose."

"I suppose." But Paul didn't sound amused. "Anyway, I was going to drop them off to you on my way to the office this morning, but I'm closing a deal on that office building on Main today, and a glitch came up during the inspection. I'll get them to you later, if that's okay?"

"No rush. I have extras."

"Um..."

"Um?"

"I meant he put *all* your reading glasses in Natalie's bag."

"All?" I blinked at Merlin, who blinked back. "You mean *all* all? All four pairs?"

"If that's how many you had."

Despite the inconvenience, my lips twitched again. "The little monkey."

"I'm really sorry, Mom. I'll bring them by as soon as I can, I promise."

On the counter, Merlin toyed with something that glinted in the sunlight coming through the window, nudging it with a delicate paw until it dropped with a clatter into the sink. Braden's magnifying glass pendant. I'd taken it off last night while I loaded the dishwasher and forgotten it there. I sighed and waved away Paul's apology.

"It's fine," I said. "I'll make do."

We chatted for another few minutes, during which I pretended polite appreciation for the birthday celebration and Paul typically didn't notice my lack of enthusiasm. Then he arrived at his destination, bid me a distracted goodbye, and ended the call without waiting for my response.

I hung up the phone and retrieved the pendant from the sink, looping it around my neck and removing Merlin from his perch. Then I poured coffee into my 'World's Best Grandma' mug and carried it and my now-cold toast to the table.

Munching on a bite, I spread out the newspaper. Merlin jumped up and took possession of the top half, and I scanned the headlines visible around him before settling on a story about the latest brouhaha in the provincial government.

It took a bit of trial and error to find the best angle for using the pendant's magnifying glass, but once I got the hang of it, it proved surprisingly effective. I alternated sips of coffee with bites of toast, moved Merlin when I needed to turn the page or see what was under him, and managed to read the entire paper more or less as I would have on any other morning.

Until I reached the personal essay page I always saved for last, and a blocky, dark-red scrawl obscured the entire first paragraph. I scowled through the lens at the handwriting. Seriously? Who would do that to someone's newspaper?

I set aside the pendant, tugged the paper out from under Merlin, and carried it to the window where the light was better. I looked again and then stared.

There was nothing there except the blurred first paragraph.

No mark of any kind, let alone blocky red letters. What the heck?

"*Hell,*" Edie's voice corrected in my head. "*What the hell.*"

I ignored her, turning the paper this way and that. The red letters didn't reappear. Had I slept so badly that I was now hallucinating? Or had Natalie's fussing about all those age-related illnesses and conditions finally gotten to me?

I sighed, poured myself a second coffee, and returned to the table to read the essay about—of all things—the quirks of menopause. The irony wasn't lost on me.

I picked up the pendant, pushed Merlin a few inches to the side, and positioned the lens over the newspaper.

13

The number floated in red across the first paragraph. My hand jolted and the pendant dropped onto the paper with a heavy thunk. Merlin batted at the chain.

The number disappeared.

I drew a shaky breath. Cautiously, I brushed my fingers across the paragraph and found nothing but the smoothness of paper. I extricated the sturdy silver chain from Merlin's claws and moved the lens over the paper again. The number reappeared.

I managed to keep hold of the pendant this time and moved it along the block letters unfolding after the number:

THE MORRIGAN'S WAY, CONFLUENCE, ONTARIO

An address? Here in Confluence? I moved the lens away. The writing disappeared. I moved it back. Letters and numbers returned. A chill slipped across my shoulders and down my spine, and I swallowed hard as I set the pendant on the table and curled fingers into palms, willing myself not to panic. I didn't take any medications, so whatever this hallucination was, it wasn't drug induced. That left what? Dementia?

Sixty years reached up and smacked me in the face. With a

rush that took away my breath, the thousand insecurities I'd pushed away or refused to consider over the last months—much like the refrigerator and Jeff's closet—flooded over me. All the signs of encroaching age: the aches and pains; the stiffness; the forgetfulness. I put a hand over the uneasy flutter of my heart. Damn Natalie and all those articles she insisted on sharing with me so I could be informed.

My health had been good so far, but I hadn't been to see the doctor in months. What if I'd missed something? Brushed it off when I should have paid attention? What if those little bouts of word-recall issues, losing my keys, forgetting to lock the front door on my way out, leaving the stove on—what if those were indications of something more? Something I was ignoring—or, worse, denying?

Dear heaven, even my four pairs of reading glasses, so meticulously never removed from their assigned places, might be a coping mechanism...a way of masking a serious decline. With no one else in the house to notice if I'd changed, could I trust my own judgment?

A dozen visions reared up in my mind. My house in flames and me trapped inside...alone. My door left unlocked and an intruder finding me...alone. The place in shambles while I shuffled from room to room in search of misplaced items...alone.

The rest of my life ahead of me...alone.

And therein lay the crux of the matter. I rested my elbows on the table, dropped my head into my hands, and closed my eyes, forcing myself to breathe through my panic. A panic that might have been precipitated by the imagined writing in the paper but had far more to do with my fear of that rest-of-my-life-alone part.

Merlin nudged me under my chin and wedged himself into the space between my arms, his purr rumbling against my chest. Little by little, the panic released its grip on my heart and lungs and, gratefully, I buried my face in the velvet of his fur. At least I had him to keep me company.

And to feast on my body if I fell down the stairs and died and couldn't feed him anymore.

A mangled chuckle-snort burst from me. Now I was being plain ridiculous. Merlin would likely be gone long before I was, and even if I did fall down the stairs in the meantime, he wouldn't starve because someone would find me long before that, too. And, as Edie had reminded me yesterday, I was only sixty, not dead. I might not have planned on living this part of my life alone, but it didn't mean I wasn't capable.

Look at Jeanne. She was three years older than me and still working full time at the hospital, for heaven's sake. And Edie was older than both of us and as fiercely active and independent now as she'd been the entire time I'd known her.

Both of them weren't just fine, they were confident and fabulous, and they had lives, and I...didn't. I hadn't worked since before I'd had Paul. Jeff had liked having me at home. Liked having me throw dinner parties for his clients and play the role of successful businessman's wife. The few times I'd suggested I might want more, the pushback from him had been so fierce that it hadn't been worth the fight. It had been easier—again—to give in. To not rock the boat. To find more acceptable ways to keep myself from going slowly mad—gardening, bits of charity work...things Jeff approved of.

By the time Jeff left me, his land development company had become the largest in the region, and under Ontario law, the divorce settlement meant my life could remain unchanged. It didn't, however, mean it *should* remain unchanged.

I pushed back my chair and stood up, meeting my cat's round, orange look of inquiry.

"I need to be more like Edie and Jeanne, Merlin," I announced. "They do things. They do lots of things. They have *purpose*. I want purpose, too."

Merlin yawned, showing a rough pink tongue and sharp, needle-like teeth more than capable of tearing chunks of flesh from a body. I shuddered, picked up my empty mug, and turned my back on cat, pendant, nonexistent address, and overactive imagination.

Purpose.

I could totally find purpose in my life.

Couldn't I?

CHAPTER 5

13 The Morrigan's Way.

TRY AS I MIGHT, I COULDN'T STOP THINKING ABOUT THE address. Every time I passed through the kitchen, my gaze strayed to the newspaper on the table. Twice, I stopped to stare down at it, wondering if I would still see the dark-red writing if I held the pendant over it again. Twice, I walked away.

I ate a late lunch at two o'clock on the front porch, preferring to swat away the yellow jackets and bottle flies than to sit at the kitchen table with the newspaper. Or even move it. I was still there at three, when Paul brought my reading glasses—all four pairs—and handed them over to me along with his apologies for not being able to stay for a visit.

Briefly, it crossed my mind to ask him to look at the newspaper, to see if he saw anything out of the ordinary. But Paul would share the odd request with Natalie, who would in turn arrive on my doorstep, tomorrow at the latest, with a stack of articles about cognitive function in the elderly and a handful of brochures from retirement homes in the area.

So I hugged my son and told him I understood, then trailed after him as he strode back to his vehicle on the street. I stood at the white picket gate while he rounded the hood of the fancy black SUV. Then, as he opened the driver-side door, I called out, "Wait."

Paul looked over the SUV's roof, one eyebrow raised.

"Have you ever heard of a road called The Morrigan's Way?" I asked, because who better to know all the streets in a town than its top real estate agent, right?

He frowned. "I can't say I have. Why?"

"I came across an address," I said. "On an old envelope I found in a book."

"Was it here in Confluence?"

I nodded.

He pulled out his cell phone, tapped on it a few times, and shook his head. "There's nothing on the map. Sorry." He climbed into the vehicle and fastened his seat belt, then gave me a wave and pulled away. A second later, he reversed to where I stood. The passenger-side window slid down. "Are you sure you read it right? There's a Morgan's Way that runs off Barrymore Street. Could that be it?"

Before I could respond, he grimaced and answered his own question. "Nope. Never mind. It's all bush along there. Although depending how old the envelope is, I suppose there might have been a house at one time. Sorry again, Mom."

Another wave, this one followed by a toot of the SUV's horn, and Paul disappeared down the street. I watched until he rounded the corner at the stop sign, and then I looked over my shoulder at the house. Morrigan...Morgan...*had* I read it wrong?

I gave myself a mental shake. I hadn't read it at all, I reminded myself, because it didn't exist. And yet...

And yet.

I returned to my porch to retrieve my lunch plate and glass, stooping to pick up the napkin that dropped to the floor. The pendant around my neck swung free of my shirt, and I watched it twirl slowly on its chain. I could still return it to Gilbert, I thought. Return it, forget about the nonexistent address, and—

Raised voices across the street caught my attention, and I straightened to peer through the maple branches at Jeanne and Gilbert's house. An unfamiliar vehicle sat parked in the driveway, and Gilbert stood toe-to-toe on their front porch with a man almost twice his size. I couldn't see Gilbert's expression from here, but belligerence marked his every line, and his head shook in the negative even as the other man towered over him. I pursed my lips. As much as I disliked the man, I had to hand it to him: he certainly wasn't lacking in bravado.

I watched as the stranger shook a finger under Gilbert's nose. Gilbert knocked his hand away and pointed at the stranger's gray sedan. The man's hands closed into fists, and more words were exchanged, but I couldn't make out any of them—a pity, because my curiosity was well and truly aroused. What *had* Gilbert gotten himself into? And did Jeanne know?

Gilbert whirled and went into the house, slamming the door behind him, and the stranger stalked down the stairs to the walkway, heading for his car. He stopped beside it, then turned his head and stared across the street. My breath caught, and an urge to run into the house swept over me, but before I could act on the impulse, a crow flapped down from the tree to land on the porch railing. It fixed me with a beady eye, and I froze. Another one? What was with me and crows all of a sudden?

For his part, the stranger didn't seem to notice the crow. He walked to the end of Gilbert's driveway and stared across at my house and yard, searching, but his gaze skipped past me, and I gave silent thanks for the maple screening me from the street. The man narrowed his eyes, then turned away and returned to his vehicle. Seconds later, car and driver departed, the crow lifted off the porch rail and flew away, and I exhaled a shaky sigh and eased my grip on the plate I held.

That had been...unsettling.

Enough so that I made a mental note to double-check the locks on my doors before bed. I wouldn't sleep otherwise. Not after that encounter. Or with all those crows hanging around.

And speaking of things standing in the way of sleep...

I marched up the walkway to my house in search of my walking shoes and hat, because *13 The Morrigan's Way* wasn't going to leave me alone until I checked it out.

And I wasn't handing over the pendant to Gilbert until then, either.

Two hours later, hot and cranky and wishing I'd brought two water bottles instead of just one, I stood in the middle of what amounted to a wide gravel path, staring at a heavily wooded dead end and guzzling the last of my lukewarm, plastic-tasting liquid. When Paul had said "off Barrymore Street," I hadn't realized he'd meant near the end of a very long Barrymore. Or that Morgan's Way itself would be so blasted long. Maybe this was why people carried cell phones with map apps.

By the time I'd realized it wasn't going to be the easy walk I'd anticipated, I was already forty minutes in and had reached the how-much-further-can-it-possibly-be point.

A lot further, it had turned out. As in a full hour and a half of walking time that included ten minutes of backtracking to find the Morgan's Way signpost I'd missed beneath a wild grapevine engulfing it. All of which entitled me to be as cranky as I wanted to be, in my opinion.

That, and the fact I'd made the trek at all, because my empty water bottle was all I had to show for my efforts. There wasn't a single trace of human habitation, past or present. No old mail-box, no hint of a driveway or path, and certainly no house.

I sighed. It was what I should have expected from an imaginary address, but that didn't stop me from feeling a pang of disappointment.

A bright-red maple leaf drifted past my nose, and I tracked its descent to the ground. It seemed jarringly out of place in the first week of September, but it wouldn't be for long. Summer was definitely on the wane. I could hear it in the drone of the cicadas above, their electric buzz more frantic with each passing day, and in the screech of a blue jay and the cheerful calls of the chickadees picking seeds off the wildflowers lining the road. And I could certainly see it in the angle of the sun, already slanting behind the trees and casting long shadows across the road, even though the watch I wore on my wrist told me it was only a little past six.

I shivered, rubbing my arms through the thin fabric of my long-sleeved blouse. It had been downright hot while walking along the open roads, but here among the trees, it was a good deal cooler, and I wished I'd thought to bring a sweater as well as a second water bottle. Although I supposed I'd warm up again on the walk home.

The long, hour-and-a-half walk home.

I sighed again, cast a last glance into the shadowed woods, and turned to retrace my steps toward civilization. A rush of feathers sounded, and I jumped back as something brushed past my nose. With one hand over the heart trying to climb out of my chest and the other clutching my water bottle, I glared at the crow that had alighted on a nose-height branch at the edge of the trees.

"What the *heck*," I growled at it. "You scared the life out of me!"

Head tipped to one side, the crow regarded me with a bright black eye and far too much intelligence for my liking. Had it followed me from the house? I scowled. I was beginning to feel like I'd fallen into a Hitchcock movie. I jumped as the bird gave a harsh caw and lifted into the air again, this time winging into the woods.

I pushed back the hair from my eyes and settled my hat more firmly onto my head. Between crows and pendants and nonexistent addresses, I was beginning to not much like being sixty. Life had been a great deal less weird when I was only fifty-nine.

A shadow moved in the underbrush to the right, huge and low to the ground, and I froze mid-step. I stared into the trees, water bottle clutched tight again. Had that been a dog? It had *looked* like a dog, but what in the world was it doing all the way out here on its own?

My imagination, which had never been particularly active

before today, seized on the question and spiraled out of control. *Unless it isn't on its own,* it whispered. *Unless there's someone* with *it all the way out here.*

In the middle of nowhere.

Where no one knew I'd gone.

Visions of everything from a wolf pack to a deranged serial killer flashed through my head. I thought about the uncharged cell phone I'd found on the shelf in my front closet when I'd gone looking for my hat. Maybe this was why Natalie thought it was a good idea to carry one? I swallowed a burble of laughter born of nerves and gave my overactive imagination a metaphorical shake. I really needed to scale back on the detective shows I'd taken to watching.

"There are no serial killers here, you idiot," I muttered under my breath. "Or wolves, for that matter."

There *had* been, however, that stranger in Gilbert and Jeanne's driveway. What if he'd followed me?

I took a deep breath and loosened my death grip on the water bottle. That was as ridiculous as my serial killer notion. *Middle of nowhere, Claire, remember? You haven't seen a single vehicle for the last half hour at least. Now get your tail-end in gear. You have a long walk ahead, and—*

The crow cawed again. My gaze swiveled back to the woods and came to rest on the bird sitting atop a half-hidden pile of stones too orderly to be natural. A breeze rustled through the leaves as my brain picked out a pillar-shaped outline...with a gate attached to it.

Tiny goosebumps lifted across my arms. So there really *had* been a house here at one time. How—

I pulled the thought up short. How *what*? Interesting? Coincidental? Downright impossible that my newspaper should know that?

I glanced around, seeking evidence of a former driveway, but there was nothing. No culvert, no vague driveway-shaped entrance hiding beneath roadside growth. My gaze sought the pillar again, and I blinked. It looked clearer than it had a second ago. Cleaner. The gate, too, as if someone had pulled away some of the vines and leaves clinging to it. And there was something else...something on the pillar that looked...

Wolves and serial killers, I reminded myself, even as my feet edged toward the brush and I scanned the woods again. *And strangers. And no one knows you're here.*

But nothing out of the ordinary moved, and all around me, the songs of cicadas and chickadees continued as if everything was normal. Ordinary.

The crow cawed again and left the pillar to fly up into the treetops where it belonged. Also ordinary.

Just a quick look, a new-to-me voice whispered in my brain, sounding a little like Edie. *You know you want to.*

I did. I set the empty water bottle at the edge of the road and picked my way through the tumble of brush. Excitement tingled in my belly. Was that a plaque of some kind? With a number on it? The flowy fabric of my pant leg snagged on a wild rosebush, and I paused to disentangle it, adding jeans to the mental list of things I wished I'd thought to bring.

I skirted a Canada thistle as tall as me, picked burrs off my sleeve when I brushed against a burdock, narrowly avoided an encounter with an enormous stinging nettle, and stumbled into a patch of vicious wild raspberry canes.

I eased myself free of the latter, nursing a scrape on the back of one hand. It had been many years since I'd been out in the woods—Jeff had detested camping—but I didn't recall them being quite this hostile. I eyed the brush still between me and the pillar and licked a trickle of blood from my wrist. Maybe I should mark the place and come back tomorrow, when I was better dressed for exploring. And when the sun wasn't slipping with such alarming speed behind the trees.

And when I had a charged cell phone with me.

I looked over my shoulder at the road. The vegetation showed no sign of my passage through it. If anything, it looked even denser and more treacherous from this side. If I wanted any skin left, it would be easier to continue into the trees, where the undergrowth thinned. As long as I kept the road in view, I could walk parallel to it until I found an easier way back.

I turned to push through the remaining dense brush and almost fell flat on my face when I met with...nothing. Arms pinwheeling, I regained my balance and then gaped at the clear trail that had opened between me and the gate.

Impossible, my brain said. My gaze flicked left, right, back to the gate. I sucked in a ragged breath and tried to quiet my thoughts—especially the inner voice that kept shouting *RUN!* But I couldn't quite rid myself of the knowledge, the panicked certainty, that paths didn't magically clear themselves because magic wasn't real.

Which left what? A return to this morning's dementia theory? But surely dementia didn't set in this fast or ferociously. Which brought me back to...

Poof! my unhelpful brain whispered, and then it giggled.

I pressed a fist against my mouth to stop an answering giggle. The last thing I needed was hysteria setting in. I took another breath and made my shoulders descend from my ears. I was a grown woman, out for a walk in the woods, and the light was playing tricks on me as the sun went down. It had nothing to do with either dementia or magic. It was that simple. That straightforward. And now, now it was time to go. Old houses and invisible addresses be damned, and—

Wait. Was that a *gargoyle* on top of the gatepost?

Squirrel! my inner voice accused. It had a point, but I shushed it because, *gargoyle*. I'd always wanted one of the stone creatures for my garden, but Jeff had thought them creepy and we'd ended up populating the yard with those ridiculous, red-hatted gnomes so I could be friends with Jeanne, instead.

Jeff hadn't wanted a cat, either, but now he was gone, and I had Merlin, and now...now I might have a gargoyle, too.

I picked my way to the gatepost and squinted up at the

figure that perched there, its heavily clawed feet clinging to a round stone ball beneath them. It had a broad head reminiscent of a mastiff's, and its mouth was open to bare four distinct, curved teeth—two on top and two on the bottom. Cat-like ears were set close to the sides of its skull; disproportionately short, muscled forelegs and haunches supported a stocky body; and a pair of stubby wings, like those of a bat, sprouted from its back.

It was as ugly as sin and absolutely gorgeous. I grinned up at it in delight. "You alone," I declared, "were worth the trek out here. And you are going to look *so* good in my garden!"

Assuming, of course, I could find a way to get it down from there. It was a lot bigger than it had seemed from further away —probably three feet tall or more. Which meant it would weigh a *lot*. Maybe I could get Paul to give me a hand on the weekend. I didn't relish the lecture I'd have to endure from Natalie when she learned how I'd found it, but that, too would be worth it.

I gave a nod of satisfaction at my plan, then stepped back. My gaze dropped to the gatepost itself, and the tarnished edges of a plaque peeping out from behind a Virginia creeper. An engraved number '1' was visible under the leaves.

Leave it, Claire, my voice prompted, stilling my hand mid-reach. *You can check it when you come back with Paul.*

Do it! my heretofore unknown spirit of adventure countered, again sounding like Edie.

I pushed aside leaves edged with the crimson of encroaching autumn and stared at the uncovered plaque. The number 13 stared back at me.

I wasn't surprised. Not really. After finding the gatepost, having the path somehow clear itself, and then spotting the gargoyle, what I felt was more a sense of fulfilled expectation than surprise. Truth be told, I would have been more surprised if it hadn't been the number 13.

Or if the words beneath the number hadn't read *The Morrigan's Way.*

CHAPTER 6

I STARED AT THE PLAQUE FOR LONG SECONDS, MY ARMS wrapped around my midsection and the hair standing on end along them. This had gone beyond weird. It was downright creepy. The address in my newspaper had been a figment of my imagination; there was no such road as The Morrigan's Way in Confluence; and a gate could not magically appear in the woods where no houses existed.

It just couldn't.

Run, my cautionary voice urged again. *Run now, while you still can. Before...*

Before what?

Therein lay the rub.

I shifted my gaze to the gate. What would I find down the path just visible in the deepening shadows? Would there be an imaginary house to go with the imaginary address that had brought me here? Did I have the nerve to find out?

One of my hands drifted out to settle on the cold iron, as if of its own accord.

Hold on, Claire. Think this through. No one knows where you are; you have no cell phone with you; and even if you leave now, it will be dark before you get home. This is not the time to be wandering off alone into the trees.

Except...

Except a gatepost with the same address on it that I'd seen in my newspaper.

Except a gate with a path on the other side.

Except what was the harm if I ventured in just a little way? Maybe to that bend in the path, just to see what was around the corner. Two minutes in, two minutes back, keeping the gate—

and the road—in sight. Surely four minutes wouldn't make any difference to the walk home, right?

I pushed against the iron. It held fast. I pushed again. Then I gripped it with both hands and pushed, pulled, pushed again. The gate didn't so much as wobble. I planted hands on hips and scowled at it. Seriously?

I heaved a sigh. Maybe it was for the best—a sign that now really wasn't the time to go exploring, and that I should stick with Plan A: mark the road so I could find the spot again, and come back tomorrow. In the daylight, preferably with Paul, and failing that, at least after telling someone where to start looking if I happened to go missing.

I nodded in satisfaction at my new-old plan and looked one last time at the plaque. At the number *13* in large numerals, with a smaller *The Morrigan's Way* in ornate lettering beneath it. And—

Was that another line of lettering below? I stooped to peer at it. Definitely letters, but they were too small to read without my glasses, and there wasn't enough light to see by if I stepped back to—wait.

"Ha!" I tugged the pendant from inside my shirt and held it over the plaque, moving it around until the letters became clear and formed words that—

Were just plain bizarre.

Knock three times on the gatepost if you want me.

I blinked. Rubbed my eyes. Repositioned the magnifying lens. Re-read the lettering. Yup. That was what it said, all right. *Knock three times*—and below that, more writing, even smaller. *Twice on the gate if the answer is no.*

I fumbled the pendant and almost dropped it. Who in the world would write words that mimicked the lyrics of an old Tony Orlando and Dawn song on a gatepost in the middle of nowhere? And why? I straightened and glared into the surrounding woods. I was the only person I knew who would even admit to liking Tony Orlando and Dawn anymore. This was a joke. A prank. It had to be. There was no other explanation.

But neither was anyone around. No one hiding in the bushes, watching for my reaction. No one recording me for posterity. No one...and no reason. What in heaven's name was going on?

Gripping the pendant in a tight fist, I stared at the plaque, at the gate, at the path beyond. Once again, caution urged me to turn tail and run. Once again, I stood my ground. Then, feeling intensely foolish, I raised my free hand, curled my fingers into my palm, and rapped on the plaque—once, twice, a third time —the words and melody of the old song looping through my brain as I did so. *Knock three times...*

Nothing happened.

I waited a full minute, counting off the seconds under my breath and flexing tender knuckles. The gate stayed closed. Nothing moved in the shadows on either side of it. The woods stayed silent but for the buzz of cicadas and chirping of crickets behind me. I tightened my lips and raised my fist again. One, two, three raps.

Another minute.

Another three raps, hard enough to make my bruised knuckles protest and the breath hiss from me.

A third minute of waiting.

My sense of foolishness increased. Was I, a grown woman old enough to know better, really standing in the semi-gloom of the forest, knocking on a stone pillar? And worse, expecting someone to answer? A breeze whispered through the trees and under my shirt, carrying with it the scent of damp earth and pine trees. I shivered in its chill. I seriously needed to get moving if I wanted any daylight left for my walk home. I slipped the pendant chain back over my head.

One last time, my inner Edie-voice insisted, *and then you can go.*

My inner Edie-voice was as much of a pain as the real thing. But I lifted my hand and knocked again. Once, twice—

"Goddess above, woman," rasped a voice like gravel scattering across stone, "I heard you the first time. It's not like I can hop down in just a few seconds after being stuck up here for decades. A little patience, please!"

I yelped, fell backward over a tree root, and landed on my rear end amid dead pine needles and twigs. My head snapped back, and my gaze zeroed in on the huge stone gargoyle slowly uncurling itself to stand upright on the gatepost—at least double in height than the mere three feet I'd thought it.

My brain froze, refusing to accept what my eyes said they saw. I blinked, squeezed said eyes closed, blinked again. The gargoyle jumped down from the gatepost, landing with a *whump* that shook the ground beneath me. Stone feet sank up to their ankles into the soft earth. A massive head tilted first to one side, then the other, as the gargoyle stretched its neck. It heaved a deep sigh.

"Better," it said. Then it stared down at me with blank stone eyes devoid of pupils. "Well?"

"Uh," I said.

The gargoyle raised what wasn't quite an eyebrow. Its stony —no pun intended—gaze raked my sprawled form from head to toe. It heaved a sigh.

"Well?" it said again, "Are you going to lie there all night, or are you going to unlock the gate?"

I looked past the hulking form to the gate. *"I don't have the key,"* I wanted to say, but no. No way was I going to start conversing with what I now had no doubt was a hallucination. I was going to pick myself up from the ground, get back to the road, and get my butt back home as fast as I could manage. And first thing in the morning, I would call my doctor and—

I squeaked and scuttled backward on my butt as the gargoyle reached for me, certain I was about to be crushed. But with surprising dexterity, stone claws lifted the chain from around my neck, and then the gargoyle turned to the gate and fitted the pendant into an indentation on a flat panel I hadn't noticed. A pendant-shaped indentation. The latch disengaged with a rusty protest, and the gate swung inward on hinges that squealed from disuse. The gargoyle looked back over its shoulder.

"You're still on the ground."

I scrambled to my feet and shot a look toward the road, which had almost disappeared in the encroaching dark. How late was it, anyway? And just how long had I spent poking about, staring at a gargoyle and knocking on a plaque inscribed with a nonexistent address? Merlin would be starving, and Edie was supposed to come by for tea on the porch after dinner, and...I looked back at the waiting gargoyle and the open gate. A faint glow, with no discernible source, illuminated the path on the other side. I swallowed.

"Keven," said the gargoyle.

"I beg your pardon?" I responded out of sheer surprise.

"My name," said the gargoyle. "It's Keven."

"Ah..."

Stone hands—paws?—settled onto stone hips. Haunches?

"Nice to meet you, Keven," it coached. "My name is...?"

I wondered what it meant when a hallucination started coaching you on manners. I sidled toward the thicket that stood between me and a pell-mell run to safety. "It's..." I mumbled, "it's...ah...Claire. My name is Claire."

"*Lady* Claire," it said, sounding very much like it was correcting me. I blinked.

"I—what?"

"You are Lady Claire now." It handed the pendant back to me, and I accepted it automatically. "You are Crone. You are Lady Claire."

I shook my head and shifted another step away. "You're mistaken. I'm not who you think I am." Belatedly, I bristled at the unveiled insult. "And I'm not a crone."

"Not *a* crone. Just Crone."

"And that's different how?"

Keven frowned and countered, "How is it *not* different to serve the Morrigan?"

Serve—I backed into a thistle and bounced forward again with a yip. I wouldn't wait until tomorrow for medical attention, I decided. I'd call Paul when I got home, and he could take me to the hospital. I was pretty sure they had a psychiatrist on call in the emergency ward. Or maybe I could ask Jeanne to take me. Having a nurse along might expedite things, get me seen faster and—

The gargoyle turned and stomped through the open gate. Despite myself—perhaps because, on some level, having an imaginary sentient gargoyle keeping me company in the shadowy gloom seemed preferable to finding myself alone—I called out, "Wait! Where are you going?"

Its gravelly answer floated back through the night. "The house," it said. "Follow or not, as you please, but I'm tired of standing around talking. I'm hungry."

Hungry.

The living stone gargoyle was hungry.

Because of course it was.

And I was a crone—sorry, I was just Crone—serving something called the Morrigan, and—and what did gargoyles eat, anyway?

I stared after the stone figure that had continued down the path and disappeared around a corner into the trees. The gate remained open. Dark crept closer, until it felt like the shadows themselves breathed down my neck. I swallowed. Dear God, when I decided to lose my mind, I didn't hold back, did I?

A twig snapped behind me and I jumped, clamping a hand over my mouth against the squawk that wanted to emerge. I needed to go home. *Now.* But while I'd stood there waffling, the moonless night had swallowed the road and woods in their entirety, and—

Something rustled in the leaves to the left.

Insects, most likely, my Edie-voice reassured me.

Or that dog/wolf you thought you saw earlier, my not-Edie-voice suggested. *The really big one that might or might not belong to a serial killer and/or want to rip out your throat.*

I eyed the faintly glowing path. The gargoyle had mentioned a house. But what kind of house? The way this hallucination was playing out, it could be anything from a door in a hollow tree trunk to a shining castle à la Disney.

The leaves rustled again, and this time whatever moved there sounded big. Huge. That did it. I skittered forward in the footsteps of the gargoyle. Any kind of house was better than staying out here in the middle of nowhere by myself. Maybe my brain would conjure a phone, and I could call Paul and have him send out a search party. I paused at the gate and wrapped my arms around myself against the chill night air.

For all I knew, I was already lying in a psych ward, hyped up on hallucinogens and dreaming this entire thing, with no idea of when or how I turned such a dramatic corner in my mental health.

And on that cheerful thought, I slipped past the wrought iron bars and onto the path.

The gate clanged shut behind me.

CHAPTER 7

THE HOUSE AT THE END OF THE PATH, AS IT TURNED OUT, was neither hollow-tree hovel nor shiny castle. Instead, it was a small stone cottage sitting in the middle of a clearing, light spilling from its windows and the open front door. It looked utterly charming, warm, and welcoming—and was it *shimmering*?

I peered at it, but the impression of a glow surrounding it had been fleeting and was gone now, leaving just an ordinary building. Albeit one that looked much like I thought Grandmother's cottage would have looked to Little Red Riding Hood.

Speaking of which...

I glanced over my shoulder into the dark woods through which I'd come. I'd halted twice along the path, my heart surging into my throat, certain that something in the shadows was moving parallel to me, but every time I tried to look closer, it was gone again. Other than the goosebumps rising along my skin, nothing moved in the night.

"In or out," bellowed a voice from the cottage. Keven the gargoyle. "I'm not keeping dinner for you forever!"

I blinked at the open front door and the invitation—if it could be called such. Dinner. My stomach rumbled. Were all hallucinations this detailed? This considerate? An idea flitted through my head and I chased it down. I'd come across an old television show a few months ago, a British series—*Life on Mars* —about a cop who was hit by a car and fell into a coma. He'd woken up thirty years earlier and lived a whole other life in the new time and place, never quite sure if it was real or all an elaborate hallucination.

I frowned. Wait. Hadn't he turned out to have a brain tumor or something? Was that what was going on? I had a brain tumor and I was lying in a coma on the floor of my kitchen, dreaming all of this?

A bulky shape filled the cottage doorway, casting a long shadow over me. "Well?"

A warm, meaty scent drifted from the house, and my mouth watered. Tumor or not, a woman had to eat.

"Coming," I said, and the doorway cleared again. After a last glance at the trees edging the clearing, I walked up the path, stepped up onto the flagstone porch, walked into the house— and came up short against a warm, broad, and very solid chest.

I froze, taking stock of this new surprise. Male, I decided. And tall. And was that chest hair tickling my nose? It smelled woodsy, like the trees I'd just come through, and—

I took a hasty step backward and tripped over the door sill. Strong hands clamped onto my upper arms long enough to steady me before letting go again.

"Milady," a deep voice rumbled as the man swept a low bow.

"Mi-what?" I squeaked, my gaze glued to tawny hair heavily streaked with gray and pulled into a man-bun at the back of his head. I abhorred man-buns.

He straightened, and I tilted my head back to look up at him. My jaw dropped. Tall was an understatement. He had to be almost six and a half feet, with a full beard as graying as his hair, the broadest shoulders I'd ever seen, and—

My gaze dropped to the blousy, snow-white shirt he wore open at the neck. And yes, that had been chest hair my nose had been buried in. I blushed.

I was sixty years old, a grandmother, and years beyond experiencing the kind of hormones that made one blush, but I still managed it. Amber eyes danced with amusement.

"Milady," he repeated, and my hormones shivered. "You *are* the Lady Claire, are you not?"

"I—I—"

"I am Lucan," he said, sweeping another low bow. "Your protector."

My gaze followed his movement, lingering on the hardened swell of shoulder muscles, then the chest revealed by the gaping of his shirt. Holy Hannah, but he was built. Maybe I didn't have to hate *all* man-buns?

"Goddess preserve us, mutt," Keven's voice grumped from somewhere behind the man towering over me. "I said show her into the dining hall *for* dinner, not turn yourself *into* dinner."

I closed my eyes against another wave of mortification. Forget the tumor. At this rate, I'd die of sheer embarrassment. I took a deep breath and curled my fingers into fists so tight that my nails bit into my palms.

The pain surprised me with its realness, and I zeroed in on it. If I could hold onto it and stay focused, maybe when I opened my eyes again...

The man regarded me, his head tipped to one side. *Shit. Shoot,* I corrected myself.

See? More proof that none of this was real, because despite Edie's efforts, I didn't swear, damn—darn it.

"You are perplexed," the man said. Dear heavens, but his voice was deep. Mind you, given the breadth of his chest, was it any wonder?

I yanked my gaze away from the latter yet again. Hallucinating or not, I had no business thinking about a strange man's chest. I lifted my chin. I was getting tired of this. I wanted to wake up, or go home, or do whatever it took to get back to reality.

"I need to use your phone," I said. In the television show, the actor had been able to communicate with his other life by phone sometimes, so it was worth a shot, right? Preferably before I resorted to hysterics.

"There is none."

"No—" I broke off. Now that I thought about it, there had been no telephone poles along the road, or any sign of wires. "What about a cell phone, then?"

"Sorry. There's no signal here."

Wonderful. Just—

"Dinner!" Keven's faint voice prompted.

"Dinner?" the man suggested, offering his arm.

I had no appetite anymore, but neither did I have any idea of what to do next, and so I nodded. But I was darned if I'd take the offered arm.

Holding my head high, I sidestepped him and started in the direction of Keven's voice—only to come up short again. Were there *no* limits to my hallucination?

I gaped at what had been hidden behind the man—Lucan, he'd called himself. My protector...from what? But no. I wasn't going there. Not now. Not when faced with this.

Slowly, my gaze panned the enormous foyer in which we stood, from soaring, vaulted ceiling supported by massive stone pillars to polished flagstone floors, oak doors that stood to the left and right, and twin suits of armor standing guard on either side of a wide, central stone staircase. Real armor. Flanking a staircase rising to a second level that had most definitely not been a part of the cottage's exterior.

Lightheadedness swept over me, rising from my toes like a hot flash but without the heat. My head spun, and I swayed on my feet. Before I could topple, Lucan took my arm and steered me toward an ornately carved bench beside the door. He pushed me onto it and ordered, "Head down," even as his hand guided me to comply. Then he crouched beside me. "Breathe."

I am breathing, I wanted to say, but the words wouldn't manifest because, nope, I actually wasn't, because I couldn't. Not past the snarl of panic that had risen in my chest, and not past the overwhelming terror that I'd been right. I had well and truly descended into madness. I squeezed my eyes shut, certain that this was it. I was going to die in a nightmare. I was going to die *because* of a nightmare.

But I didn't.

Instead, a gentle hand rubbed circles on my back between my shoulder blades, and bit by bit, the knot behind my breastbone eased. I tried a tentative breath, then another, then a third. My head stopped spinning. The panic receded. And the madness...

I forced open an eye. An amber gaze met mine, warm and concerned.

The madness remained.

Lucan frowned. "You weren't expecting any of this, were you?"

I considered him for a moment, then opened the other eye. "Expecting...this?" I gestured at the foyer. "What reason could I have possibly had to expect a talking gargoyle and a cottage that's like the Doctor's phone booth?"

He glanced over his shoulder, then put the back of his hand to my forehead, as if feeling for a fever. His frown deepened. "This looks like a phone booth to you?"

I pushed away his hand. "Of course not. It's just—oh, never mind. It was a television reference."

His brow cleared and he nodded. "Doctor Who. I remember. But you were saying about not having expected this...?"

I snorted. "How could anyone expect to go insane in the middle of a walk in the woods? Although it actually started this morning, I suppose. With the newspaper."

"This morning," he repeated. He exchanged a glance with Keven, who had somehow managed to approach without my notice—an interesting trick for an enormous stone creature—and now hovered a few feet away. The gargoyle's head shook, and massive shoulders lifted in a shrug. Lucan cleared his throat. "Ah... are you saying this is the first magic you've encountered? That you've never...?"

"I've never what?" The rest of his words registered, and my voice rose in pitch. "First *what*?"

Man and gargoyle both stared at me, their expressions thunderstruck.

I stared back. A bubble of hysteria replaced the earlier panic. Lucan had *not* just said what I thought he—

"Well, isn't this just fecking grand," muttered Keven. "She knows *nothing*? Has no training, no history? She should be a midwitch by now. What, by the goddess herself, are we supposed to do with her?"

Midwitch. Training. History. My head went woozy again.

"I haven't any idea." Lucan sighed and climbed to his feet. "I say we start by feeding her, and then you can explain—"

"Oh, no. You're her protector, *you* explain."

There was that *protector* word again. I looked back and forth between them. I knew my mouth was hanging open, but darned if I could make it close. This was too much. *They* were too much.

"I want to go home," I said, my voice little more than a whisper. Man and gargoyle ignored me.

"Are we certain she's the one?" Lucan asked, examining me now as if I were some kind of specimen.

"She's here, isn't she? By the Morrigan's own magic, no one but a Crone could even find this place, let alone summon me," Keven retorted. "Or you, for that matter."

"True," Lucan agreed, "but still. Mistakes happen."

A part of me bristled at being called a mistake. A greater part of me snarled at the first to shut up. I ignored both and said again, louder, "I want to go home."

"Mind your words!" the gargoyle growled at Lucan. "The Morrigan doesn't make mistakes."

"Fine." Lucan crossed his arms and glared at Keven. "And what if she *is* Crone? You said yourself you don't know what you're supposed to do with—"

"I want," I bellowed over them, "to go *home*!"

Silence dropped over the great hall, deafening in its totality. I glared first at Lucan, then Keven, then Lucan again. They stared back. I pushed myself up from the bench, twitched my flowy pant legs into place, and smoothed the front of my shirt. For a fourth time, and with as much dignity as I could muster, I repeated, "I want to go home. To my house. Now, please."

Two heads shook as one.

"You can't," said Keven.

"It's not safe," said Lucan.

"Fuck that," said I, who had never so much as spoken the word *damn* aloud. And with Edie's voice cheering in my brain, I marched past Keven, grabbed hold of the handle, and pulled open the heavy oak door.

A shrieking black form hurtled out of the dark, straight toward me.

I barely had time to register its slitted, glowing yellow eyes and razor-sharp talons before a four-legged shape shot past me and launched itself into the air with a snarl that turned my blood to ice. Feathers and fur dropped to the ground and rolled out of the light, with a duet of screeches and snarls, punctuated by screams of pain. A massive, clawed hand grasped my shoulder and yanked me back into the cottage.

House.

Castle.

Oh, hell.

The heavy oak door slammed shut.

CHAPTER 8

THE STONE HAND THAT PULLED ME TO SAFETY TURNED ME this way and that, as it might have a rag doll. Which was how I felt as I stood paralyzed by the horrible sounds filtering through the door, every bone in my body about as solid as an overcooked noodle.

"You're *certain* it didn't touch you?" the hand's owner fussed for at least the fourteenth time. "Not even a feather?"

My head flopped in a nod, also for the fourteenth time. I flinched from a shriek outside the door.

"I'm fine," I croaked. Because apart from losing the capacity to stand on my own, I was. I might be stark raving mad, but thanks to whatever had shot past me to attack the other whatever, I would at least live to tell the tale. I swallowed a burble of hysteria. Sucked in a breath. Wrapped trembling arms around a shaking body. I had questions. So many questions.

I shrugged off the gargoyle's touch, relieved when I didn't fall flat on my face as a result, and opened my mouth. But another shriek cut me off, and then—

Silence.

My heart lodged in my throat and, involuntarily, I stepped closer to the gargoyle's hulking stone presence, stumbling as my feet tangled in something soft. I looked down at a pile of vaguely familiar clothing: dark pants, a white shirt—

Lucan. My head snapped around in search of the man I'd all but forgotten. He was nowhere to be found.

"Kev—"

Something thudded against the door, and my intended query ended in a wheeze. The gargoyle crouched in front of me, muscles bunched and ready to spring. Heavy oak swung inward.

A bloodied and very naked Lucan swayed on the doorstep,

man-bun gone and long hair in disarray about his shoulders. He braced one hand against the doorframe. The other, he pressed against a gash in his belly.

"It's dead," he announced, "but there were two, and one got away."

"Damnation," muttered Keven, straightening up. "How did they find her here?"

"I don't know. But they'll be back." Lucan stepped into the hallway. Blood seeped between his fingers and dripped to the flagstone floor. "I'll need healing."

"Of course." Keven turned to me. "See him into the parlor"—a clawed hand pointed at the door to the left of the staircase—"and seat him by the fire. I'll be back in a few minutes."

"What? No! He needs to go to a hospital," I objected. "He needs stitches—and antibiotics—and there may be internal damage, and—"

Keven's broad head shook. "You really don't know anything, do you?" the gargoyle muttered. "See him to the fire. I'll be back."

"But—" I tried again, but Keven had already lumbered away, down the dark hallway beside the stairs. I stared after the retreating form, trying to gather my wits and sort through what had just happened—including why Lucan's clothes sat on the floor at my feet, while he stood naked and bleeding by the door. Because what I thought might have happened—what it looked like had happened—

It just couldn't have.

"Milady?" a deep voice prompted.

I didn't want to respond—and I really, really didn't want to turn around to face him again—but the man was injured. And he'd maybe had something to do with saving my life just now, although I had no idea how he fit in with what I thought I'd seen go past me into the night, and—

I stooped and picked up his clothing, then thrust it at him.

Or at least in his general direction, because I refused to look at him again in his current state. I was no prude, but neither was I comfortable with casual nudity, especially when it came packaged in the kind of muscled hardness that—injury or no injury—made a long-dormant libido sit up and take notice the way mine was doing.

"Press that against the wound," I ordered. "It will slow the bleeding."

The clothing left my grasp, and I marched over to the door Keven had indicated and tugged it open. The room beyond was spacious, but without the cavernous feel of the great hall. With dark wood paneling lining the walls and a fire crackling in a stone fireplace between two overstuffed couches, it felt downright cozy. Welcoming. Familiar. I shook off the last, stray thought and stood back for Lucan to precede me into the room, careful to stay out of touching distance—for all the good it did.

I could have been blind and still been aware of the masculinity passing me. Hyper aware, because holy Mother of God, that man packed a powerful presence. And was he *laughing* at me?

He stopped halfway through the door, inches away. He'd pressed the clothing bundle against his belly as directed, with the happy bonus of covering at least part of his nether region. Not that I was looking, I reminded myself.

"I don't bite, you know," he said, amusement lacing his rumble. "At least, not unless I have to. Or unless I'm asked."

My gaze flew to meet his, skimming powerful shoulders and the woodsy-smelling chest hair along the way. A wave of heat climbed up from my toes. "You should sit," I said, ignoring the innuendo. "Like he said."

"He?"

"The gargoyle."

Lucan blanched and shot a look down the corridor—a look that could only be described as panicked. "Ssh!" he hissed. "By the Morrigan's own magic, don't let her hear you!"

"Let who hear me?"

"The gargoyle!"

I blinked. "Keven is female?"

"And extraordinarily touchy about being called male." Lucan still watched the hallway down which the gargoyle had disappeared. "She also has an impressive temper. You wouldn't want to see the last person who made that mistake."

I tried to process this new information. "But Keven is..."

"A male name? I know. So does she. But she insisted on choosing it. It's a long story." He winced and clamped the clothing a little tighter against his belly. Fresh crimson bloomed through the white shirt.

Guilt stabbed at me. He really should be off his feet. I could reconcile the idea of a female gargoyle named Keven later.

My inner voice snorted. *A walking, talking, living female gargoyle named Keven*, it corrected. *Who chose her own name.*

"Fine," I said. "Then you should sit down the way *she* said."

Lucan's tawny, gray-streaked head shook, and my fingers itched to straighten the tangle of hair. I put my hands behind my back.

"Actually, she said you were to seat me," Lucan corrected, "which means you're supposed to help."

Even though my hormones did cartwheels at the thought of offering my body as support for his very naked one, I lifted my chin and replied tartly (and wisely, I thought), "I'm quite sure you're capable."

"Perhaps. But I did just save your life."

I opened my mouth to argue that it had been no man who had gone past me into the night, but my gaze dropped to the clothing he held instead of wearing, and the words died on my lips. Impossible...

Lucan chuckled and made his own way to a sofa, treating me to a well-muscled rear view. I blushed again. Dear Lord, I'd had more licentious thoughts in the past half hour than I'd had in my last twenty years of marriage—and about a man many years my junior, no less. I really needed to get my mind back on more important matters. Such as the brain tumor that might be killing me even as my imagination ran wild.

On the other hand, if you're going to go anyway, at least you'd go happy, my less-than-helpful Edie-voice suggested.

I told it to get stuffed and, on my way to join Lucan, grabbed a blanket that was folded over the back of the couch. I shook it out and draped it over his half-prone form. When I'd covered as much of him as I could without touching him, I turned to the fireplace, prodded the embers to life with the poker, and added a log to the flames. Then I took a seat on the edge of the opposite sofa, grasped my courage in both hands, and met his gaze. It was time for answers.

"What was that thing outside?" I asked. "And what attacked it?"

"Later," Keven said, stumping into the room with a bowl clamped in one hand, a steaming mug in the other, and a towel draped over one bulky shoulder. "He needs rest."

He—she handed the mug to Lucan, who slanted an oblique look at him—her.

"She needs to know."

"And she will. But not now." Keven set the bowl on the low table between the couches.

I leaned over to peer at the dark green mash in the bowl, wrinkling my nose at the stringent odor rising from it. "What is that?"

"Heal-all," Keven said. "You may know it as woundwort."

I didn't. "You're going to put that on the wound? But infection—" I fell silent under the stony gaze.

"You have much to learn," the gargoyle said. "But for now, watch and let me work."

Keven peeled away the blanket from Lucan, then the bloodied bundle of clothes, *tsking* as the wound was exposed. "How bad is it?"

The question seemed an odd one, given the obvious severity

of the injury. Lucan's cryptic, tight-lipped answer was even more so.

"I suggest you double up on the good stuff."

Keven nodded and stretched a heavy hand over the bowl. Eyes closed, she murmured unintelligible words. The air in the room changed. Shifted. Thickened. My gaze flicked over the wood-paneled perimeter, but I saw nothing. Only felt it as it lifted the hair on my arms and turned my breathing shallow. The bowl's contents glowed neon and bubbled thickly, spattering onto the table. I scooted back on the couch seat, as far away from it as the leather would allow.

Keven opened her eyes. She sniffed the bowl and gave a grunt of satisfaction. "Better," she said. She scooped up a handful of the goop and turned to Lucan. "Ready?"

Lucan nodded, his expression grim. Keven put her free hand on his shoulder and, before I could muster another objection about infection, slapped the green sludge onto his belly. Its effect was instantaneous.

The open flesh of the wound smoked and sizzled, and Lucan's entire body convulsed as he tried to lunge to his feet. The gargoyle held him in place, her expression impassive. A snarl filled the room, deep, guttural, inhuman—and unmistakably coming from the man on the couch. A man whose body shifted and dissolved into smoke and, for the space of a single, staccato heartbeat, became...something else.

Something other.

Something four-legged and fur-covered and...

At last, hysteria won.

Wolf! I thought. *He just turned into a wolf!*

And then Lucan the man returned, the amber gaze met mine, and what little remained of my normal turned inside out and upside down.

CHAPTER 9

I REGARDED THE MUG KEVEN HELD OUT TO ME FOR A LONG moment before I poked a hand from under the blanket to accept it. A faintly floral scent rose from the pale liquid within.

"Chamomile," Keven said, her voice gruff. "For calm."

Calm. Still laced with traces of hysteria, my inner voice (the Claire one, not the Edie one) laughed at the idea. *As if.*

I sipped the herbal tea anyway, and a heavy sweetness curled over my tongue, washing away the remains of the bowl of stew Keven had insisted I eat.

"And honey," the gargoyle added. "For shock."

Now that, I could get on board with.

"Thank you," I said. I sat at a rough-hewn wooden table in the center of a large kitchen, where Keven had brought me after settling Lucan into bed upstairs. Dried herbs hung from the rafters above the table, whose knife-scarred surface marked it as a well-used workspace. A wood-fired stove sat against one stone wall. A long counter ran along the length of another. Above it, a window was flanked by open shelves filled with dishes.

Almost everything in the house was built of either stone or wood, and while steady light glowed from an iron chandelier suspended in the middle of the herbs, I had yet to see a light switch or other evidence of wiring. I gripped the mug with both hands, trying to use the heat against my palms to ground my rampant thoughts and quell the flicker of uncertainty at my core. Clinging to the cup as I did to the shreds of my sanity, I closed my eyes.

Lights with no electrical source. An address that didn't exist. A house that was bigger on the inside than out. Winged creatures that attacked in the night. A man who shifted from human form to wolf and back again. Herbal mixtures that bubbled and smoked and healed almost on contact. A walking, talking, living gargoyle named Keven. Tea hot enough to burn my hands.

One of those things I knew to be real. And if one was real, then the others...

I squeezed my eyelids together, setting off tiny sparks of light behind them. "I'm not crazy, am I?" I murmured. "This—all of this—it's real, isn't it?"

"It is." Keven's voice was quiet, too.

"But how?" I opened my eyes to find the gargoyle shaking her head at me.

"Not tonight, milady. There's much to tell, and you've had enough for one day."

With a suddenness—and violence—that shocked me, I decided I was tired of having others direct my life. I'd been putting my own questions and concerns on hold—putting *myself* on hold—for as long as I could remember. I'd been the good daughter, the good wife, the good mother and neighbor and churchgoer and committee member and citizen and everything else that had been required of me, all as expected. All without asking questions.

And where had it gotten me? A divorce from a husband who'd cheated on me, a son I'd trained not to listen to me, a level of invisibility that was downright depressing, and a life so routine that the slightest deviation from it terrified me.

I banged the mug onto the table hard enough to slosh liquid from it. Cool air slithered across my shoulders as the blanket dropped from them.

"No," I said. "I want to know."

Keven reached over to tuck the blanket over my shoulders again. "You're sure?"

Not even a little.

"I'm sure."

A slow incline of the wide stone head. "Very well. Ask your questions."

Where did I even start? I studied the worn wooden tabletop.

Looked at the woodstove. The chandelier. Gestured at the room in general. "The house. The gate. The address. You."

Keven pondered for a moment, then said, "Address first. The number thirteen is the return of the divine feminine—you—to the service of the goddess Morrigan. Morrigan's Way. Thirteen is a prime number, and so it is incorruptible. It helps to protect the house. Your house."

My—? Goddess—? My brain balked again at too much information. I took a mental breath. First things first. "How did it get into my newspaper?"

"It was made visible to you as Crone now that you've come of age."

"Come of *age*?" I laughed without humor. "I'm sixty years old!"

Keven nodded. "Yes. The age of wisdom and power."

There was too much to argue with in the idea, and so I waved it away with a vague sweep of my hand. "Whatever. Go on. The gate next—and you."

"The gate is just a gate, but it can be seen only by a Crone, and it can be opened only by a pendant. Just as the address can only be revealed by a pendant."

"And no one else can find it?" *No one but a Crone.*

"Not without your will."

Another too-big idea. "And you?"

"I am part of the house. I look after it. I look after you. And because you have been given no knowledge..." Keven trailed off, scowling. Then she sighed. "I will teach you what I am able to."

"Teach me what?"

Keven sighed again, with the sound of wind whistling through a canyon. "Magic," she said. "I will teach you magic."

That word again. It hung in the kitchen between us, as if strung up with the dried herbs above the table, silent, waiting for me to react. I stared at Keven. Keven stared back. The herbs waited some more.

I shook my head. "No," I croaked. I cleared my throat and

repeated in a firmer, albeit somewhat high-pitched, voice, "No. Magic isn't real. It's illusion. Sleight of hand. Pretend."

"Not that kind of magic," Keven said. "Magick with a 'k.' This." She waved from side to side in a gesture that encompassed the kitchen in a house in the woods that no one else could find. "Lucan. Me. You. The ones who have come before you."

I clung to the mug of chamomile tea with both hands and gazed down at the sediment in its depths. *No. It has to be something else,* my panicked Claire-voice insisted. *It has to be dementia...brain damage...anything except what she's saying.*

A giggle burbled up inside me and escaped before I could stop it. Right. Anything except what the talking gargoyle said. Because that totally made more sense than accepting what the talking gargoyle *did* say.

"Are you in distress?" Keven asked.

"I—" I looked up from my study of the tea's sediment, which had gathered into the vague shape of two numerals in the bottom of the mug, a one and a three. I swallowed. "I don't know," I whispered. "I honestly don't know."

The massive head shook. "I knew it would be too much tonight. Come. I'll show you to your room, and we can talk more in the morning."

I wanted to object, wanted—desperately—to stand up and run home to my own bed, to my cat, to my nice, safe reality. But Lucan's words from the great hall whispered through me, holding me back.

"There were two, and one got away."

"Lady Claire?"

I flinched from the name, but I couldn't find it in me to object. To anything. Not anymore. Not tonight.

I nodded. "Yes," I said. "We'll talk in the morning."

Keven led the way up a set of stairs hidden behind a door just outside the kitchen—because what seemingly tiny cottage in the woods didn't need two sets of stairs to a second floor that shouldn't exist? We continued down a hallway past several doors.

Wall sconces lit up along the walls as we approached and extinguished as we passed, but I couldn't be bothered to wonder why or how.

Any brain cells that remained after turning sixty had been fried by the day's events, I decided. Perhaps they would recover after a good night's sleep; perhaps they wouldn't.

Turning sixty had apparently killed my ability to care, too.

By the time Keven opened the last door on the right, all I could think about was the oblivion that came with unconsciousness. And then I stepped past the gargoyle and into the room, and found a home I had been missing all my life.

The room was both massive and intimate at the same time, with a soaring, coffered ceiling and walls of stone and wood paneling that should have made it dark but didn't. An enormous four-poster bed stood to one side, flanked by two nightstands with glowing lamps on them, and a plain, uncarved chest at its foot. Opposite the door, the stone wall held a large, recessed window with a cushioned seat running its length and heavy, green velvet drapes hanging on either side. A leather wingback chair to my right sat before a crackling fire in a floor-to-ceiling fireplace.

With its bare floorboards, unadorned walls, and simply built furniture, the room was almost austere, but it drew me in and wrapped around me with a comfort that encouraged me to breathe deeply for the first time since—

Well. I couldn't even remember.

"You like it," Keven said, and she sounded pleased.

"I do," I responded, surprising myself by smiling at the gargoyle. A genuine smile, not one of the ones I'd perfected to fool others—and myself—into believing I was happy even when I wasn't. "Very much," I added.

The gargoyle lumbered into the room and opened the mirrored door of a wardrobe near the bed.

"There are night things here for you," she said, one claw pointing to a white cotton nightgown hanging from a hook in the back. "And a change of clothes for morning if you wish it." The claw indicated a garment on the next hook that looked to me like a dark blue version of the nightgown.

She crossed to the bed and pointed to a rope that emerged from the wall over one nightstand. "Ring the bell when you wake, and I will bring your tea and breakfast."

I doubted I would stick around long enough in the morning for tea or anything else—because surely whatever had come at me out of the night would have disappeared by daybreak and I could go home, right? But I suspected telling Keven so would precipitate another conversation I didn't want to have right now. So I made myself smile again, not as genuinely this time, and nodded. Then, for good measure, I added a thank you, even as my gaze drifted toward the bed with its simple white draperies drawn back and a veritable cloud of a duvet spread across it.

"You're tired," Keven's voice was gruff. "I'll leave you to your sleep." She turned to go and then paused to indicate a closed door beside the fireplace. "I almost forgot. Your personal facility is through there. If you need anything, the bell will summon me."

Bidding me a good night, she stepped into the hallway and closed the door behind her.

I stared after her, breathing in the faint smell of woodsmoke and thinking about the day that had brought me here. To a house in the woods where time seemed to have frozen centuries ago, where a gargoyle lived with a man who could turn into a wolf and lights went on and off by themselves, and winged creatures lay in wait for me in the night. My mind skipped from one thing to another like a little metal ball in a pinball machine, changing direction with dizzying speed and careening off metaphorical barriers and bumpers as it set off lights and bells and—

I exhaled a long, slow, shaky breath. Keven was right. I needed sleep. But first, a visit to the personal facility, which I hoped meant what I thought it did, because I suddenly, desperately needed to pee.

Not without trepidation—because what kind of facilities had existed at the time this house was built?—I crossed the room to the door beside the fireplace, twisted the knob, and pushed it open onto another shock.

No dark and primitive corner, the bathroom gleamed and sparkled with white and chrome and glass. A porcelain sink in a granite countertop beside a modern, low-profile toilet; a claw-foot tub cozied up to a separate shower stall, thick white towels hanging from a towel bar...

I waited for astonishment to set in, but my brain shrugged, my inner voice mumbled, *"Huh,"* and that was it.

I really had run out of reaction capacity.

I regarded my reflection in the mirror over the sink. The same lines I'd studied this morning were still there, as were the gray hair and the softness around my jawline. *It's me,* I thought. But it wasn't. Something had changed. Something I couldn't put my finger on.

That would also have to wait until tomorrow.

I used the unsurprising toilet, washed my hands in the unsurprising sink, gave the unsurprising tub and the thick white towels a long, wistful look, and then returned to the bedroom to collapse, still dressed, on top of the cloud-like duvet.

Not until sleep closed over me did I register Keven's word to me in the kitchen: *a* pendant. The gate could be opened by *a* pendant.

As in, I didn't have the only one.

CHAPTER 10

I WOKE ONCE DURING THE NIGHT, WHEN A NOISE IN THE hallway penetrated the haze of sleep and prompted me to stagger out of bed and crack open the door. A single sconce came on as I did, casting a pool of light over the wall and onto the floor. The corridor stretched beyond it, dark and empty.

I started to close the door, but the noise came again, like the shifting of someone—or something—against the floor. I stared into the shadows outside the sconce's pool of light. Then I saw them.

Unblinking amber eyes, watching me.

Adrenaline jolted through me. I caught my breath, stumbling a half-step back, my grip tight on the door, braced for attack. But the eyes remained where they were, and slowly I picked out the shape behind them. A wolf shape, curled up in a ball, tail tucked around its legs.

Lucan? The name hovered on my lips, but I couldn't bring myself to speak it. I held the wolf's gaze for another moment, then closed the door and padded back to bed. Again I stayed dressed, but this time I slipped off the pendant and placed it on the night table, removed my shoes, and crawled beneath the duvet instead of lying on top of it. Then, feeling oddly safe, I went back to sleep.

When I woke again, the fire had gone out, the bedroom was cold, and the promise of daylight crept in around the edges of the curtains pulled across the window. For the breath of an instant, in the stillness of early morning, I almost believed I was at home, in my own house, with Merlin on the front porch, waiting to come in for his breakfast.

My heart contracted at the latter thought. The poor cat had already missed yesterday's dinner. He would be frantic if I didn't open the door at the usual seven a.m. Not to mention seriously annoyed.

And Merlin could hold a grudge for days.

I steeled myself to abandon the duvet's fluffy warmth for air chilly enough to make my nose cold to the touch. If I was quick, I could leave before Keven and Lucan woke and derailed my going-home plan with more weirdness. And when I got there, I could call Gilbert and tell him to come pick up his damned pendant. Better yet, I'd just drop it in his mailbox on my way.

I threw back the covers and swung my feet out of bed. Then I stopped. Wait. What about the wolf outside the door? What if it was still there? And what if it was really Luc—no. No, in the cold light of day and with a good sleep behind me, I was willing to accept that I might have seen a dog—maybe even an actual wolf—but I drew the line at the idea that it was man who could turn *into* a wolf.

Right, Claire, chided my Edie-voice. *Because that's so much more far-fetched than the walking, talking gargoyle.*

I wanted to tell it to shut up, but arguing out loud with an inner voice—no matter who that voice belonged to—seemed right up there on the best-avoided-because-maybe-dementia list. So I ignored it instead and, grimacing at hips stiff from yesterday's extended walk, reached for my running shoes. I tied them onto my feet, slipped the pendant's chain over my head, and tiptoed to the door. I needed to pee something fierce, and I could just imagine what my hair looked like, but every passing second increased the chances of Lucan and/or Keven getting in the way and—

"Good morning, milady," rumbled a voice.

I yelped in surprise, berating myself even as the sound emerged. I really wished I could stop squeaking like some damsel in distress. I glared at Lucan. "*Must* you do that?"

He looked down at himself, then over each shoulder. "Do what?"

I flapped an irritated hand at him. "Sneak up on me like

that."

"By waiting outside your door?"

I scowled, remembering the wolf that had been there last night. "That's even worse. It's...stalking."

He shrugged. "I can't protect you if I'm not here."

There was that word again: *protect*.

Nope. Not asking.

I pointed at his belly. "How is it this morning?"

Lucan hiked up his shirt to expose his wound and the six-pack I had seen last night. Or was it an eight-pack? I ignored my Edie-voice's suggestion that I count to be sure and focused on the wound itself, or what remained of it. The thin line, edged in a healthy pink, looked nothing like the gaping slash that had been there last night. I frowned. "But it—it looks healed."

"Keven is very good." Lucan let the shirt fall into place. It was another like he'd worn the day before: loose, with an unlaced v-opening instead of buttons, a wide collar, and full, drop-shoulder sleeves that ended in cuffs at his wrists. A poet's shirt, I thought it was called, though Lucan didn't strike me as the poetic type.

I wrenched my attention back to him as he continued, "And speaking of Keven, I've been sent to see if you want breakfast served in your chamber or the dining hall."

I shook my head. "I'm not hungry, thank you. I'll eat when I get home."

"You are home."

"Wh—" I clamped my lips shut. *Not asking*. "I meant my own home. Where I live."

"You live here now."

My heart stuttered. Was Lucan saying what I thought he was? I remembered how no one knew where I had gone. In a voice I couldn't quite keep from trembling, I asked, "Are you telling me I can't leave? That I'm a prisoner here?"

His guffaw made me blink. "Of course not. This is your house, milady. You may come and go as you please."

My knees wobbled in relief. I gripped the door handle and made myself stand straighter. "Then it pleases me to go," I said. "Now."

He shrugged. "As you wish. I'll let Keven know, and I'll meet you in the great hall."

"Meet—?" I began, but he was already gone, disappearing through the door to the back stairs. I stared after him for a moment, then galvanized myself into movement. I hadn't liked the sound of that *meet you* part, and I had no intention of sticking around to argue it.

Still needing to pee—more now than ever—I closed the bedroom door and scuttled down the hallway toward the other stairs, the ones that descended into the front entryway. I was determined to be out the door before Lucan got there. And trying hard not to think about what had been waiting outside for me the night before.

Daylight, I reminded myself, running down the stairs as fast as I dared. It was daylight now, and whatever that thing had been, it was almost certainly long gone by now.

Two of them, my memory whispered as I reached the flagstone floor of the enormous foyer. I shrugged it off. The smell of bacon drifting down the corridor from the kitchen was a little harder to ignore. I salivated. Then I squared my shoulders, crossed to the door, and twisted the knob. I'd pee under a tree along the deserted road, if I had to, but I wasn't staying here any longer. I eased open the heavy oak.

"Lucan says you want to leave." Keven scowled at me from the sunlit walkway outside.

I managed to hold back the squawk of surprise this time—barely—and stepped out onto the porch. "I *am* leaving," I corrected. "I'm going home. To *my* house."

"You saw what tried to attack you last night. One survived. It will bring others, and it will find you."

"I'll stay inside after dark."

Keven crossed her arms across a carved torso. "Your house is not warded. This one is."

"My house is fine."

She scowled. "I cannot teach you there."

"I don't want to learn anything."

She sighed. "You must learn. You are Crone."

"I am a sixty-year-old woman with a home and a family and a life," I corrected, ignoring the whispered *"Liar!"* in my brain that followed my declaration. Living with Edie's voice inside my head was becoming seriously annoying. "And I want to go back to them."

Keven's massive head moved from side to side, and I would have sworn the gargoyle was sad—if gargoyles could be sad.

Or alive.

"You cannot run away from this, Lady Claire. You are Crone, whether you wish it or not. The magick in you cannot be stopped; it can only be directed. Trained."

I took an involuntary step back, and now my own head shook in denial. "I have no magick."

The gargoyle's mouth stretched into a grimace that may or may not have been a grin, and she rumbled with something that may or may not have been amusement. A large, clawed hand waved in a gesture that encompassed our surroundings. "Milady, you have found your house, brought me to life, and called your protector to you. What do you call that, if not magick?"

My lips compressed, and I crossed my arms. "I didn't do any of those things," I retorted. "At least, not on purpose."

"Exactly," agreed Keven. "Now imagine what you could do *with* purpose."

"I can go home."

The gargoyle regarded me for a long moment before heaving a sigh. "Very well. If you insist, I cannot stop you. You may return here each day for lessons, beginning tomorrow."

"Fine," I said, having no intention of doing so. The sooner I dropped the pendant in Gilbert's mailbox, the better.

Shaking her head again, Keven stepped aside, her feet

sinking into the grass. Her gaze shifted to above my shoulder, and she said, "You'll need to be extra vigilant."

"Of course," came Lucan's deep voice, and my mouth dropped open.

"No," I sputtered, whirling to face him. "Absolutely not. You are *not* coming with me."

"I must, milady," he said. "I am your—"

"I don't want a protector." I fought hard not to sound like a petulant five-year-old. Or to stamp my foot for emphasis. A bumblebee droned past my nose, its body heavy with pollen. The morning was already warm, and I wanted to be back at my house before the real heat of the day.

I wanted to be back at my house, period.

By myself.

"I'm afraid that part is not negotiable, Lady Claire," Keven said. "Your protector has no choice but to follow where you go. It's what he does. What he *is*."

I wanted to refuse. Wanted to argue. Wanted to throw a temper tantrum, if necessary. But looking between the implacable gargoyle and the equally implacable Lucan, I knew there was no point. Whatever I said or did, Lucan would be coming home with me, and if I didn't let him into the house, he would sit on the porch where my neighbors and family could see him, and...

"Fine," I snapped. "But you stay out of sight, understand?"

He smiled and bowed. "As you wish, milady."

And stop bowing and stop calling me milady, I wanted to add, but then what would he call me? Claire? I eyed the broad shoulders beneath the poet's shirt, remembered the ten-pack and the tickle of woodsy chest hair against my nose, and—very wisely, I thought—kept my objection to myself as I turned and stalked back into the house.

"I'll be back in a minute," I growled over my shoulder. Because if I wasn't going to escape unnoticed, I might as well pee before I left.

CHAPTER 11

I ALMOST GOT LUCAN INTO MY HOUSE UNSEEN. ALMOST.

I retrieved the key from its hiding place under a potted plant, inserted it into the lock, twisted it, and—

"Claire!" The exclamation stopped me mid door-push, and I bit back a groan. If I had to get caught sneaking a man into my house, why couldn't it at least have been Edie who did the catching, instead of Jeanne?

At least Edie might approve of the idea. Jeanne, on the other hand...

Play it cool, Claire. I withdrew the key from the lock and turned, smiling my best at her and angling my body in front of Lucan. I didn't have a hope of hiding someone that much taller and broader than me, but...well, I could dream.

"Jeanne," I said cheerily. "Hi. How have you been?"

I knew the question was wrong the second I uttered it. Even before Jeanne peered over her glasses at me or the crow sitting in the maple beside the porch *haw-hawed* in rusty amusement. I shot it a baleful look; Jeanne seemed not to notice it.

"Since the day before yesterday, you mean?" she asked.

"Ha! Of course. It was just then, wasn't it? Silly me." *For God's sake, Claire, stop babbling.* "Did you need something?"

Jeanne crossed her arms. "You're kidding, right? You do know that half the neighborhood is out looking for you, *right?*"

"I..." I trailed off, taken aback by the announcement. I honestly hadn't thought anyone would notice my absence that soon. Did Paul know, too? I groaned inwardly. If he did, then so did Natalie, and—God, I'd be in a long-term care facility by sundown, if she had her way.

The crow in the tree ruffled its feathers. My across-the-street neighbor tapped the fingers of one hand against the tanned skin of her other forearm, waiting for me to continue. Not for the first time, I thought about how she would have been as good a high school principal as Edie, just with a different approach. Where Edie had ruled with iron, Jeanne would have relied—effectively, I might add—on sheer guilt. I pitied the poor nurses who worked under her watchful eye at the hospital.

"Well?" she asked, and I jumped a little.

"I'm fine," I said. "As you can see. There was nothing to worry about."

Jeanne's sharp gaze flashed fire. "Nothing to..." She reached out, seized my arm, and towed me to the end of the long porch, turning her back to Lucan. "Nothing to worry about?" she hissed. "You *never* stay out all night. Of *course* we were worried. Gilbert and I both were. And so were Edie and Paul and Natalie, when I called them to ask if they'd seen you!"

Which answered my earlier question. My groan this time was audible. "You didn't have to call them, Jeanne. I am a grown woman, you know."

As for Gilbert, the only thing he would have been worried about was the pendant.

"Claire. *You stayed out all night.* And then you brought home a *man*." The queen of dramatic emphasis dropped her voice to a whisper, but the curve of Lucan's lips told me he'd still heard her. Awesome. "A *strange* man."

Lady, you have no idea.

"He's a—friend," I said.

"A friend," she echoed. "From where?"

"Um..." *Dear God, Claire, think! House, trees, woods...* "Camping!" I said triumphantly. "I met him while we were camping once. He was in town and looked me up."

"You haven't been camping in more than twenty years. What was he, fifteen at the time?"

Ouch. I scowled at her. "Shouldn't you be calling off the search?"

"What search?"

"Half the neighborhood?"

"Oh. That. I may have exaggerated a little. But we were going to get one going if you hadn't come back by this afternoon. I told Paul he should file a missing person's report. You need to call him. *Now.* And then you need to tell me what the heck is going on." She jerked her head in Lucan's direction. "Where *were* you?"

"I—" I stopped. It hadn't occurred to me to come up with some kind of story on the way home, and I was a lousy liar at the best of times—which this was not. I had no idea what to say.

"She was with me," Lucan said, crossing the porch to join us. He smiled down at Jeanne, his manner easy, eyes crinkling at the corners. He held out his hand as he introduced himself. "Lucan."

He didn't give a last name, and a bemused Jeanne didn't ask for one as he lifted the hand she gave him and bent low to kiss it. Jeanne gaped. So did I. *This* was how he greeted people? I definitely had to keep him out of sight. I wedged myself between them and guided Jeanne toward the stairs.

"I'd better call Paul," I said, by way of excuse. "I'm sorry I worried you, but I really was fine."

My neighbor snorted at me. "There's no way you're getting off that lightly, Claire Emerson. This—that—" She waved a hand in Lucan's direction and dropped her voice. "A strange man? Out all night? You're behaving as oddly as Gilbert, I swear."

The crow cawed again.

"Gilbert?" My voice was sharper than I intended, the kitchen incident from my birthday still fresh in my mind. "What does Gilbert have to do with this?"

She drew back a little in surprise. "Nothing, really. He's just...antsy, I guess is the word. And he *hates* cats."

I liked Jeanne. Or at least, I tried to. Most of the time. But sometimes, trying to follow her line of thought was rather like trying to catch a ping pong ball that had spiked in an unexpected direction. "Cats?" I echoed.

"What?" She was back to eyeing Lucan in semibemusement.

"You said Gilbert hates cats." This wasn't news in and of itself; all the neighborhood felines knew to avoid the Archambault yard or risk having unknown projectiles flung at them. "What's odd about that?"

"He insisted on coming over to feed yours this morning and spent a half hour visiting with it."

"Inside my house? Alone?"

"Well, he couldn't very well feed him anywhere else, could he? And I didn't have time to come with him." She glanced at the watch on her wrist and *tsked* under her breath. "Speaking of time, I'm going to be late for my shift. You're sure you're all right?" She tipped her head toward Lucan and waggled her eyebrows at me.

My brain was still dancing around the idea of Gilbert coming into my home uninvited. Had he gone through the house, looking for Merlin? Been upstairs? In my room, even? My skin crawled. I was going to need my key back from Jeanne. Soon.

"Claire?" Jeanne prompted. "*Are* you all right?"

Lucan had come to stand at my shoulder, a solid presence that managed to somehow be both annoying and reassuring at the same time. I nodded, trying not to act as distracted as I felt, lest Jeanne report my behavior to Paul. But it was hard to get past the Gilbert-in-my-house idea because seriously...ick.

"I'm fine," I said. "Really. This is a whole lot of fuss about nothing. Now, you get off to work, and let me call Paul before there really is a search party out looking for me."

"If you're sure..." She trailed off, still not convinced. Then she brightened. "I'll let Edie know you're home, and that you have...company. At least then you'll have someone keeping an eye out for you." This last part was addressed more as a warning

76

to Lucan than a reassurance to me, and it almost made me smile.

Almost.

But in the same instant, the crow moved in the tree, drawing my attention to it. It watched me, the expression in its beady black eye seeming expectant, as if it waited for something. Waited for me. But to do what? My fingers found the pendant hanging from my neck and closed over it. I couldn't shake the feeling I was missing something. Something obvious. Something—

I stared at the bird. Then at the living room window overlooking the porch. The one where Merlin sat when I went out, watching for my return—always. But not today. A slither went down my spine. If Merlin wasn't in the window, he wasn't in the house. And if he wasn't in the house, then Gilbert—

The pendant's edges bit into my fingers as realization dropped. Gilbert hadn't been here for the cat at all. The snake had been after the pendant because I'd refused to sell it back to him. And here I'd been planning to give it back to him. I'd almost followed through on my plan to drop it in his mailbox, but I'd been too concerned about someone seeing Lucan.

The little creep.

Gilbert, not Lucan. I'd sooner—

"If you don't say goodbye," Lucan's deep, warm voice murmured in my ear, "she'll never leave."

I jolted back to the present and found Jeanne staring at me in concern. Her head shook.

"I'm not sure I should leave you like—"

"Jeanne, I'm fine. Seriously. I'm just a little tired. It was—" *Don't say it, Claire. You know she'll take it the wrong way.*

On the other hand, it would ensure her swift departure, too.

"It was a long night," I said. "You know."

Poor Jeanne. Her eyes went wide, her jaw went slack, and her mouth formed a perfect 'o' that told me I'd offended her every fiber. Our tepid friendship had barely survived my divorce as it was. I wasn't sure it would withstand my becoming a loose woman.

On the other hand, if she was going to make a habit of allowing her husband to go into my house uninvited, I wasn't sure I wanted it to.

I wasn't sure about a lot of things anymore.

"I see." Jeanne's tone was clipped. "Well. I'll get out of your way then, shall I? I'm so sorry to have bothered you."

I watched her stiff figure descend the stairs and march across the street. I had a momentary urge to run after her and explain that it wasn't how it sounded—wasn't what I'd meant. But I didn't. This new sixties' lack of giving a darn was growing on me. Edie would be pleased.

With a last harsh caw, the crow left the tree and winged its way down the street.

CHAPTER 12

INSIDE THE HOUSE, I UNTIED MY SHOES AND KICKED THEM off, then dropped my keys on the front hall table and went through to the kitchen, leaving Lucan to follow or not, as he pleased. He did, and I ignored him as I let in an indignant and very hungry Merlin through the back door. As suspected, Gilbert had absolutely not fed him.

The orange cat sashayed into the kitchen, wrapped once around my ankles, and then noticed Lucan. With an unearthly yowl, he made a beeline for the top of the refrigerator. A copper bowl of fruit went flying in his wake, and an overripe banana plopped onto the counter while apples, oranges, and bowl rolled across the floor in all directions.

"Seriously, dude?" I picked up the dented bowl and collected the scattered fruit, scowling up at the animal. Twice his usual size, Merlin growled in reply, then spat at the stranger in his house for good measure.

Lucan looked equally unimpressed. He handed me an apple. "Is he always like this?"

"Actually, no. I'm not sure—" The phrase "fight like cats and dogs" popped into my head, and I stopped. My scowl deepened. *Still not going there*, I reminded myself. I picked up the banana, now mushy within its skin, and dropped it into the compost bin. "He's probably just mad at me for not being here to feed him."

"Your neighbor said—"

"I know what she said," I snapped. Then I sighed. I put the bowl of fruit on the counter, out of the path of Merlin when he decided to descend from his perch. "I'm sorry. I didn't mean to bite your head off. It's just—Jeanne's husband and I..."

"You don't like him."

"Not even a little. But it's more than that. I don't think he was here to feed Merlin. I think he was looking for this." I withdrew the pendant from beneath my shirt and held it up. It twirled gently from the chain still looped around my neck. Lucan's gaze locked on it, then lifted to meet mine.

"How does he know about it?"

"He has an antique shop of sorts. Mostly junk. He buys estate lots from all over. This was in one of the lots, and Braden —my grandson—bought it from him as a birthday gift for me. Gilbert wants to buy it back from me. He says the estate heir didn't mean to sell it."

"But you don't believe him."

"Not that story, no. I think someone offered him a lot more money for it than what he got from Braden, but I don't think it has anything to do with an estate heir. Gilbert is..."

"Opportunistic?"

"Slimy." I crossed my arms over myself and leaned back against the counter, debating the wisdom of telling him more.

"Out with it," he said.

I traced a ceramic floor tile with the toe of one foot. "A man was here yesterday afternoon, before I went—before I found— well. Not here, exactly, but at Gilbert's. They were arguing. Gilbert slammed the door on him, and when he was leaving— the man, I mean—he stopped at the end of the driveway and stared across at my house. It was...unsettling."

Lucan seized my elbow and started out of the kitchen. "We need to leave."

"What? But we just got here!" I wrapped my fingers around the door frame and planted my feet against the floor.

Lucan glared over his shoulder at me, continuing to pull. "That was no ordinary man, milady. It was a Mage. Which means they know you have the pendant, and they know where you live. They followed you to the woods. That's how the shades found you there, and they'll find you here, too."

I put my full weight into resisting his tug on my arm. I was under no illusion that I could stop him from hauling me out of my house, but if he insisted on trying, I could at least make it hard enough that someone would notice. And, with luck, call for help.

"Stop," I said. "You can't possibly know who he was. Gilbert is less than popular in town—it could have been anyone with a bone to pick. Besides, if it were a Mage, why wouldn't he have just come over and demanded the pendant for himself?"

"A Mage on his own is no match for a Crone, milady. He would need ten times his number to even consider going up against one of you."

"But I can't—"

"They don't know that. You should—you were supposed to —" Lucan broke off and frowned, obviously looking for a gentle way to state the obvious.

"I'm a mistake," I said.

"An anomaly," he hedged.

I wasn't sure that was much better. I tugged my arm free. "Well, regardless, if they can find me in either place, I choose here. Go if you want, but I'm staying in my own home. I'm going to call my son, and then I'm taking a shower and getting changed, and then I'm going to have breakfast and go work in my garden."

He towered over me, glaring down. "You don't understand. I cannot protect you here. Not without your magick."

"No, *you* don't understand. I'm staying in my own house, Lucan." His name felt foreign as it rolled off my tongue, and I realized it was the first time I'd used it. I stepped away from the distraction, back to my argument. "A lot has happened in the last couple of days, and I need time to think. To process. And you just said that they won't attack me directly."

"I said one wouldn't attack you on his own," he corrected. "Who knows how many reinforcements he's gathered since yesterday?"

I considered the possibility, then shook my head. "Even if

there are others, I've never even heard of Mages or magick before yesterday, so I'm guessing they like to stay under the radar. And if that's the case, do you really think they'll attack me in broad daylight in my little suburban neighborhood?"

Lucan scowled at me in a way that made me think he didn't much like losing arguments. I scowled back because I'd recently discovered that I didn't like losing, either. And I really didn't like being ordered around in my own home.

"What about tonight?" he demanded. "When it's dark?"

"Suburban neighborhood," I repeated, crossing the fingers of my free hand behind my back. "And I'll stay inside with the windows and doors locked."

"And you won't change your mind." A statement rather than a question. He was finally getting it.

"No."

"Fine," he growled. "We stay one night. But you go nowhere without me."

"Except the shower."

"I'll wait outside the door."

With our parameters drawn, I followed through on my plan. First, a call to Paul to assure him I was fine, had spent the night at a friend's, and didn't need Natalie to come check on me. Then, upstairs to wash away the prior twenty-four hours. At least from my body.

True to his word, Lucan followed me and paced outside my bedroom door while I showered in the attached bathroom, dressed, and brushed my teeth. When I emerged in fresh linen slacks and a sleeveless navy blouse, he followed me back down to the kitchen to watch while I made coffee and tried—very hard—to go about my daily routine.

He didn't make it easy.

When I went to take out the blueberry jam for my toast, he opened the fridge door wider and leaned around me to peer at the contents and wrinkle his nose.

"That's a lot of vegetables."

I ducked under his arm, away from his too-closeness and a warmth that had no business fluttering in my sixty-year-old chest. "They're good for you."

Lucan grunted. "For you, maybe. What am I supposed to eat? If we were at Morrigan's Way, there would be meat."

"Feel free to leave anytime," I retorted, "given that I didn't invite you here in the first place." I didn't tell him about the freezer full of beef in the garage because yes, I was that petty right now.

"I told you, I go where you go." Lucan closed the fridge door and leaned against it to watch me, arms folded over his chest. "It's not a choice, it's a binding."

"A—" I clamped my lips shut against the question that almost escaped and turned my attention instead to the toast. In the shower, I'd re-re-thought my decision not to give Gilbert the pendant. If he wanted it badly enough to break into my house, and the Mages were willing to kill me for it, and I *didn't* want it, it was time to let go of my affronted senses and hand the darned thing over.

I didn't even want anything in return. I just wanted it out of my life. Gilbert would be happy; I could get my key back; Braden would recover; the Mages would go away; Lucan and Keven would have no choice but to find a new Crone; and I...I could return to my tidy and blessedly uneventful life, purpose be darned.

Boring life, my Edie-voice corrected.

Better bored than dead, my own voice retorted, scooping a glob of jam from the jar and plopping it onto my toast. Lucan leaned past my shoulder, picked up the toast and sniffed it, then took a large bite and chewed.

"It's not bacon," he said around the mouthful, "but it's not bad."

I compressed my lips and put two more slices of bread into the toaster. I'd have salad for lunch. Lettuce, tomatoes, cucumbers, and no dressing. Heck, I'd even skip the cream in my coffee and go vegan, if I had to.

But I wouldn't have to, because somehow, some way, I would rid myself of—

"You can't escape it, you know." Lucan took another bite of toast and turned to rest against the counter, uncomfortably close both in physical proximity and in terms of gleaning my train of thought.

I refused to give way. I stared out the window over the sink at the vegetable garden in the back yard. More tomatoes had ripened on their vines. I'd pick them after breakfast.

"You are who you are," he continued between bites. "You're not the first to resist your calling, and you won't be the last. Like it or not, the house is still yours, the shades will still come for you, I will still protect you with my life, and sooner or later you will still need to learn to control your magick."

A shiver danced its way down my spine. *Magick*...with a 'k.' I hadn't been entirely honest with Lucan and Keven about never encountering it before. The idea of it had fascinated me all my life. The possibility that one could exert power over it, direct it, use it. When Paul had been young, I'd turned to herbs to ease his coughs and colds, and ventured briefly into the study of Wicca, but a couple of inexplicable outcomes to the spells I'd attempted had scared the crap out of me.

And now a man who could turn into a wolf stood in my kitchen, telling me that *magick* was my calling? That scared the crap out of me all over again.

But I'd be lying if I said it didn't intrigue me at the same time. I'd also be lying if I said I didn't wonder about the training Keven had mentioned.

"Shades," I said, because that seemed a good place to start with my many, many questions. I played with the braided rope of hair that fell over my shoulder, still damp from my shower. The aroma of fresh-brewed coffee drifted from the pot, but it was on the other side of Lucan. "Was that what attacked last night?"

"They were."

His affirmation in the plural was a not-so-subtle reminder that there had been more than one.

"It looked like a bird, but...not." I shuddered at the memory of outstretched talons and glowing yellow eyes.

"They're bird-like," Lucan agreed, plucking the new toast from the toaster and dropping it onto the plate. "But their feathers are barbed and toxic. As soon as one brushes your skin, it releases from the Shade and embeds itself in you. If it's not removed immediately, the toxins can be fatal."

Involuntarily, I glanced sideways, my gaze landing on his belly. "Is that what...?"

He shook his head. "The feathers can't penetrate my fur. That was a lucky talon strike. Painful, but not fatal."

Fur.

I turned back to the window. Lucan buttered the toast, the scrape of knife against crusty bread loud in the kitchen, underscored by Merlin's continued growls from the top of the fridge. He added jam, then nudged the plate toward me.

"Eat," he said. "It will help."

I laughed at that. A short, disbelieving *ha!* that made Merlin hiss and back up against the cupboards. I sent him a sympathetic look. *You and me both, buddy*, I thought, and he replied with a plaintive yowl.

"Is his name really Merlin?" Lucan asked. He opened random cupboard doors until he found the mugs and took two down.

"It is."

"Your choice?" He poured coffee into both mugs and slid one my way, then sipped from his own.

So. Gargoyles ate dinner, and wolf-shifters drank coffee. Got it.

"Yes...why?" I'd renamed the cat when I'd brought him home

from the shelter because I refused to stand on the porch and call for a cat named Gonzo. Edie had suggested Rover, but I'd vetoed that for the same reason.

"Have you never wondered why you chose it?" Lucan watched me over the rim of his cup as he sipped again.

"I read a lot of books about King Arthur when I was young. Merlin was one of my favorite characters. I liked—" I broke off.

"The magick?" Lucan suggested.

I picked up the toast and took a bite, so I wouldn't have to answer. It tasted like sawdust. I made myself swallow anyway, and then lifted it for another bite.

"He wasn't anything like the stories, you know."

I glanced at him, my teeth still sunk into the bread. Amber eyes met mine, their expression flat.

"Merlin," he clarified. "He wasn't the good guy."

My world, already seriously off-kilter, tipped a little more sideways under my feet. With great care, I finished biting off the toast, chewed, swallowed, and placed the remainder of the slice back on the plate.

"Merlin wasn't real," I said. Was it just me, or was my voice pitched higher than normal? And louder, too. I tried to rein it in. "None of them were. I mean, some historians think they might have been, but most don't. Not anymore. Arthur...Camelot—they're just legends." But my objections felt automatic, as if they were expected, and I was already bracing myself for Lucan's rebuttal.

Lucan.

I blinked as childhood memories of books flooded back. I'd meant it when I said I did a lot of reading about Arthur when I was young. I'd been more than a little obsessed by the mythical king and his wizard, and I had devoured every book I could lay my hands on, down to the most obscure. And now I was remembering the stories—and the names within them. Names like Sir Lucan of the Round Table, servant to King Arthur, loyal until the very end when he died trying to save his king's life...

There was no reason for my brain to make the leap it did. No catalyst. It was just a sudden, random thought—a connecting of dots. On the other hand, there had been no good reason for me to suddenly come into the possession of a pendant that showed me the invisible, either, or for a gargoyle to come to life at my apparent summons, or for the existence of what Lucan called shades, or—

My breath snared in my throat as I looked into the calm, steady depths of a gaze that seemed to wait for my acceptance.

An understanding too ancient to be my own tugged at the edges of my mind, but before I could grasp it, Merlin meowed, breaking the silence. Lucan slanted him a look.

"You might want to change his name before you bring him home with you," he said, "or Keven won't let him into the house."

I set the remains of my toast on the plate, brushed off my hands, and headed out to the back yard in search of tomatoes and sanity. Lucan's words went with me, replaying over and over again and destroying the peace I sought.

"Not the good guy."

"Home..."

Magick.

CHAPTER 13

LUCAN SHIFTED INTO WOLF FORM TWICE IN THE SPACE OF
as many hours that afternoon. Smoothly, seamlessly, and with
none of the contortions or snapping of bones imagined by
Hollywood. It was more like watching a cloud change shape—
but faster. One moment he stood tall and man-bunned and
broad-shouldered, and the next, in the blink of an eye and a
wisp of fog, a wolf had replaced him, lean and thick-furred and
lethal, crouching over a pile of clothing no longer needed.

The first time was when Gilbert knocked at the door, osten-
sibly to deliver a casserole from Jeanne, but no doubt more interested in resuming negotiations for the pendant he hadn't been
able to find in my absence. Before I could decide how to greet
him, his startled gaze dropped from me to the beast crowding
my side, and his eyes went wide.

"Is that—that's not a—is it?" he stammered.

"A dog?" I supplied, trying to shove Lucan out of the way
with my knee. "Yes. He's—he belongs to..."

I trailed off and Gil's gaze returned to me—mostly. But he
kept a wary eye on the bristling animal.

"Your guest?" he prompted. "Yes, Jeanne told me you
brought someone home with you." He sniggered like a twelve-
year-old and shoved the casserole at me. "So? Did you think
about my offer?"

I hip-checked Lucan aside and, with a throaty growl, he
retreated a few steps and sat down. I turned back to Gilbert,
holding the warm casserole like a shield between us. The
pendant's weight pulled at the chain around my neck. I'd tried
several times through the day to lift it from my neck, but to no
avail. And even if I had been able to take it off, Lucan's words
about not being able to escape my fate remained uppermost in

my mind. I didn't want the thing, but the fact someone else did—badly enough to send a shade after me—made me nervous.

Plus, I really didn't like Gilbert.

I eyed him up and down. "What's the matter? Couldn't find it when you searched my house this morning?"

A dull brick red crept up his neck to stain his cheeks. His gaze slid to the right. "I don't know what you're talking about. I came over to feed your cat, but he wouldn't come in."

His gaze returned to land on my neck and the chain there. He rubbed his fingertips together at his sides, and my own hands tightened on the casserole dish.

He wouldn't—would he?

A low growl rumbled behind me. Gilbert's hands became fists and he shuffled his feet. "I meant what I said, you know. About taking anything you want in exchange."

My head shook. "Thank you, but no. I'm not interested."

Irritation flared in Gilbert's face, and he took an aggressive step toward me. "Damn it, Claire—"

His words ended in a high-pitched shriek as Lucan lunged past me with a snarl and reared up. His front feet landed against Gilbert's chest, and Gilbert stumbled back and fell to the porch, then scrambled on hands and knees toward the stairs. He staggered upright and glared over his shoulder at me and the still-snarling Lucan. "The offer won't remain open forever, you know. You'll be sorry you didn't take it when you had the chance!"

And with that, he turned tail and ran, his comb-over flapping in the breeze.

For long, long, *long* moments, I stood in the open doorway, staring at the door Gilbert slammed behind him across the street. A tantalizing aroma drifted up from the covered dish: chicken, broccoli, and sharp cheddar cheese.

Jeanne's casserole was legendary on the street, but she'd been on her way to work and wouldn't have had time to make it for me. I suspected it had been intended for her own dinner rather than mine, which meant I should probably return it. But she was at the hospital, and the thought of facing Gilbert again—

The casserole was lifted from my grasp, and I jumped. Lucan —fully dressed again, thank goodness—took the glass lid from the dish, sniffed at the contents, and grunted. "Still not quite what I consider meat," he said, "but it's better than what's in your fridge."

I crossed my arms and lifted a thumb to my mouth, nibbling absently at the cuticle as I looked across the street again. "Lucan?"

Lucan replaced the casserole lid. His gaze met mine, anger simmering beneath its surface. "Yes," he said. "That was definitely a threat."

THE SECOND TIME LUCAN SHIFTED, HE WAS HALFWAY through devouring the greater part of the casserole for his dinner, carefully discarding the broccoli pieces as I pushed my own share around my plate. I heard nothing, but his head snapped up and his gaze narrowed, and then *poof*, the change was upon him and he was upon the clothes upon the floor.

By the time the doorbell rang, he stood in the front hall, and his low, throaty rumble made the hairs on my arms stand on end as I joined him. I peeked through the window at the side of the door and met the steely gaze of Edie, who wore purple-flowered leggings, an orange plaid shirt, and her best *you're going to tell me everything and don't you even think of lying* expression, perfected over her high school principal career. I bit my bottom lip. Edie pointed at the doorknob. I sighed and reached for the deadbolt.

"She's a friend," I told Lucan over my shoulder. "Please go away?"

The request was made without hope, so I was neither surprised nor disappointed when he didn't move. Any more than I was surprised when Edie's gaze zeroed in on the animal the second the door opened. "Jesus," she said. "Gilbert was right. That really is a fucking wolf!"

"It's not really," I mumbled. "It's—"

"It's a fucking wolf," Edie repeated. "Why do you have a fucking wolf in your house, Claire?"

I hesitated. Edie was my closest friend—my only friend, really, now that Jeanne and I no longer had Jeff shoving us together. If I were going to tell anyone my story, it would be her. But where would I even begin? If I showed her the pendant, would it reveal its magic to her? And if I told her about the shade that had come at me last night, and the wounded Lucan, and Keven the gargoyle, would she believe any of it? Or would she back away slowly and go home to call Paul—or an ambulance?

"Well?" the stout, gray-haired woman on my porch demanded.

I blinked and pulled my attention back to the present. "Sorry, I was wool-gathering. What did you say?"

Edie scowled, but despite the fierceness of her expression, her brown eyes gentled with concern behind her glasses. "What's going on, Claire? We've been friends for thirty years, and you've acted more bizarrely in the past twenty-four hours than you have in the rest of that time put together—including the times when you had every right to act bizarrely. Are you feeling okay? Do you need to see someone? I'm happy to drive you, you know that."

Edie, my voice of adventure, thought I was losing it? That wasn't a good sign. My dementia and/or brain tumor theories resurfaced, and I hesitated, considering her offer. But the fact that Jeanne and Gilbert and Edie had all seen Lucan—in one form or another—told me that he, at least, was real. And if he was real, it stood to reason that the rest of it, impossible as it seemed, was real, too. And if the rest of it was real...

"Claire?" A gentle hand touched my arm. "Hon, seriously, are you okay?"

If the rest of it was real, that would include the shades that had been at the back of my mind all day.

I shivered, and my gaze went past Edie to scan the sky beyond the porch. The sun already sat low behind the trees. What would happen when it set? Would the shade that got away find my house in the dark? Would it find me? Would Lucan have to protect me again? What if he failed this time? What if—

"Claire!"

The sharpness of Edie's voice jolted through me, and I pulled my scattered thoughts back together. "I'm fine," I said. "I just—I'm going through some stuff right now, that's all. I just need some time."

"Stuff." One of Edie's eyebrows hovered above the rim of her bifocals. "What kind of *stuff*?"

I waved a vague hand, grasping for a response that would put my friend's mind at rest. Or at least get her off the porch before sunset and the possibility of another shade. Suddenly— desperately—I wanted to talk to Lucan about maybe returning to the house in the woods after all.

"You know," I said. "Turning sixty. The divorce. Stuff."

"Jeff has been gone for a year, the divorce was six months ago, and despite still not being able to swear, you were coping just fine with turning sixty until now." Edie crossed her arms. "What happened? You know you can tell me anything, right? And I mean that. *Anything*."

Sheer willpower kept me from glancing at Lucan. "Nothing happened. I've just been thinking since we talked, that's all."

"About?"

"I don't know. Needing a change, maybe."

"A change like staying out all night and bringing home a strange man and his wolf."

I lifted my chin and crossed my own arms. "Maybe. Why not?"

Edie's eyes narrowed, and I braced for the forthcoming tirade. I loved my friend to death, but when Edie went into lecture mode, she could make the strongest of souls wilt into cowering, abject shadows. She called it her superpower. I would have given my right arm to possess a tenth of the confidence behind it—and both arms not to be on the receiving end of it. Especially when it was prefaced with that look of disappointment I saw gathering on her face.

But to my surprise, the disappointment evaporated and Edie grinned and reached out to pat my cheek. "It's about time," she declared. "Good on you!"

"What?" I gaped at her. "But—"

"Seriously. I told you, remember? You're sixty, woman, not dead. You deserve a little fun after putting up with that deadbeat for all those years. I'll tell Jeanne and Gilbert to mind their own damned business, and you *enjoy*. You can tell me all the details over wine one night." For a brief instant, she hesitated, as if she wanted to add something more, then she gave an almost imperceptible shrug, delivered another pat on the cheek, and turned to trot down the stairs.

"*All* the details, mind," she called over her shoulder as she reached the gate. "I don't get much excitement of my own these days."

CHAPTER 14

SLEEP WAS ELUSIVE. BETWEEN THE KNOWLEDGE THAT Lucan lay curled in wolf form outside my bedroom door and the possibility that a shade might crash into the unprotected house at any moment, I lay wide-eyed and staring at the dark ceiling.

Merlin's insistence on lying on my chest while growling in the direction of the door didn't help. I sighed and moved him aside for the third time.

"Would you *not*?" I grumbled. "Why can't you just go outside for the night like you always do?"

The cat turned his head toward me, eyes glinting in the faint light filtering through the blinds from the streetlamp outside. Then he returned his attention to the door and resumed the low, throaty rumble he hadn't let up on since finding Lucan in the house.

I sighed again and went back to staring at the ceiling and going over the conversation with Lucan after dinner.

"The shades—what are they, exactly?" I'd asked, returning to my unanswered questions from the afternoon. I'd set my cross-stitch on my lap and pushed my reading glasses up onto the top of my head to watch him where he stood guard at the window.

He hadn't turned. "Creatures caught in the ether. The Between."

"Between what?"

"Earths."

"Ear—you mean planets?"

He'd crossed his arms as he leaned a shoulder against the window frame and frowned at me. "No, I mean Earths—or more accurately, slivers of Earths."

"Like a multiverse?" I'd gaped at him. "Seriously?"

"Not the kind physicists imagine, but yes."

I digested the revelation in silence for a moment. The idea of a multiverse itself wasn't that shocking, but I wasn't sure how I felt about Lucan's cryptic explanation of it.

"How many?" I asked finally.

"How many what? Shades?" He shrugged. "Countless."

I shook my head, even though I wanted to know more about the shades, too. *One impossibility at a time*, I told myself. "No. Earths. How many Earths?"

And why slivers? I held back the second question because it was also another impossibility.

"No one knows. We think one or two per century, but we've only accurately tracked them for the last five or six."

"Divisions?"

"Centuries."

Math wasn't my strong suit, but if I was right, and Lucan had been around since King Arthur's final battle at Camlann— surreptitiously, I used my fingers to count fifteen centuries. Then I clenched those same fingers into fists atop my cross-stitch. Fifteen to thirty divisions? That was—

Lucan shifted his position at the window then, and the fabric of his shirt pulled across his broad shoulders. With no other encouragement whatsoever, my brain was suddenly far more interested in other matters. Such as how much difference in age there actually was between me and Lucan in the face of fifteen centuries, and if it mattered.

Slow heat had suffused me, and I plucked at the collar of my shirt, blaming it on the start of a hot flash as I wrestled with mortification at my wayward imagination.

Lucan didn't help.

"It doesn't," he said, without looking at me. A quiet rumble of amusement underlined his voice.

"I beg your pardon?" I squeaked.

"You're wondering if the difference in our ages matters," he said. "Aside from the fact that you know I'm considerably older than I look, it doesn't. But the fact that I'm your protector does.

As attractive a woman as you are, milady, I need a clear head around you. I cannot allow myself to be distracted by your...charms."

I left the room then. Without a word, I dropped my cross-stitch and my glasses on the chair I vacated, and took my fiery-hot body upstairs to my room.

Lying in bed now, I still hadn't cooled off. Neither had my questions. *How had he known? Did I project that much desperation? Had he said the same thing to all the Crones he'd protected?*

And my favorite one: *How can I change his mind?*

Groaning, I flopped over in bed and scowled at the empty pillow beside me. I couldn't remember the last time I'd even thought about sex, let alone practically been consumed by the idea. Jeff and I...well, we hadn't been that interested in one another for a long time. He because of his affair, it had turned out, and me—well, I'd put it down to age, but something about Lucan made me feel years younger. More vital. More—

A shadow passed across the pillow, there and gone in the blink of an eye. I rolled over to stare at the window. Long seconds ticked by, marked by the sturdy wind-up alarm clock on the bedside table. Steady, faint light from the streetlight filtered around the blind and between the horizontal slats, the same way it had done for thirty years. Merlin, a comforting lump beside me, still growled deep in his throat. Nothing else moved.

I sighed into the dark and pushed the duvet away from my chest. My internal heat, helped by my lascivious thoughts, had become an all-out hot flash, and internal combustion seemed imminent. God, I hated my hormones sometimes.

The room went black.

My gaze jerked back to the window. The faint light from behind the blinds had been cut off. I bolted upright, then, instinctively, I dived off the bed and onto the floor, away from the window, sucking in a breath to scream for Lucan.

Before I could make a sound, glass exploded inward. Outlined against the streetlamp outside, a shrieking shape thrashed in the blinds—a shape with slitted eyes that glowed yellow as they zeroed in on me. My limbs turned heavy. The world slowed. The heat from my hot flash pooled in my chest and radiated outward. My head swam and the room wobbled around its edges, and I fought off the desire to close my eyes and ride out the wave. Dear God, not now. Not when—

Ice-cold clarity washed over me.

Merlin.

I lunged upward and grabbed for the cat on the bed, but my fingers barely brushed short, sleek fur as he leaped toward the shade, hissing and spitting. I screamed for him, but splintering wood and a savage snarl drowned out my voice as the massive wolf that was Lucan crashed through the bedroom door and joined the attack. Yowls and snarls and shrieks blended together in a cacophony of sound. I struggled to rise and go to their aid, but my body's temperature continued to climb, the worst it had ever been, pinning me in place on my knees with its ferocity, threatening to consume me.

My fingers dug into the sheet-covered mattress as I hovered on the edge of unconsciousness. The fire in me gathered and liquified, rolling out from my center and down my arms. My fingers splayed wide. Without conscious thought, I turned my palms toward the window just as brilliant white fire flashed from them to envelop shade, wolf, and cat alike. Horror filled me.

Merlin. Lucan.

An unearthly screech pierced the snarls and howls. More glass shattered, and the shape that was the shade retreated into the night, taking the white flames with it. A small, four-legged shadow streaked from the room through the broken door. A larger one morphed into two legs and came to crouch beside me.

I stared at the streetlight outside.

"Milady," Lucan's voice was rough, "are you injured?"

He pushed back the hair from my face, his heat mingling with my own. I swallowed against a tongue that felt three times its normal size, trying to form words. To reassure him. I could do neither. Shock held me immobile. I stared at the window where half the horizontal blind hung in tatters.

Concern puckered between Lucan's brows. He cupped my chin in a gentle hand and turned my head one way, then the other, searching for damage. His touch set off a vibration that started in my core and worked its way through me until my teeth chattered, my body shook, and my muscles screamed with the effort of trying to keep me from flying apart.

Lucan growled under his breath and pulled the duvet off the bed. He wrapped it around my shoulders, tucking it around my legs and under my chin. It didn't help.

"We should be at the house," he muttered. "The gargoyle would know what to do."

I knew what to do, too, but the bottle of whiskey I kept for medicinal purposes was all the way downstairs, which meant it might as well have been on another continent at the moment. Or another sliver of Earth. Across whatever the hell the Between was.

I closed my eyes and focused on taking a breath. A single, shallow inhale. An exhale. Another inhale.

Were those voices I heard? I frowned at the break in my fragile concentration. Yes, those were definitely voices out in the street. Jeanne and Gilbert and—

A pounding sounded on the front door below my window, Lucan morphed into a wolf again, and Edie bellowed, "Claire! Claire, for God's sake, open the door! Claire? She's not answering. Jeanne, how far away are the police? Can you see anything at her window? Gilbert, for chrissakes, stop gawking and go get the key! Claire? Help is coming, sweetie—hold on!"

I threw off the duvet and lunged for the snarling wolf beside me, wrapping my fingers in his thick ruff to keep him from leaving, smelling the singe on his fur. Had that been my doing? White fire. How—?

I shook off the question.

"No," I croaked. "Lucan, no! It's just my friends. They heard the noise. They're worried about me, that's all."

He fought my hold for a second before subsiding with a final throaty snarl. Then he vaporized and reformed as Lucan the man, still on all fours, and my fingers were wound not in his ruff, but in the long hair released from the man-bun that never managed to survive his transformation. With a startled inhale, I released my hold, and he turned his head to me. The savage amber eyes met mine, gentled, turned somber.

"You cannot tell them, milady," he said. "They wouldn't understand."

No shit, Sherlock. I bit back the words—and the burble of misplaced hilarity that wanted to accompany them—and shook my head. "Of course not. I'll—think of something." Anything, really, because anything would be infinitely more believable than a creature from a place called the Between, a wolf-shifter, and fire streaming from my fingertips.

Lucan rose to his feet, lithe and muscled—and dear God, still naked—and held out a hand to help me to mine. I pulled away when I was upright and wobbled toward the door as the pounding below continued. A siren wailed in the distance, coming nearer.

"I have to go downstairs," I said, "so they'll know I'm okay."

"I'll come with you."

"You can't—not like—" I waved a hand at him. "Do you really need to do that?"

He looked down at himself and grinned at me, amusement dancing in his eyes. "My wolf finds it easier to run without pants on, so yes. But I'll get dressed, on condition that you wait for me."

His tone brooked no objection, and I waited on the stairs while he dressed. It took him only seconds—perhaps because he'd had so much practice?—and we descended together. Lucan insisted on opening the door, just in case, and did so with a suddenness that had Edie toppling across the doorstep and into his arms with a startled, "Oh my!"

She stared up at him in consternation for an instant, then her gaze found me. "You're alive."

I hadn't even formed an agreement before my friend extricated herself from Lucan's hold and gripped my shoulders, turning me one way and then the other, and then back again as she examined me.

"What in hell happened? Your window—the noise—I thought for sure you were dead."

"An owl," I blurted the first thing that popped into my head. The siren wailed closer. Edie stopped manhandling me and stared.

"At least, I think it was an owl," I amended, running through my limited knowledge of birds. Was there another nocturnal one big enough to crash through a window? A bat, maybe? No, too small. I nodded at my friend. "Yes. An owl. It hit the window and broke it and got tangled in the blinds."

Edie frowned. "That was no owl. The noise. It was..." She shuddered. "I've never heard anything like it."

I met Lucan's gaze over my friend's shoulder. He shook his head. "Merlin, maybe?" I suggested. "He went after whatever it was."

But Edie wasn't buying it. "It was no cat, either." She peered around me. "Where's the wolf?"

My mouth opened, but nothing emerged. I was fresh out of ideas. Outside, a police car skidded to a halt in front of the house, splashing blue and red light over the little cluster of people gathered outside the front gate. I looked to Lucan for help.

"He's locked in one of the bedrooms," he told Edie. "To keep him out from underfoot."

Edie cocked her head to one side. "He's very quiet."

"He's well trained."

"But not legal."

Lucan half smiled, a slight upward tilt of his mouth that made the corners of his eyes crinkle and my toes curl against the floorboards. "Difficult to explain," he allowed.

Edie snorted. "I can imagine. But don't worry. Your secret is safe with me as long as you treat our Claire well."

Our Claire choked. "Edie!"

Without the slightest remorse, Edie shrugged. "You know I don't beat around the bush, hon. Now do up those buttons on your pajamas before you flash the nice police officers."

I looked down to find my pajama top gaping wide, almost to my belly. I clutched the two sides together, mortification scorching my cheeks as Edie turned to greet the female cop coming through the door.

Lucan sidled over to join me, keeping his gaze averted while I fumbled the buttons closed. I glowered at him, demanding under my breath, "Why didn't you tell me?"

The half-smile returned. "I said I couldn't allow myself to be distracted by your charms," he murmured. "Not that I couldn't enjoy them."

The top button I wrestled with popped off the fabric and dropped to the floor, skittering across the tile entrance to come to rest against a booted foot. The police officer bent down to retrieve it. She held it out to me.

My mortification ramped up a thousandfold. I stepped forward to accept it, one hand still clutching the pajamas closed. Dear Lord, would this night never end? Or this night*mare*?

Because aside from the sexy wolf shifter who thought I had charms (Seriously? Me? A sixty-year-old grandmother?), that's what this was: a nightmare. One filled with things I didn't understand, things that attacked me in the night, and things an inexplicable, foreign, impossible part of me just...knew. The way my hands had known to throw the fire. The way I had known to find the house in the woods and rouse the gargoyle. The way I knew I had to go back there.

"Ma'am?"

I blinked at the police officer, who regarded me expectantly, pen poised above a notebook. On her jacket, a rectangular pin proclaimed her to be *Cst. K. Abraham*, and I wondered what the 'K' stood for. She didn't look like a Kimberley or a Karen. Maybe a—

Edie nudged my elbow. "She asked your name."

Lady Claire of the Morrigan, a voice whispered in my brain. Not mine, not the one that sounded like Edie, but a whole new one that I most assuredly did not need.

I took an involuntary step back but came up short against the solid chest that was unmistakably Lucan's. His hands settled onto my shoulders, squeezing gently. I closed my eyes, allowing his strength to seep into me. Then I gathered myself, straightened my spine, and met the police officer's frown with a steady gaze and lifted chin.

"Claire," I told Constable Abraham. "My name is Claire Emerson."

I would answer their questions, everyone would leave, and I would return to my bed—or at least *a* bed, preferably in a room with an intact window. And then, in the morning, when it was light outside and the things that went bump in the night were no longer a threat, I would return to the house in the woods.

And to the answers there.

CHAPTER 15

THE HOUSE STOOD AS IT HAD WHEN WE'D LEFT IT: SOLID, too small to contain all that it did, and filled with questions. Or was that just me?

I walked out of the woods and started up the path toward it, Lucan's clothes held against me as he trotted alongside in wolf form. We'd driven most of the way this time, and I'd left the car parked on the road near the gate. Lucan hadn't been happy with the idea of marking our whereabouts so clearly, but since the Mages already knew where to find me, he hadn't argued for long.

Neither of us had wanted to converse beyond that. We hadn't even bothered with breakfast. I hadn't offered, he hadn't asked. We'd left the house in silence a little past six, just as the sky grew pale. As we pulled away, I glanced at the gaping hole above the porch where my bedroom window had been, wondering if I should do something about it before we left, but with no clouds in the sky, it seemed safe to leave it as it was. I made a mental note to call a contractor later, and continued down the street.

Lucan seemed content to stare out the window as I drove, and I hadn't had the wherewithal to string words together after a mostly sleepless night. He changed to wolf form as soon as we were out of the car, and I picked up his clothing, still warm from his body, and tucked it under my arm.

Now, midway across the clearing as the sun set the treetops alight, he changed back again and held out a hand for my bundle. I passed it to him and turned away while he dressed.

"The shade came through the window at my house," I remarked to the trees, "but not here. Why?"

"Wards," Lucan answered. "This house is protected. Your other is not."

"Wards—like magick spells?"

"Wards like wards," he said. "Did you not see them?"

"That would depend on what they look like?" I wasn't in the habit of ending statements with question marks, but it seemed warranted.

"The lights," he elaborated. "Around the house."

"Like a glow, you mean? I thought I saw something when I found the house, but it didn't last. I assumed it was my imagination." Along with a lot of other things.

"On the contrary. Wards are very real. And very much alive. They're sometimes mistaken for fireflies, but they're smaller. When they come together, they can form a barrier that deflects magick and protects whatever is behind it."

Well, that fit with absolutely nothing I'd ever thought I knew about magic. But I liked the idea of protection. "I've decided to stay here for the time being. Until we—I—figure out what to do next."

"A wise plan." I couldn't see Lucan's expression, but his voice held no note of the *I told you so* that I richly deserved after putting him in the path of the second shade the way I had.

I did have one proviso I hadn't yet mentioned, however, which involved returning for Merlin, who hadn't come out of hiding before we left. Lucan wouldn't like the idea, but it was non-negotiable. I would not—could not—leave the cat to fend for himself. I cleared my throat to tell him, but a low, keening cry in the woods behind the house cut me off.

Forgetting Lucan's state of undress, I whirled. His head emerged from the neck of his shirt, and he tugged the garment into place. Frowning, he scanned the forest that surrounded us. I sidled closer. The shiver that traveled down my spine underscored the sense of vulnerability fast becoming part of my life.

"That was no shade," he murmured, answering my unspoken question.

"You say that like it's a bad thing."

"Not bad. But definitely not good. We should go in."

As if on cue, the front door of the house opened, and squat, solid Keven filled the doorway, disquiet stamped across her face. She sniffed the air, then looked at Lucan. "Gnomes."

"We heard. The wards will hold?"

"For now. But I can only do so much to keep them here. The sooner she learns to call them herself, the better. Especially if *he* is involved." Keven's gaze settled on me with the weight of expectancy behind it, knocking the idea of gnomes—and the question of *he who?*—from my head.

"I—uh—" I stammered. "Me?"

"That's why you're here, isn't it? To learn?"

"Um..." *Well, yes, but maybe a cup of coffee and a chance to catch my breath first?*

"We had an incident last night," Lucan said, forestalling my suggestion. "Another shade."

Keven's expression hardened at the words—no pun intended, I thought—and she stood back to hold the door wide.

"Inside," she directed. "Now."

Not until I stood in the massive entry hall did it occur to me that I could—and probably should—object to being ordered around that way, but the gargoyle had already closed the door and crossed the foyer to the hallway leading past the stairs. "This way. You will work in the cellar."

She grunted the words over her shoulder as if it were a given that I would fall in behind her. Out of pure contrariness, I did not. Instead, I crossed my arms, scowled, and waited. And waited.

Lucan chuckled and strolled past me to climb the stairs with an amused, over-the-shoulder, "Good luck with that."

And then I waited some more.

After ten minutes as marked by the grandfather clock beside the sitting room door and an eternity as marked by my impatience, I caved, conceding that Lucan was right. Keven had no intention of coming back for me, damned impertinent gargoyle.

I would have to go in search of her if I wanted my answers. Wistfully, I eyed the front door.

Gnomes, whispered Keven's voice in my head.

Shades, whispered Lucan's.

"Damn it," I muttered, then told my gleeful Edie-voice to shut it. I stomped down the hall in the gargoyle's wake. The cellar, Keven had said. So where would a cellar door hide in a place like this? It would make sense to have it off the kitchen, but between the impossible vastness of the house and things like non-electrical electricity and modern bathrooms, *sense* wasn't a word that much applied.

Sure enough, no door led off the kitchen. Or the enormous dining room. Or a smaller room also set up for eating. Or the massive storage cupboard under the stairs. Or the hallway itself, which I had now reached the end of.

Perplexed, I stared at the paneled wall in front of me, then turned and looked back down the flagstone passageway. Keven had most definitely walked in this direction, and she was too big to have overlooked in passing, so where in the world had she gone?

"Oh, for heaven's sake," I growled under my breath. I cleared my throat and called, "Keven? Keven!"

A faint response rumbled behind me, and I turned again, this time to face the wall.

"Keven?" I asked it doubtfully.

I wouldn't have been in the least surprised if it had answered, but the wall stayed silent. I narrowed my eyes. I was *sure*...

I put a hand against one of the panels and pushed. Nothing. Another. Still nothing. A third. A fourth. My temper edged up a notch, and I pushed hard with both hands. Without warning, the wall gave way. I flailed like a windmill, then toppled into dark, shadowed emptiness and landed with a muffled thud on my hands and knees. Sharp pain streaked through my limbs. My eyes watered.

"Cheesy rice on a cracker!" I snarled. My Edie-voice sighed.

"Well?" came Keven's gravelly voice from what sounded like the bottom of a distant barrel, "Are you coming, or not?"

I stared into the dark to my right. Slowly, the lines of a wall emerged from the shadows, curving down along the edge of what looked like a stairway. I contemplated the choice facing me. Retreat? Or get up and descend the dark, creepy stone stairs into an unknown cellar?

If I were watching the situation unfold onscreen, I'd be yelling at the heroine to run, to get out while she still could. Faced now with my own spooky scenario, however, I was beginning to understand the curiosity that drove almost all of them to make the choices they did.

I looked over my shoulder at the passage leading to the great hall. I thought about how I had once again wandered off without letting anyone know where I was going. Then I closed my eyes and sighed.

If I lived through this, I promised myself, I'd be a lot kinder to all those onscreen characters.

I pulled myself up, using the rough stone wall for help, rubbed my bruised knee, and dusted off my hands on the seat of my pants. I thought about the many articles Natalie had printed off for me in the weeks leading up to my birthday—the warning signs of every possible age-related illness that might lead to an early death. I snorted. All that research, all that concern, and I'd bet she never imagined I'd go like this.

And I'd bet double she never dreamed that the prospect of my potential demise would make me feel more alive than I had in years.

"You're a weird woman, Claire Emerson," I muttered under my breath. "Weird."

I began my descent.

The light below grew brighter with each step, and despite two unexpected twists, no handrail, and a narrowness that made me wonder how the bulky Keven had navigated the stairs, I made it down unscathed. Rounding the final corner, I found myself in a small room carved out of solid stone.

Its ceiling was so low that the gargoyle waiting for me had to hunch her head between her shoulders, giving her the appearance of having less neck than usual. Sconces lined the walls, again with no light switch in sight, and a wooden table stood at the center. A bench had been pushed to one side, and a massive wood cabinet, closed, took up most of one wall.

Keven stood beside the latter.

"It's about time," she grumped. She turned her back on me and opened the cabinet's double doors. Its shelves overflowed with papers, dead plants, and dust-covered jars and bottles. Muttering under her breath, the gargoyle rummaged inside and emerged with a book and a triumphant, "Ha!"

She wedged the doors shut again and dropped the book onto the table with a thud muffled by the smallness of the space, then pointed a claw at it. "Page one," she ordered. "We start at the beginning."

I eyed the book. Bound in leather and held closed by a knotted leather tie, it had bits of yellowed paper sticking out from its edges, and I could smell its mildew from across the room. It looked ancient—and intriguing. I wrestled with my curiosity and reminded myself I'd come back to the house today for answers, not more questions. I crossed my arms and stood my ground.

"Who am I?" I asked. Then I blinked. That was *not* one of the questions I'd intended to ask, but now that it was spoken, neither did I want to retract it. Keven straightened the book on the table, centering it carefully. At last she looked up at me.

"Why do you hide your magick?" she asked.

The question hit me like a shove to the middle of my chest, and I staggered back a step. "I—I—"

I can't hide what I don't have, I wanted to say, but memories rose again, ensnaring the words, twining with them, accusing them of being lies. A cold heaviness—a dread—settled into my belly. Panic licked through my veins. I knew no magick—*had* no magick. I was just Claire. An ex-wife, a mom, a grandmother, a friend...

A woman who had dabbled in the study of Wicca until inexplicable things had begun to happen around me, linked to rudimentary spells I'd attempted.

Things like crotchety old Mr. Nicholls spraining an ankle on our porch stairs—stairs under which I'd buried a charm against negative energy—when he'd come to complain about Paul playing street hockey.

Things like finding a portrait of my father, covered in the green cellophane of a color-magic healing spell, face down on the sideboard one morning—with no physical reason for it to have fallen. Mom had called later that day to tell me Dad's cancer was back, and I could still feel the sensation of the air whooshing from my lungs as the implications had pressed in on me. Terror at the idea of losing my dad. Terror at realizing the magic—magick—had known.

It had told me. It had worked, even if not as I had intended —and it had scared the living daylights out of me. The potential power. The overwhelming responsibility. The certainty that if I continued, there would be no turning back. No more pretending I was normal.

That afternoon, I had taken my books and my notes and my tools and buried everything in the far back corner of the garden. Jeff, who had never been happy with my pagan altar, discreet as I'd made it, had filled the empty space on the living room mantel with his collection of model cars and stuck one of his garden gnomes on top of the burial site. "About time," he'd said, and that had been the end of it. Much like almost all our disagreements had ended during our marriage, when I thought about it. But that was a topic to ponder another time. Right now, Keven waited for my answer.

I raised my chin. "Fear," I said. "I was afraid."

"Of...?"

"Opening a door I wouldn't be able to close again. Tapping into something I couldn't control."

"But you were at least intrigued by the idea at some point in your life."

I swallowed. "Yes."

"And now?"

My gaze dropped to the book on the table between us. I couldn't read the title from here, but I wanted to. More, I wanted to know what was in it—what was in me. I took stock of my reaction to the idea. There was no doubt that a part of me was repelled—a still-afraid part that whispered to me that it wasn't too late, that I could still run away, still go back to what I'd always been.

Except I'd been a lie—a collection of pretenses carefully cultivated to reassure others in my life that I belonged; that I was satisfied with my place as wife, mother, upright citizen; that I could be counted on to do the right thing and not rock the boat; that I would follow the rules and live up to the expectations. I'd been a lie, I'd lived a lie, and now...

Now I wanted to know what was in that book—and what was in me. I met Keven's patient, implacable gaze.

"What do I do?" I asked.

Keven pointed a claw at the leather-bound book. "Read. Everything you need to know is in there. Your history, your purpose, the spells you will need. Everything."

I craned my neck to read the simple block letters: *The Crone Wars: A Compleat History and Grimoire*. Goosebumps rose along my arms. A grimoire was a book of spells. I could handle that. But *Crone Wars*? Kevin had called me Crone when we first met.

The thrill of anticipation that had carried me through the dark and down the stairs disappeared with a *poof* so loud in my head that I was surprised the gargoyle didn't hear it. Cold pooled in my belly—the kind of cold that snaked out like tentacles from a core of absolute ice and wrapped around my heart, my lungs, my throat.

"Wars?" I asked. I swallowed. "As in more than one?"

"Read," Keven repeated, turning toward the stairs. "And then we will practice."

"I can't."

The gargoyle swung back to face me.

"I don't have my reading glasses with me." And no way was I attempting to read an entire book with the pendant's magnifying lens.

Keven scowled. "It would be a simple enough spell if you knew magick."

"But I don't. You'll have to give me the Cliffs Notes version."

Her scowl deepened.

"A synopsis," I said. "Just give me a synopsis."

Keven regarded me for long seconds, then she shook her ponderous head. She sighed. "Very well," she agreed. "I will answer your questions. But afterward, the mutt will take you to fetch your reading glasses, and you will read the book."

"Agreed." I had to go back for Merlin anyway.

"And first," she said, sweeping the book off the table and replacing it with a bundle of dried grass, "We train."

"But—"

"We train," she repeated. "Because you will hear my words more clearly through the connection to your magick. And you need to hear them."

CHAPTER 16

TRAINING TURNED OUT TO BE A MISNOMER FOR WHAT
Keven had in store.

"Again," she demanded, clapping her hands together with a
thunderous *crack* of stone on stone. "*Feel* the energy, milady.
Summon the heat. *Use* it."

I dropped my hand to my side and flexed stiff fingers that
had gone numb from holding my arm outstretched for endless
minutes. The only thing I *felt* was tired, achy, hungry, and frustrated beyond measure. I rubbed at my bursitis-prone shoulder
and glared across the table at the gargoyle. We'd been at this for
more hours than I wanted to calculate, and I was no closer to
setting fire to that bit of tinder-dry grass now than I had been
when we started.

"I *can't*," I snapped at Keven.

"You *can*," the gargoyle growled back, "if you stop fighting it
and accept that you can."

My fingers tingled with returning sensation and the desire to
throw something at the scowling stone visage. Unfortunately, the
only object within reach other than the table—too heavy to lift,
let alone throw—was the damned dried grass I was supposed to
set fire to. And the only heat I felt was the result of irritation.

I planted my hands on my hips. "Fine. Then I *won't*. Not
until I've had something to eat. And drink. If I don't sit down
soon, my knees are going to seize up permanently."

"I'll give you a lotion for them," Keven said. "Now try
again."

"Your sympathy is overwhelming."

"Your efforts are less than so."

"Oh, for—" I glowered at my tormentor. "Damn it, Keven,
I'm tired! I'm tired, I've only just learned that magick exists,

never mind that I'm supposed to be able to do it, and I'm standing here talking to a gargoyle, and I have way more questions than answers, and—"

"And you will try again," said an implacable Keven, folding her arms across her torso. "And you will keep trying until—"

My temper flared. The fingers of my right hand twitched at my side, and without warning, the wood table lifted from the floor, flew across the room, and smashed into the gargoyle, knocking her into the cupboard. All three crashed to the floor, cupboard on top as books, herbs, and shards of broken glass scattered across the room. A silver goblet rolled across the flagstones into a corner. Utter silence descended.

Dumbfounded, I stared at the fallen stone figure, limbs splayed beneath the mess. The dried grass that had stubbornly refused to ignite settled on a granite shoulder. The shoulder didn't move.

Shock, horror, and disbelief churned together in my chest, squeezing the air from my lungs and pressing against my heart. I held up trembling fingers and stared at them. The treacherous, traitorous fingers that I had barely moved, hardly twitched...

The wooden cupboard shifted and slid sideways off the gargoyle, landing with a thud that made me jump. Keven sat up, stout forearms resting on raised knees, and surveyed the damage surrounding her. Without speaking, she picked up a chunk of rock from beside her foot and held it against her other hand—a hand now missing one of its claws. She heaved a sigh, then set aside the broken fragment of herself and looked up at me.

"There's stew keeping warm on the stove," she said. "You may eat while I clean up here. After dinner we'll work on your control."

"Keven, I'm sorry," I whispered. "I don't know what happened."

"Frankly, I don't either," Keven said. "Fire magick doesn't usually move things. But you're right. You need to eat before we go further."

I swallowed hard, feeling as if I should object. Apologize further. Grovel. But Keven's implacable gaze invited none of those responses, and so I nodded. But I didn't move.

I *couldn't* move.

I regarded my feet in vague puzzlement and then growing concern as I tried—and failed—to lift first one and then the other.

"Milady?" Keven levered herself upright and cocked her head to one side.

I looked up at her. "My feet." I gestured at them. "They're stuck."

Keven frowned. "Stuck?"

"I can't move them."

The crease in Keven's brow deepened. "That's odd," she murmured. "The mutt said you threw fire at the shade."

"White fire," I agreed. "But what does that have to do with stuck feet?"

"Fire means—at least, I assumed it meant..." Keven trailed off, and her gaze narrowed. "When you threw the table just now, did you feel warm?"

"Not particularly. Just annoyed." I tried again to lift a foot. Nothing. I spread my hands wide and met Keven's puzzled gaze. "What's going on?"

Keven circled me, sturdy arms crossed, staring at my feet. "What do you feel now?"

I huffed. "Irritated again because you're not answering my questions."

"Your feet. What do your feet feel?"

"I told you. Stuck."

Keven flashed me her own annoyed glance, and I sighed.

"Fine," I said, focusing my attention on the feet in question. They were warm enough, I supposed. And the floor was solid beneath them. And—wait. That was odd. No. Not odd. Weird. A creepy, holy-hell-what-in-the-name-of-heaven-*was*-that level of weird.

My chin jerked up, and I stared at Keven. "Something is holding them," I whispered.

"Holding them? You're sure? Focus on it. What is it?"

I swallowed a bubble of panic. I really, really didn't want to return my attention to whatever had hold of me, but I wanted even less to remain held. I gritted my teeth, closed my eyes, and focused again on my feet and the stone beneath them. On the nameless, formless *whatever* that connected them. That ran from the stone itself—no, from deeper than that—my eyes popped open.

"Roots. It's like I've grown roots into the earth. Keven, what the hell is going on?"

"Huh," said the gargoyle. "I'll be damned."

I couldn't decide if I was more flipped out by the idea I'd grown roots or by Keven *not* being flipped out by the idea I'd grown roots. I glared at my stone companion. "You'll be more than damned in a minute if you don't start talking."

"Apologies, milady. I'm just surprised. When the mutt told me about your fire, I assumed it meant the Fire element was your source of power. But this"—she waved a hand at the floor —"this is Earth power. And it's very strong."

No kidding. I tugged again at my feet, to no avail. I opened my mouth to demand Keven tell me how to free myself, but something in the gargoyle's expression stopped me, sending a frisson of unease down my spine. Concern?

"What?" I asked.

"It's just—" Keven broke off and shook her head. "It's nothing. We'll talk later. Right now, we need you to release your hold on the Earth."

"*My* hold? I'm not the one—" I put all my strength into jerking one foot from the floor, then squawked in surprise when it lifted and I did a faceplant against Keven's chest. "Ouch!" I pulled back and blinked away tears as I rubbed a skinned and tender nose. "What the hell! How...?"

Keven shrugged. "You understood the connection was at your end, so you were able to let it go."

"But I didn't. I don't." I didn't understand any of this, and freaking hell, my nose hurt. Had I broken it? "I have no idea what you're even talking about."

"Perhaps not here"—Keven placed a heavy hand on my head, compressing the vertebrae in my neck—"but you do here.." The hand moved to my belly and nearly knocked me off my feet again. "The more you think about it here—"

I ducked the return of the hand toward my head, and a flash of sadness crossed the gargoyle's visage. She dropped her hand back to her side with a scrape of granite on granite.

"The more you think about it," she said, "the harder it becomes. Your mind wants concrete evidence of magick's existence. It wants to see it, to touch it. But magick is ephemeral. It cannot be held or captured or studied. It does not require proof. It just is. Acceptance of that is found in your core, not your mind."

I felt the stir of something in the pit of my belly. *Truth*, whispered my third inner voice. *She speaks truth.* But when I tried to seize the something, it dribbled away like water through my fingers. I stamped a recently freed foot in sheer frustration, not caring that I was sixty years old rather than six.

But dear God, I *was* sixty, and I was far from inept. I'd raised a son, run a household, taught myself to cook and sew, to knit and crochet, to paint and garden—hell, I'd even learned how to plumb and tile when Jeff had ripped out the main floor bathroom and then lost interest in the project. I'd lost count of the number of challenges I'd overcome and the skills I'd acquired. A lifetime of them. So why was this magick thing so difficult? Now that I was willing to learn—heck, part of me even *wanted* to learn—what was the stumbling block?

Keven's hand bumped against my shoulder, making me stagger. "Go," the gargoyle said gruffly. "Eat some stew. Let the idea settle. We'll try again later."

I wanted to argue, to insist on trying again now and figuring out where I was going wrong, but the rumble of my belly stopped me. Keven's words made sense. Besides, if I was this frustrated by my lack of learning, the gargoyle had to be even more so. No doubt a break would do us both good. My stomach growled again. Food, too.

I sighed and nodded. "All right. But let me help clean up here, first."

"Milady, my purpose is to serve you. Yours is to serve the Morrigan. I will clean. You will eat. We will resume your lessons."

The old part of me that had been cleaning up after others my entire life wanted to object. The new part that wanted—desperately—to explore my roots to the ground helped me to nod instead. I crossed to the foot of the stone stairs, pausing to cast a last look over my shoulder as Keven picked up the stone claw again and held it in place against her hand. Then she sighed, righted the cabinet, and tucked the claw into the back corner of the top shelf. I started up the stairs.

CHAPTER 17

"SO. A SYNOPSIS." KEVEN SAID, HANDING ME A BASKET, A ball of twine, and a small knife. She'd brought me out to the kitchen garden after lunch instead of resuming our lessons. I was grateful for the reprieve, though I suspected it was as much for her own benefit as it was for mine.

I nodded. "Yes," I said, "but first, can I ask why you call Lucan *mutt* the way you do?"

She grunted. "Ours is a long history, milady. We serve on the same side now, but we didn't start out that way. And not all wounds are easily forgotten."

"You were enemies?"

"His kind was created by evil. I was brought to life to fight them. Others got in the way."

"Merlin—"

"Do *not* mention his name!"

I stumbled backward into a patch of strawberry plants, shocked by the gargoyle's swift anger—and the pain underlying her snarl.

"I'm sorry," I whispered. "I didn't mean..."

Keven shook her head and scuffed a foot on the ground, leaving a furrow six inches deep and a foot wide. She scraped the soil back into place and pressed down on it. "It is I who should apologize, milady. You meant no harm."

She drew a breath and hunched her shoulders. "You know of the Battle of Camlann?"

"The war King Arthur was killed in."

"A war that had nothing to do with king or kingdom," she grated. "The wizard brought it about in his quest to destroy good—to destroy Morgana."

"Morgana? But she was—"

"A servant of the Morrigan, like you," Keven said. "Rewritten by history, as all witches and their kin have been."

Oh.

"Shall I continue?"

"Please."

"When the wizard realized he was losing, he employed the darkest of magick to change his soldiers into wolves. Morgana countered by bringing me and my kin to life and sending us after the wizard. Many died. Too many. Some were innocent."

The pain had returned to Keven's voice, along with a rawness that sounded like grief. This time, I waited for her to finish.

"I found him. The wizard. But the mutt's—" she stopped, curled her free hand into a fist, and corrected, "*Lucan's* family stood between us. His wife and son. I didn't even hesitate."

Oh God. I stood in the middle of the strawberries, clutching at my basket, unsure how to respond. What did one say to a story like that? What *could* one say? I put out a hand and patted tentatively at a rough granite arm.

"I'm sure you..." What? Didn't mean to?

Keven looked down at my hand. "He says he has forgiven me," she said gruffly. "But I haven't. Keeping distance between us, continuing to think of him as my not-friend—it makes it bearable. Most days."

She straightened her shoulders, shrugging off my touch in the process, and pointed at a patch of basil. "You may gather that. Small bundles, or it will mildew before it dries."

She moved a little way beyond to the yarrow growing along the garden's stone wall. "As for your synopsis, it is simple. You are a witch. You have always been a witch. And now you are chosen as Crone."

Having so decreed, she squatted down and sliced off a handful of tiny yellow flowers on long, feathery stems.

Seriously?

I stood with hands on hips, knife angled away from me, and

rolled my eyes at her. "Can I have a little more than that, please?"

"Such as?"

"How can I be a witch when I never practiced witchcraft?" Well, not much, anyway. "What does it mean to be Crone? And chosen how? By whom?"

"All women are witches. Or at least, they have the capacity to be so. Some feel a stronger call to the craft; others have lost their connection. It depends on how far back their own ancestors practiced." Keven tied a length of twine around one end and laid the bundle in her basket.

I blinked my surprise. "My ancestors practiced witchcraft?"

"All women did at one time." She cut another handful of yarrow. "Herbs. Healing. Raising the divine power. The fortunate ones grow up in it. They're taught by their mothers and aunts and grandmothers. The less fortunate…"

"Like me."

"Yes. The less fortunate must seek the tutelage of women outside."

"Covens."

"Or midwitches. Women of great learning who become teachers to others. You likely crossed paths with at least one in your lifetime, but you chose to ignore her offerings."

"I—" I broke off my objection. Had I? But when? And who? The only person I'd ever even remotely broached the subject with outside of Jeff had been…

Edie?

I almost dropped the knife in astonishment because, of course. Edie, who had loaned me books on gardening and herbs and always seemed to know just when I needed to talk, and—

"So you do know one." Keven grunted. She sliced off more yarrow.

—and who had seen the dozens of crows in the tree on my sixtieth birthday when no one else had mentioned the oddity.

"I think I do," I murmured, "but I didn't—"

Didn't what? Realize? Want to know? I stooped to cut a handful of basil and give myself time to process my revelation. Could Edie really be a witch? All those years of living next door. All those years I could have been learning. How much different would my life be now? If she'd taught me the craft, would she have known that I was to be the Morrigan's servant? *Did* she know?

I paused in tying my bundle of basil and looked over at Keven. "When was I chosen?" I asked. "As Crone, I mean. And why? Why me?"

Keven shrugged as she stood upright and moved along the row. "Both are up to the Morrigan. Crones are chosen by their pendants when they are needed, and when they are *who* is needed."

Honestly, getting answers around here was like pulling teeth. I dropped the basil into my basket and tried another route. "Fine, then tell me about the others. Who are they? Where are they? And what happened to the one before me?"

"If you're getting your glasses this afternoon, you can read all of this in the book later."

"Humor me."

"Lady Akira died of old age." Keven moved along the row and squatted again. "She was a hundred and three."

I brightened a little. That was the most encouraging news I'd heard in days. It didn't last.

"As for how many, there are four in total. One for each of the elements: Earth, Air, Water, Fire. We know only that the others will have been chosen at the same time as you, or near to it. It will be up to all of you to find one another."

"And then? When we do find each other, what do we do?"

"You divide the Earth."

"We—what?"

Divide? As in splinter? *Crones* had created the multiverse? I mentally kicked myself for letting my blasted hormones sidetrack me last night the way they had, when I should have been asking Lucan more questions instead of—

The same keening cry I'd heard earlier echoed through the woods. Keven pushed upright and lifted her basket from the ground.

"We should go inside," she said. "You need to leave if you're to return with your reading glasses before dark, and I must feed the wards."

I wondered what wards ate, but filed the question away in favor of a more important one. "Are those really gnomes?" I asked.

The irony was almost too much for words. I seemed destined to be plagued by the things in one iteration or another. First a ceramic collection foisted on me by my neighbor and my ex, and now a gathering of—what? Little forest creatures calling to one another in the shadows, their clothes woven from grass and leaves? I almost smiled at the image—one likely pulled from a childhood book, though I couldn't recall which one.

"They are. Nasty little creatures, too," she said, and the little forest creatures in my mind grinned evilly. "That is their call to gather." She prodded me in the back to hurry me along, but I resisted.

"Wait," I said. "Why are Crones supposed to divide the Earth? And how?"

"How is something known only to Crones, milady." She prodded again, harder this time, and about as easy to resist as a landslide. "As for why, you'll find that in the book after you fetch your glasses. Now, hurry."

DESPITE THE LOOMING THREAT OF GNOMES, I REMAINED focused on other concerns as I followed Lucan through the woods to where we'd parked the car.

Because *divide the Earth*? Even if I read the book from cover to cover, managed to find the others, and somehow mastered the whole not-sticking-to-the-ground thing, the idea was insane. Four women attempting to add to the magickal multiverse would not—*could* not—end well. Not by any stretch of my imagination.

"Milady?" Lucan's voice broke into my thoughts in time to stop me from running into his chest. He'd stopped at the gate and was frowning at me. "Are you sure you're up for this? You need to pay attention."

"I'm fine," I said. But was I? I eyed the half-open gate. I was sixty years old, for Pete's sake. Life was supposed to get simpler at this age, not throw existential decisions at me that demanded I choose between pretending ignorance or stepping into the role of world-splitter.

Divide the Earth. Tear it asunder. And hope to hell we didn't destroy it in the process.

Not quite what I'd envisioned as a retirement plan.

"Perhaps we should do this tomorrow." Gruff concern underscored Lucan's words. "We can leave early in the morning."

I took a deep, albeit less-than-steady, breath and drew myself tall. "No. I really am fine, and I want to go home. I need my reading glasses for the book. And clothes. And Merlin."

Lucan inclined his head and stood aside for me to precede him through the gate.

The drive was uneventful, and soon we turned onto the street I'd lived on for thirty years. My gaze traveled down the block as we passed familiar houses and yards. I knew every single one of them. Every occupant. I'd watched the spindly trees planted on each lawn mature into towering maples and oaks that shaded the homes. Seen thirty years of children and pets and parents come and go.

The entire neighborhood was home for me. It was—

My mouth dropped open. It was on fire?

I slammed my foot onto the brake pedal and the car jerked

to a stop. I stared at the emergency vehicles clustered in front of a smoldering, vaguely house-shaped black ruin. I looked at Jeanne's tidy blue bungalow across the street from it, then Edie's solid red brick rancher next door, then the ruin again. Shock gave way to disbelief.

"My house," I whispered. My movements automatic, I slipped the gear shift into park and switched off the engine. For long moments, I couldn't think. Couldn't breathe. Couldn't believe.

"Lady Claire, we need to turn around. We need to go back."

"My house," I said again.

"Lady Claire!" Lucan's voice turned urgent and his hand closed over my arm. Numbly, I shook him off, trying to unravel the scene before us. To make sense of it. I reached for the driver's door handle. From a great distance, a tiny segment of my brain noted Lucan's dissolution in the seat beside me and the appearance of his wolf. I got out of the car.

Lucan's wolf jumped down beside me and whined, pressing against my leg. I ignored him.

Two police officers conferred with a heavily geared firefighter who shook his head in the negative at the rear of the ladder truck. Other firefighters rolled up their hoses and gathered equipment. A handful of neighbors—because most were at work at two in the afternoon—clustered together on the opposite side of the street, staring at the devastation that had once been my home.

Lucan whined again and nudged my hand.

"We should go," the whine said.

I climbed out of the abyss threatening to swallow me. Down the block, I watched my son Paul run a hand through his hair as he stood to one side of the barrier set up across the street. Dear lord, he'd be worried sick, wondering if I'd been...

I dug my fingers into Lucan's thick ruff. He pushed again. My heart kicked against my breastbone. "No," I said, my voice a bare thread of sound around the constriction in my throat. I blinked back a sheen of tears. "No. We're not going back. Not yet. I need to tell them I'm okay."

Lucan growled disagreement, and I shivered at the threatening rumble. I eyed him. Just how far would a Crone's protector go to keep her safe? As if sensing my thread of uncertainty, he licked my free hand and gave another whine. Soft, this time. Reassuring. I disentangled my fingers from his fur and patted his head.

"I have to do this. I can't let Paul think I was in the—" I broke off, wrenching my gaze back to the smoldering wreckage. Horror gripped me. Merlin. Dear God, Merlin had still been in the house when we'd left this morning, and—

I shoved Lucan away and broke into a jog down the middle of the street, adrenaline driving muscles that hadn't been asked to move that fast in years. The wolf loped beside me, grumbling his disapproval, then veered left and slipped between two houses and out of sight. I focused on the remains of my home, trying to remember if I might have left a window open, an escape route available, a—

A shout went up from the gathering of neighbors, and a half dozen people ran toward me, their cries mingling together. "Claire!" "Oh, thank God!" "You're alive!"

Paul whirled, closed the space between us in a handful of strides, and pulled me into the kind of bear hug he hadn't given me in years. "Jesus, Mom, you scared the living daylights out of us! When Jeanne called, I thought—we thought—Christ, where *were* you?"

"Out," I mumbled into his shoulder, struggling against his hold. "And I'm fine. But Merlin—"

The crowd reached us, and I was passed from hug to hug, buffeted by my neighbors' anxiety and need for reassurance. Jeanne was the last to hold me, her arms strong and fierce, refusing to let go.

"You gave us *such* a fright," she whispered against my ear, her voice shaking. "I was terrified we'd lost you."

Jeanne was neither the sentimental nor the panicky type—a byproduct of being an emergency room nurse, I'd always supposed —and so the genuine terror rolling off her in waves hit me like a tsunami. I stopped trying to push away and allowed myself to be held as I absorbed the collective relief of the group surrounding me. Let it soak in. Only then did I face the horror that loomed behind it.

I stared at the dark plumes of smoke drifting from the blackened wreckage a few houses down and across the street. My home had burned to the ground, and I could have been inside when it did. *Would* have been inside, if it hadn't been for the house in the woods...and Lucan...and Keven.

One of the police officers strode down the sidewalk toward me, accompanied by a firefighter, their faces somber. They would ask the questions they needed to ask, and there would be an investigation, but I knew already they would find nothing. No reason for the fire. No fault in the wiring. No appliance left on. Nothing that could have sparked an inferno. Nothing, that was, that could be identified or traced.

Paul moved to intercept the first responders, giving me time to pull back from Jeanne and gather myself. A movement between the houses on the left snagged my attention, and my stomach lurched as I recognized Lucan. His raised hackles and lowered head signaled his disquiet. Annoyance with me, or something else?

I half-listened to Jeanne babble on about the fire as I scanned street and lawns, rooftops and trees. But nothing else moved. All the activity was here, between me and what remained of my house, and a little of the tension left my shoulders.

"I should talk to them," I said to Jeanne, pointing toward Paul and the first responders. And then I remembered and clutched her arm. "Merlin?"

A plaintive yowl answered me, and I whipped around to find Gilbert clutching an indignant ball of orange fur liberally smudged with black. My heart stuttered, then swelled with relief and gratitude as I took the cat from his arms and buried my face in sooty fur, not caring that the cat stank of smoke. Or that Gilbert had been his rescuer.

"You made it," I whispered. "I can't believe you made it."

The cat sank his claws into my shoulder and hissed at Gilbert in response.

"He survived," Gilbert agreed, "but I'm pretty sure he used up most of his nine lives. By the time he came sailing out of that broken window in your room, the whole place was ablaze. I have no idea how he made the jump or survived it. I saw him go under the Jacksons' porch. It took most of a can of tuna, but I managed to coax him out."

"Thank you, Gilbert. Truly. Thank you *so* much."

"It was nothing. I—" His gaze darted left, then right, then slid past his wife. He shuffled a few steps off, and jerked his head in invitation for me to follow.

I hesitated. Was he going to ask for the pendant as a reward? I wouldn't put it past him. Shifting my grip on Merlin so he wouldn't escape again, I sighed and followed.

Gilbert shoved his hands into his pockets and dug a toe into the lawn we stood on. "I just..." he began. Then he stopped and cleared his throat before continuing in a rush, "You need to be careful. There are people—that necklace I sold Braden—I think they're—"

"I know," I interrupted. But I wanted to confirm anyway. "There are no estate heirs, are there?"

Gilbert shook his head, his comb-over flapping with the movement. "No. He—they—"

"They?" I asked sharply. There was more than one? How many?

"There were two of them. They saw the pendant on my website and came into the shop on the morning of your birthday party, just after I sold it to Braden."

"How much did they offer you?"

"A lot." His voice went hoarse. "Jeanne could stop working. We could retire."

My palms went damp against Merlin's fur. If I'd had any doubt before that 'they' knew what the pendant was, I didn't anymore. A glance toward Paul found him leading the first responders toward me, his face somber. Great. This was going to be more difficult than I'd hoped.

"Thank you for your honesty," I said to Gilbert. "I appreciate—"

"Claire, be careful. I don't know who they are, but they're—I think they're dangerous. I told them I would get the pendant back for them, but they said they'd—I think they might have..." Jeanne's husband trailed off and nodded toward my house.

"They came to my house to talk to me. I told them you wouldn't sell the pendant back to me, and they wanted me to tell them where to find you so they could negotiate with you directly. I refused because—well. I just did. And then I saw you come out onto your porch, so I went inside, hoping they'd leave. But I think I might have tipped them off somehow, and now— after what happened to your window last night—and then this—"

So Lucan had been right. It *had* been a Mage who had watched me from Gilbert's driveway—and there had been another one. Cold trickled down my spine. And if Lucan was right about that, he was probably right about why they hadn't come after me right then and there.

Magick.

I was supposed to be able to do magick. They thought I *could* do it. I took one hand from Merlin and slapped it over my mouth to hold back a honk of laughter. Oh God. If they only knew.

"Mom?" Paul's voice cracked on the word behind me, and I turned to look up at him, sobering as my eyes searched his face. I'd been wrong. His expression wasn't somber, it was...stricken.

The cold in my spine spread through my belly. My gaze flicked from my son to the police officer at his shoulder.

Paul cleared his throat. "Mom, they found someone. In the house. A body."

Horror unfurled in my chest. I stared past him toward the black, smoldering shell that had been my home. Someone...in *there*? Dear God, no.

And then it hit me. The neighbors.

I whirled, and my frantic gaze raked over the clusters of people standing on lawns and in the street, searching for the one face I already knew was missing.

Edie.

CHAPTER 18

I SHIVERED IN THE AFTERNOON SUN. THE BLANKET A firefighter had put around my shoulders was no match for the ice that had enveloped me and claimed my core. Someone had brought a pet carrier for Merlin, and the cat now sat contained at my feet, his howls punctuating the conversation happening above his head. The questions. So many questions.

They came at me from a distance, and I answered them there, too. As if the concerned, responsible citizen part of me had stepped away to handle the situation while the friend part of me sat, stunned and hollow, on the side step of a ladder truck. The police officer asked. The citizen answered. The friend tried desperately to make sense of what had happened.

When had I left the house?

Around seven this morning. I'd gone to see...a friend.

Edie.

Did I know why Edith James would have been in my house?

No.

Funny, blunt, pulls-no-punches Edie.

Did she have a key?

Yes, of course. She was my friend.

My best friend.

Had I asked her to check on something for me?

No.

Had I left the stove on? Was this my fault?

There would be an autopsy. And a full investigation. Did I understand?

Of course.

Why in God's name had she been in my house?

Paramedics rolled a gurney down my front walk to the street, a long, black bag strapped to it. Another police officer stretched

130

yellow tape around the perimeter of the picket fence after they left. She looked over at me and nodded, and I recognized her as K. Abraham from the night before. She must be pulling a double shift; she would be tired by now.

I stared at the remains of my home. My mind separated a little more from my body. So much was gone. Erased. Could never be retrieved. Paul's baby pictures and his first lock of hair, his report cards, the artwork that had decorated my refrigerator over many years. My wedding dress, remade from my mother's and saved to one day pass on to another bride. Photographs that captured decades of memories. Financial records and personal papers.

Edie.

"Ma'am?"

I blinked up at the officer standing over me, his notebook in hand. "Pardon?"

"I asked if you have somewhere to stay. The Red Cross has someone standing by if you need accommodation. They can help with clothing and food, too."

"She'll stay with me," Paul interjected, and I gave a little start. I'd forgotten he was even there. He started giving his particulars to the officer—Constable Charbonneau, I thought he'd said, or maybe that was his partner?

I let myself leave the conversation again, absently hushing Merlin at my feet. Most of my neighbors had dispersed, with a few still standing further down the street and only Jeanne and Gilbert nearby. Gilbert watched me with the kind of caution one gave to an explosive that might detonate at any second. As well he might, because he had information in which the police would be most interested, if there was any point in them having it.

But there wasn't, and telling them would only open the door to more questions for me. Awkward ones I couldn't answer even if I wanted to.

I thought of the unread book waiting for me in the stone cellar. *The Crone Wars: A Compleat History and Grimoire.* When I was finally able to read it, would it explain why Edie had died? Or would it simply confirm what I already knew—that it should have been me? I curled my shoulders around the ache in my chest. If I'd given up the pendant and turned my back on all of it, the Mages might still have come after me, as Lucan had said. But it would have been me they'd found in my house. Me that they killed, and not Edie. And then all this would have been over.

Instead, my friend was dead and the Mages were still out there. Still wanting the pendant. Still looking for me.

My gaze left Gilbert and wandered over to Jeanne, who stood talking with Natalie while Braden rolled around in the grass beside them. Huh. I hadn't noticed their arrival. Had they said hello? Had I answered? I suddenly longed for the feel of my grandson's warm little arms wrapped around me, but I couldn't find my voice to call out to him and didn't trust my legs to carry me that many steps.

Oh, Edie.

I swallowed against the lump in my throat and blinked back the hot tears that made Braden hazy. Over my head, Paul agreed to bring me to the police station the following day to sign a statement. Unease unfurled in my belly. Something was wrong with that idea. But what?

I frowned, trying to concentrate. Paul. Statement. No, that wasn't it. Paul, Natalie, Braden—

My head snapped up. Utter terror filled my soul. I couldn't protect them. I'd already lost Edie, and if Keven and Lucan were right and the Mages wouldn't stop coming after me, and if I went with Paul and Natalie and Braden—

A crow glided in over our heads and landed on the fire truck roof above me. It cawed once. A harsh, guttural sound that underlined my thoughts.

"I can't protect you," I whispered.

Paul and Constable Charbonneau looked down at me.

"Mom?" Paul put out a hand as I struggled to my feet, but I avoided his touch.

"I can't protect you," I said again, my voice stronger this time, bordering on hysterical even to my own ears. Frantically, I searched for Lucan, but I found neither wolf nor man. Panic licked through my veins. I tried to rein it in. *Get a grip, Claire. He's just hiding.*

Both Paul and the cop looked alarmed now, and I gritted my teeth and balled my hands into fists.

"I can't stay with you because I can't protect you," I told Paul. So much for reining it in. I turned to Constable Charbonneau and repeated, "I can't stay with him."

"Mrs. Emerson—"

Lady Claire, the third voice that was neither mine nor Edie's corrected him in my head. Because sure, on top of everything else, I totally needed three-way arguments in my head.

I tuned back into Constable Charbonneau's words. "—active investigation," he was saying. "Maybe it's best if you let your son—"

"You," I snapped, "have no idea what's best."

"Mom!" An appalled Paul turned to Charbonneau, hands raised placatingly. "I'm so sorry. I don't know what's gotten into her. She's not usually so rude—it must be shock or something."

Or something.

In the shadow between the houses near where we stood, a shape moved, low to the ground. Lucan. I hoped.

I hoisted the cat carrier in one hand and tugged Paul's sleeve with the other. "I have a friend," I told him. "I'll stay with him. Take Natalie and Braden home."

Paul stared over his shoulder at me, his mouth hanging open. He snapped it shut. "Mom, be reason—"

"Freaking hell, Paul, for once just do as you're told," I growled, and his jaw dropped again. "Oh, for—" I pushed past him and the cop, and with Merlin banging against my leg in the carrier, headed across the lawn toward Natalie and Jeanne.

Natalie would understand. I would make her understand.

"All women were witches once," Keven whispered in my memory.

Jeanne reached out in an effort to fold me into another hug when I got to them. "Poor Edie," she blubbered. "Poor, poor Edie."

All women except Jeanne, perhaps. I evaded her grasp, ignoring the pain that shafted through me at the sound of Edie's name, and set Merlin on the ground. I put my hands on either side of Natalie's face, commanding her attention.

"Take Braden home," I ordered. "Now."

My daughter-in-law stared at me. "What? But why? What's wrong, Maman?"

"Just do it, Natalie. I can't explain"—well, I could, but then she would have reasonable grounds for worrying about all the age-related illnesses she was so afraid of—"but it's not safe for him here. Or you."

Natalie pulled away from my hold with a nervous laugh. "What on earth are you talking about? We have three cops and half the fire department here. We couldn't be safer. Besides, you're coming home with—"

"No. I'm not."

"Of course you are. You have nowhere else to go, and it will be fun for Braden to—" She broke off, her expression clouding over as she remembered my circumstances. "I mean..."

"I'll be fine. I have a friend I can—"

A howl cut me off. A long, low, unmistakably wolf howl. *Leave*, it said. *Now.*

Shit, I thought, but no Edie-voice crowed its delight. I pushed down my grief again and looked around, my sense of urgency ramping up at Lucan's warning. Was something coming? Was it already here? Were the Mages watching even now? If they were, would I be able to summon the magick I was supposed to have? Somehow, I'd hurled white fire at the shade. Maybe if I could—

But I couldn't, because I hadn't the faintest idea how to recreate what I'd done that night. Or what I'd done in the cellar with Keven.

My stomach churned, edging toward nausea. And if I did manage to accidentally conjure something again, I couldn't control it. I was just as likely to take out someone on the street —or another house—as I was to hit my target. I needed to learn how it worked.

I needed Keven.

And Natalie and Braden and Paul needed to get away from me before the Mages made the connection between us.

Lucan's howl had stunned bystanders and first responders alike into silence. Everyone stood as if rooted in place, their expressions varying only in degrees of shock and doubt. Natalie was the first to move, seizing Braden and lifting him off the lawn to hold him close. Jeanne was next, crossing herself as her lips moved in prayer and she edged toward Gilbert.

"Was that a *wolf?*" Natalie squeaked, her eyes round as her gaze darted over the street.

"Yes. But he's not the one—" I broke off. Too much information.

"Not the one what? That I should be afraid of?" She tightened her grip on her son, who was trying to squirm out of her arms so he could look for the wolf. "*What* is going on, Maman?"

"I can't tell you. I just need you to trust me. You need to get away from me, Natalie, and stay away. For Braden's sake. Please."

My daughter-in-law shook her head. "You're not making sense," she said, but her voice lacked conviction, and her eyes darted toward her vehicle parked down the street. My *"for Braden's sake"* had struck a chord.

Still she hesitated, loyalty warring with her desire to flee. "What about you? Where will you go? You said you have a friend...?"

"Yes. And I'll be fine," I told her again.

"You're sure..."

"I'm sure. Go. Please. And take Paul with you."

"You'll be careful?"

"Of course."

You, too, I whispered in my head as I watched her head toward Paul, her heels sinking into the grass with each step. *Please...you, too.*

She was halfway across the lawn when she set Braden down, held up a finger warning him to stay where he was, and made her way back to me. She pulled her wallet from her purse and took out a credit card.

"You'll need clothes and things," she said, handing it to me. "The fire—you've lost everything, Maman."

Edie. I lifted my hand through a fresh haze of pain to accept the card.

"The password is Paul's nickname for Braden," Natalie said, "and there's a five thousand limit, so get whatever you need."

"I..." I swallowed hard against a sudden thickening in my throat. Every unkind thought I'd ever had about my daughter-in-law vanished. I'd been underestimating her for years. "Thank you, Natalie. I'll pay you back."

She flapped a hand at me, digging through her purse with the other. "Whenever the insurance comes through is fine." She pulled out her cell phone. "Take this, too, so we can call you."

"But don't you need it? Your business—"

"Only answer if it's from Paul's phone, and let everything else go to voicemail." She pushed the phone at me. "I want to be able to make sure you're okay. I imagine yours was in the house somewhere."

I managed a watery smile as I accepted the phone. "Guilty."

"I figured. I'll pick up another for you, and we can exchange." Without warning, Natalie stepped in and gave me a quick, tight hug. "I don't know what's going on, but look after yourself, okay?"

She picked her way back to take Braden's hand and join Paul. They were too far away for me to hear them, but I watched their discussion take place in body language. The vehement shake of Paul's head, the touch of Natalie's hand on his arm and the lift of her shoulders, more talk, his arms thrown wide in a *whatever* gesture accompanied by a scowl. Paul started in my direction, but another touch on his arm stopped him. He scowled again, this time at me, and then turned on his heel and stalked away.

I watched him and Natalie get into their respective vehicles and turn them around. As they pulled away, Paul following Natalie and studiously ignoring my wave, Lucan's wolf howled again. It was closer this time, and unmistakably more urgent. As it faded away, the same keening cry I'd heard twice before in the forest floated across the neighborhood.

It, too, was close.

And it was enough to propel Jeanne toward her house at a dead run, calling on her Lord to preserve her and Gilbert to follow. Pale-faced, he did, avoiding my eyes as he passed me. The few other neighbors who remained did likewise, and one of the police officers still on the street shouted directions at the others. They fanned out in search of the cry's source. I hoped to hell and back they didn't find it.

And that *it* didn't find *them*.

Or me.

I wasn't too confident about the latter.

Using the cops' distraction to my advantage, I returned to the car, scooped up Lucan's clothes, and half-walked, half-jogged to the back of the only house I knew would be empty.

Lucan waited under the trees in Edie's back yard, morphing back into human form as I approached. I held out the clothes to him without speaking and turned away while he dressed. After a moment, his hand rested gently on my shoulder.

"The woman they found—she was your friend."

My best friend, I wanted to say, but the words wouldn't leave my throat. I nodded.

"I'm sorry, Lady Claire, truly." His hand fell away. "But we have to go."

I swiped away an escaped tear. "Gnomes," I said. "Keven said it was the call to gather."

"Yes. They'll keep to the trees, so we're safe in the open like this, but we could have trouble getting to the house. And the sun is low, which means we may have shades to deal with, if we don't hurry."

Awesome.

I looked past Edie's house to the street, where I'd left my car. The Mages might already know where I was, but Paul didn't—and I didn't want him to. The car needed to stay here. A shadow passed over me as a single crow flapped by overhead and joined a dozen others circling silently over the smoking remains next door. What could they see that I couldn't? The gnomes gathering? The shades waiting in the shadows for dark to descend? If only—

"Lady Claire," Lucan urged.

The edges of Natalie's credit card bit into my fingers, and I held it up along with her cell phone.

"A cab," I said. "We should call a cab."

"Agreed," said Lucan. "But *now*."

CHAPTER 19

THE CAB DRIVER DEPOSITED US AT THE SIDE OF MORGAN'S Way, processed Natalie's credit card, and handed it back to me through the open driver-side window.

"You're sure this is where you want to be?" he asked, waving at the dead end. "There's nothing out here but trees, and it's getting dark."

"I'm sure," I said, trying not to think about the lengthening shadows or the way the sun had slipped to the very edge of the horizon. We should have been back hours ago. "Thank you."

"Suit yourself." The driver gave the shrug of someone who had obviously seen his share of strange fares, rolled up his window, and executed a neat, three-point turn before driving back the way we'd come.

I hunched my shoulders against the evening chill and the almost too-quiet. Merlin had ceased his protests at last, we'd heard no cries from the woods, and not even the usual crickets sang.

I shifted the cat's carrier to the other hand and took a deep breath. Thoughts of Edie skated along the edges of my mind, but I held them at bay. I would take time to sit with my grief soon. But not now. Now, Lucan and I needed to get back within warded walls, and I needed to get back down into that cellar and figure out how to protect my family.

Magick 101: the crash course.

Crickets.

The thought popped into my brain, demanding my attention. I frowned at its randomness. Then I went still. Unease returned to unfurl down my spine and raise the hairs along my arms. I held my breath and strained to listen.

There were no crickets singing.

And the trees on both sides of the road were filled with silent bird silhouettes. Crows. How had I not noticed them when we pulled up?

I whirled to face Lucan and stumbled when I found him standing close enough to touch, his expression grim.

"They're coming," he said.

"I know," I said, because I did. Somehow. "How many?"

On the other side of the bramble thicket, the iron gate at the edge of the woods swung open, as if to hurry us along.

"I don't know. Wait here. I'll be back."

He dissolved into wolf-form and loped into the forest. Merlin moved restlessly in his confines, tipping the carrier back and forth in my grasp and growling low in his throat. Long seconds ticked by. They became a minute, then two, then—

Lucan reappeared at my side and morphed into his naked man-self, making me jump. "Hundreds," he announced. "Run."

I blinked stupidly. "Hundreds? But how—"

He grabbed my arm and shoved me toward the thicket.

"I'll hold them off as best I can, but if they get too close, sacrifice the cat, understand?"

I clutched Merlin's hard plastic case to my chest. "What? No! He's—"

"Expendable," Lucan growled. He seized my shoulders and put his face close enough to mine that I could feel the warmth of his breath on my lips. "And you're not. Sacrifice the cat, milady. Now *run*."

He turned me and pushed. I stumbled, found my footing, and forged blindly through the brambles, one hand groping for the carrier's handle. My fingers closed around it, and I let the cat's weight drop to my side. Lucan's presence disappeared. Without looking, I knew he had shifted again. Knew he'd gone.

I was alone.

The shadows closed in.

Run, Lucan's voice echoed in my brain. I pushed harder against the thorns snagging at my shirt and pants and scratching my hands. I broke through on the other side, and the carrier bounced off the stone pillar as I passed through the gate. The path to the house lay before me, glowing faintly. Something snarled in the trees to the left. Lucan?

A snarl sounded and grew to a roar of fury.

Lucan.

I trotted down the path as fast as I dared. Tripping over a tree root now would not be in my best interests. Leaves rustled in the undergrowth on both sides. Dry branches snapped. A faint drumming in the distance drew closer and became the march of dozens of footsteps converging on me from all sides. I sped up. Adrenaline shot through me, making my pulse race but my limbs turn leaden. Inside the carrier, Merlin growled. Hissed. Spat.

I tightened my grip on the carrier's handle, filled my lungs, and bolted toward the faint light filtering through the trees, aiming for the house I knew to be there. For Keven. For safety.

With my cat.

And then I stumbled to a halt and gaped.

The path had become a gauntlet of waist-high, red-capped, blue-coated figures. They smiled at me with their normal, cheery expressions, and I blinked, not quite believing my eyes. When Lucan had said gnomes, I hadn't expected the garden variety. Where in God's name had they all come from? This was—

The nearest Gnome stepped out of the shadows to reveal a weirdly familiar half-head with a half-smile. Instantly, I flashed back to cleaning ceramic shards and vanilla buttercream from between my floor boards. My jaw dropped. Seriously? My own gnome collection? This was—

The gnome's half-mouth opened wide on two rows of needle-sharp teeth, and my palms turned slick. Shock became terror. This was going to kill me.

The Gnome launched itself at me. Instinctively, I swung my fist and knocked it, howling, into the undergrowth. A half-dozen others marched in its footsteps, hands outstretched toward me. I dodged left, then right, high-stepping over legs stuck out to trip me and refusing to be diverted into the trees—a move I knew without doubt would be catastrophic for both me and poor Merlin.

More red-capped, blue-coated bodies emerged from the woods. They crowded onto the end of the path, standing shoulder to shoulder with arms wide and faces stretched in awful, snarling grimaces—a solid, three-foot-tall mass of hostile intent.

Heart thudding, I looked over their heads at the house in the clearing. Despair settled, bitter on my tongue. It was no more than a hundred feet away, and yet so impossibly—

Wait. The clearing. I blinked. None of the gnomes stood in the clearing. It was as if an invisible barrier sat at the edge of the woods. Had Keven been able to call more wards and expand their protection? Whatever the reason, Lucan had been right. The gnomes were confined to the trees, and the clearing was...what, only thirty feet away? Hope surged in me. Then it tanked. It was still thirty feet filled with too many tiny bodies to count, all out to get me.

Me...and the carrier that weighed me down.

Sacrifice the cat, Lucan's voice returned to whisper in my ear. And as I listened to his distant snarls and the drumming foot-steps of the countless other gnomes he kept from me, I felt their wisdom. Their inevitability.

My hand loosened, and the carrier handle began to slide from my grip. The wall of gnomes advanced toward me, their guttural growls underscoring the steady tramp of feet on the hardened path. With my free hand, I reached for the catch to open Merlin's carrier door. If I released him, he might at least have a fighting—

Horror flooded me. But what if he didn't? What if the gnomes caught him?

My fingers clamped onto the handle again, and I blinked back a hot prickle of tears at the thought of what might happen to my sweet ginger boy. Anger began a slow boil in the pit of my belly. First Edie, and now my cat?

"I don't think so," I growled at the approaching mob. I tucked the pendant inside my shirt, swiftly checked the latches on the carrier door, and shifted my grip on the handle to make room for both hands. "Hold on, pretty boy. It's going to be a rough ride."

I lunged forward with a bellow, and for a split second, the startled gnomes hesitated. It was long enough for the carrier's first blow to connect with two of them—and for me to identify the sound of shattering ceramic at the impact. They could still be broken. That was good.

And then I was in the thick of them and swinging the other way, with no time for thought as another gnome head shattered. I bellowed again, swung again, and moved a step forward, toward the house.

The solid phalanx facing me began to break apart, the closest gnomes scattering left and right to escape my makeshift club. In the back of my mind, a voice warned that they would form again behind me, but I couldn't fight on two fronts, so I shut it down and forged ahead, doggedly gaining a step at time.

Inside the plastic confines of his prison, Merlin bounced from side to side, his weight lending force to my blows. Together, we moved one foot forward, another, two more. My attack settled into a rhythm: yell, step, swing, shatter, yell, step, swing, shatter. Pray the carrier handle and door would hold. Repeat.

Seconds became an eternity, and my focus narrowed even further. I shut out all but the jar of each strike traveling up my arms and into my shoulders. Ignored the hands pulling at the back of my shirt and catching at my arms.

Yell, step, swing, shatter.
Don't look at how much farther.
Pray.
Needles sank into the back of my thigh, and I stumbled. The

carrier flew from the grip of one hand; the other saved it. I recovered, fury overwhelming the pain, and twisted at the waist to slam the cat carrier against the Gnome latched onto me. Its half-head shattered and ceramic shards flew into the trees. I returned to my attack on the others—and almost fell flat on my face on the grass when the carrier met with air.

Chest heaving, I staggered to a halt and stared at the lawn between me and the house. At the light streaming through the open front door and Keven lumbering down the walkway toward me. At the wolf racing out of the woods to the left and morphing into Lucan. Slow realization dawned. I'd done it. I'd cleared the woods. I'd escaped.

A hundred tiny voices outside the clearing howled their displeasure and defeat, barely audible above the boom of blood pulsing against my eardrums. My ragged gasps. Lucan skidded to a halt on the grass beside me.

"I did it," I puffed, pride swelling in my chest. I held out the carrier. It wobbled precariously in the hand shaking at the end of my arm. "I did it. *And* I saved the cat."

"So you did." Gently, he pried the carrier from fingers only too ready to relinquish their hold and handed Merlin over to the hovering gargoyle. He smiled down at me, his amber eyes glowing with warmth. "So you did," he said again.

And then the world turned upside down, and I slid to the ground.

I SURFACED INTO CONSCIOUSNESS FACE DOWN ON THE SAME sofa by the fire where Keven had tended Lucan's wound two nights before. I blinked into the soft leather. A blanket had been tucked around my shoulders, but judging by the cool draft across the backs of my legs, it didn't extend that far.

I frowned as I came more awake. Actually, I could only feel the draft on one leg. The left one burned like blazes. I wriggled my arms under my chest and pushed myself up. A firm hand on my back countered the attempt.

"Rest, milady," Lucan's voice rumbled above me. "The gargoyle is mixing a poultice."

I froze, contemplating my situation. Given that cool draft, my legs were almost certainly bare, which meant my pants had been removed. By Keven? Lucan? The latter seemed more likely, but oh, how I wished for the former. And wished even harder that the latter would go away. I grimaced at the couch. First the open pajama shirt, now this. The most attractive man I'd laid eyes on in years—or ever, if I was to be completely honest—and I seemed destined to have him see me in nothing but the most embarrassing of predicaments. How very—

My breath hissed out and tears sprang to my eyes as the muscle in the back of my thigh gave a vicious twist and turned white-hot. Teeth gritted, I rode out the searing pain. When I could breathe again, I turned my head to the side, seeking Lucan and finding him crouched beside me.

"Poison?" I croaked, trying not to panic at the memory of the Gnome that had latched onto me. Lucan had said a shade's feathers were toxic. Were a Gnome's teeth, too?

Lucan shook his shaggy head. His hair had escaped the man-bun again—as it did every time he shifted—and I wondered why he even bothered with it. Surely it would be easier to just have it cut—although not nearly as sexy. I swatted away the thought, reminding myself I loathed man-buns. Or at least, I used to loathe them.

This one didn't seem so bad now that I'd gotten to know the man attached to it. A man who was bound to me by magick through no choice of his own, but who still made me feel like I was the most important thing in his—

Lucan brushed a strand of hair from my face and my bones dissolved. It had been a long time since I'd felt like the most important thing to anyone.

"Gnomes aren't poisonous," he told me as I wrestled my

hormones under control. "But their teeth are like razors. There's a lot of damage to your muscle and a risk of infection."

Awesome.

"Then you've encountered them before."

"I have. Once." His face closed and his lips went tight. "It was the only time I lost a Crone under my protection. You did exceedingly well tonight, Lady Claire."

He'd lost a Crone? That meant he wasn't infallible. I shivered. I could have done without the knowledge right now. I tried to distract myself.

"When you and Keven said gnomes, it never occurred to me that they'd be the garden variety. How—why—?"

"The why is easy. They're ubiquitous. They span continents and generations. They're everywhere, which makes them easy to access and..." He trailed off.

I rested my head on my folded arms and looked sideways at him. "And?"

"And that leads us to the how." His lips took on a grim line. "But let's get you patched up before we get into that."

I wanted to insist, but my leg gave another spasm, and I closed my eyes and gritted my teeth. What was taking Keven so long with that poultice? What was she doing, growing the damned herbs from seed?

I groaned into the soft leather, and Lucan's hand rubbed my shoulders as the pain crested, then receded. I put a hand over one of his and gave it a grateful squeeze. Whether he was with me by choice or not, his presence was fast becoming all that kept me grounded in this new world of mine. A good reason to stop putting the poor man in danger, now that I thought about it.

The heavy tread of Keven's footsteps sounded in the hall. I lifted my head and peered over the arm of the couch as the gargoyle came into the parlor. Then I blinked.

Merlin had draped himself across the gargoyle's shoulders, hind legs hanging on one side of Keven's neck and front legs on the other side. His purr was audible even across the room, and his half-closed eyes signaled utter contentment with his situation. My mouth dropped open. After the house fire, taxi ride, gnomes, and, now, new surroundings, I hadn't expected to see him for at least a week. Especially given his skittishness around strangers.

"Good. You're awake," Keven said.

I nodded, then jutted my chin toward the cat. "You—he doesn't usually like new people."

Keven gave Merlin a sideways glance and shrugged. "I'm not people," she said. "And I like felines. They're interesting. Much better than canines, who just pee on everything."

Honestly, the bickering between her and Lucan reminded me so much of Jeanne and Edie—

The thought blindsided me. Edie. I'd forgotten. How could I have forgotten?

Through a haze of tears, I watched the gargoyle scoop Merlin off her shoulder with a massive hand and plunk him onto the back of the couch. "Stay."

Merlin yawned, stretched, and settled into a loaf to watch the proceedings. I blinked again.

"Does it have a name?" Keven asked, setting the bowl she carried on a side table.

"Mer—" Even as Lucan's hand tightened on my shoulder, I remembered Keven's reaction in the garden to Merlin's name. I scrambled for an alternative I'd be able to remember—and that wouldn't confuse the heck out of the cat—and seized on the only thing I could think of.

"—gan," I finished.

Keven paused in the task of squeezing excess blue goop from a cloth over the bowl. "Mergan?" she echoed. "That's an odd name."

The fire had started in my leg again. I couldn't decide whether it was better to have the conversation as a distraction from the pain, or the pain as a distraction from the conversation. To my relief, Lucan cleared his throat.

"Her leg?" he prompted the gargoyle.

"Of course." Keven cupped a hand under the still-dripping rag and carried it toward the couch. I eyed the rather brilliant color with skepticism.

"Is it supposed to be that blue?"

"Only if you want it to work." Keven nudged Lucan out of the way, and I braced for whatever effect the potion might have when it touched my skin. Instant numbness was not what I expected.

"Ohh," I breathed. "That's *so* much better."

"I should hope so." Keven fussed over the poultice's arrangement and stepped back with a grunt of satisfaction. "Ten minutes on, then change it to a fresh one," she instructed Lucan. "There's another cloth in the bowl. Burn them when you're done, then carry her to her room. I'll bring up soup and tea. Mergan, come." The gargoyle snapped her fingers—a loud striking of rock against rock—and lumbered out of the parlor with my cat trotting after her like a well-trained dog.

Silence fell when they departed, and then Lucan chuckled, a deep rumble of amusement. "Mergan?" he asked.

And, splayed like a spatchcocked chicken on the couch, with one leg growing more numb by the second, I—a sixty-year-old grandmother who had just used her cat as a sledgehammer to run a gauntlet of gnomes—giggled, chortled, outright guffawed, and then dissolved into tears.

Oh, Edie.

CHAPTER 20

SUNLIGHT STREAMED THROUGH THE WINDOW WHEN I woke the next morning. It danced across the wooden floor and the foot of the bed, filling the room with a bright warmth at odds with the dreams that had plagued my sleep. And with the events of the previous day.

I pulled the duvet up under my chin and eased onto my side. My entire body protested. And my heart—oh God, how my heart hurt.

Edie.

Beautiful, vibrant, kick-ass Edie. I couldn't believe she was gone. Because of me. The sheer volume of loss was overwhelming. Who would inspire me now? Who would waltz into my kitchen in the morning, uninvited and unannounced and—

A second wave of loss washed over me.

No one. Because my house was gone, too. Cheesy rice on a cracker.

I waited, but no Edie-voice corrected me. She really was gone, even from my head. I snuffled my despair—mixed with a healthy dose of self-pity—into my pillow. The Mages had killed my friend, and now they threatened my family, and I was the only one who could stop them, but I could only do that with magick, and I didn't know how, and I couldn't—

Panic bloomed in my chest, and I struggled for air. I squeezed my eyes shut. A glimmer of anger surfaced in me. *God damn it, Claire, enough!* my inner voice scolded. *Your family is in danger—Braden is in danger. Are you really going to lie here whining about how hard your life is? Jesus Christ on a cracker, woman, get over yourself and do something!*

I blinked into the duvet covering my head, swiped the back

of my hand across my nose, and rolled onto my back. I stared at the ceiling. My voice was right.

The magick was in me. I knew that. I'd felt it. Seen it in action. I had no idea how to make it work for me, but I could learn. I had to learn. It was time.

Determination surged through my veins. I pushed back the covers, sat up, and swung my legs over the bed.

And that was it.

That was as far as I could go, because one leg simply refused to cooperate further. I stared down at where my nightgown—had I put that on?—had ridden up to reveal the bright red puffball that had replaced my thigh overnight. That couldn't be good. And if the front of the leg looked that bad, what on earth did the back and the actual bite from the Gnome look like? I chewed on my bottom lip and eyed the distance between bed and bathroom door. If I cruised the perimeter of the room and used various bits of furniture as support—

A knock sounded at the door, and I hastily pulled the nightgown down to cover myself as Lucan barged in.

"You *could* wait for an invitation," I grumped.

"I have been waiting," he said. "I've knocked five times over the day without response. The gargoyle told me I shouldn't wait this time. I'm to report back to her on your condition, on pain of bodily harm being done if I fail."

Despite myself, I found my lips twitching. Yes, I could imagine Keven issuing just such a threat. But wait—five times? I glanced at the sunlit window, trying to think which direction it faced.

"West," said Lucan, as if he'd read my mind, "and it's two o'clock."

Okay, later than expected, but not too bad, I supposed.

"On Friday."

My brain did a quick series of calculations starting with my birthday on Sunday, finding the house on Monday, the shade attacking my home on Tuesday, that same home burning down and the Gnome gauntlet on Wednesday, and—I gaped at him. "*Friday*? But that's—I slept almost two days? Paul will be frantic!"

And the police would probably have a warrant out for my arrest because I hadn't turned up to sign that statement.

And the Mages. What about the Mages? Had they gone after anyone else? My family?

Cheesy—no, *Jesus*.

Sheer panic drove me to my feet, and Lucan caught me as I toppled. Strong, warm hands guided me back down to the side of the bed. He crouched in front of me and pushed the nightgown and my weak protests aside. His face turned grim.

"That doesn't look good."

It didn't feel particularly good at the moment, either, but I had more important things to worry about. I flapped an agitated hand at him. "It's fine. Just a bit swollen, is all. But Paul —Braden—"

"That's more than a *bit* anything," he retorted. He rose to his feet again and placed a hand on top of my head when I attempted to follow suit. "Sit still or I'll tie you to the bed." Seeming to take it for granted that I would obey, he pulled the bell-cord over the bed and then strode to the bedroom door and bellowed, "Gargoyle! You're needed!"

"You're making a fuss about nothing," I said. "It's not even that painful anymore." Mostly because I couldn't feel it at all, but I didn't think I needed to add that part. Or the part about the fuzziness beginning to fill my head. I forced myself to focus. "My family—"

"I spoke to your son yesterday and again this morning," Lucan said over his shoulder. "They're fine. I told him you were upset over the fire and your friend, but you were recovering, and that I'd keep him updated."

They're fine. The relief made my bones turn to rubber. That was what I blamed it on, anyway. I pushed through the encroaching fuzziness.

"And he was okay with that? Paul, I mean?"

"I put on my best suit and gave him my business card. He seemed content with my... pedigree, so to speak."

Lucan had a suit? And a business card?

He turned back to the hallway. "Gargoyle!"

"Keep your shirt on, mutt!" came a distant return bellow. "I'm coming."

I opened my mouth to ask what, exactly, he'd told Paul, but my tongue seemed to have fused to the roof of my mouth, and I couldn't make it move. Or feel my lips anymore. Or either of my legs. Or my hands. Or...

Panic began a slow build in my chest, filling the cavities that should have held air but didn't.

Freaking hell.

I couldn't breathe.

Lucan looked around again, and his amber gaze narrowed as it met mine. Then went wide.

"Milady, are you—" He sucked in a quick breath, roared, "*GARGOYLE*!" one more time, and covered the distance to the bed in three long strides. He caught my shoulders and laid me back, then gently cradled my face as he stared down at me. At least, I assumed he was being gentle, because I couldn't feel his touch, either. Red crept around the edges of my vision as I watched his lips form the word 'milady' again. Watched, but couldn't hear, because the buzzing in my ears drowned out all other sound.

Good God, I thought with surprise. That nasty little Gnome had done it. I was dying.

The red around my vision turned black and became complete.

I slipped into nothingness.

If this was death, it was nothing like I had expected.

Darkness sat around me, quiet and still...but not empty. Disquiet crawled over my skin, but the panic I thought I should feel didn't manifest. Instead, my uneasiness faded and curiosity took its place. Something—or someone—was definitely here with me, but who or whatever it was, it wasn't threatening. At least, not yet. It just...waited.

I uncurled my fingers from my palms and flexed my hands. I cleared my throat and opened my mouth, but a sudden light flared in the inky blackness, cutting off my words. I threw up a hand to shield my eyes, squinting into the glare of a—torch? The reflection of flames danced across the dark granite ceiling and walls. Oh, yes. That was a torch, all right. In what appeared to be an underground cavern, no less.

Nope. Not at all what I'd expected death to be.

I blinked away the spots floating before my eyes. My gaze met that of a woman holding the flame aloft. A woman, but not entirely.

She had straight black hair, darker than the darkest corners of the cavern, that fell from a severe part in the center of her head to frame a narrow, sharply featured face with skin so pale, it seemed translucent. Beneath her chin, the skin gave way to what looked like black feathers, which in turn became a long gown made of the same feathers. She held a staff in one hand and torch in the other, and beneath the gown, her feet were bare.

I couldn't help but stare. And then stare some more. The woman was far from beautiful in the accepted sense, but neither was she ugly. She was too...commanding for that. Too present. Too powerful. My unease returned, and a shiver rippled over me as the woman tipped her head to one side and returned my study. There was something about her eyes...

"Crone," the woman said, her voice a harsh rasp.

"I—" I stopped. I'd been about to deny the title, as usual, but found I couldn't. Didn't want to. Something stirred deep in my center, wanting to accept the name. To own it.

I nodded.

The woman raised the torch higher. The feathers along her neck shifted with the movement, and I gave a start. Those weren't feath-

ers, they were crows. Beady-eyed, sleek-bodied, whole crows, clinging to her and—

"I am the Morrigan," she announced.

I forgot about the crows. The *Morrigan*? The goddess *Morrigan*? The Morrigan *Morrigan*? The—

I slammed the brakes on my runaway brain and snapped my mouth shut. Was I supposed to curtsy? Bow? Kneel? How in heaven's name did one greet a goddess, anyway?

"Sit," said the Morrigan. She placed the torch in a holder on the wall and pointed the end of her staff at a rough-hewn table half hidden in the shadows. A wooden chair was drawn up to it and a single, carved wooden cup sat on its surface. "Drink," she added.

Sit before a goddess who was more bird than human? And accept an unknown drink from her? My sense of self-preservation didn't think so. "I—"

The table shot out from the wall, leaving the cup hovering in the air, and stopped in front of me. The chair followed, bumping roughly against the back of my knees.

"The Morrigan does not repeat herself," the bird-goddess rasped.

I swallowed hard and sat, then edged forward until the throbbing fire of the Gnome-bite on the back of my leg didn't rest on the chair. The pain wasn't altogether a bad thing, I supposed. It proved I was still alive. Or at least not altogether dead. Yet.

The cup floated over and settled gently onto the tabletop.

"Drink," the Morrigan said again.

I was just delirious, I assured myself, eyeing the cup filled with a dark, murky liquid. This was all in my imagination, a hallucination brought on by the infection in my leg, no doubt, and how dangerous could hallucinated poison be?

Or maybe I really was dead, in which case, poison couldn't kill me again, so...

I lifted the vessel and put it to my lips. The stench of rotten flesh and vegetation permeated my nostrils and crawled down the back of my throat. I gagged and put the cup down, pushing it away. "That's awful!"

The Morrigan's thin lips curved beneath a beak-like nose. She studied me a moment longer, then nodded. "You'll do."

Eyes still watering, I held a hand over my mouth and tried not to puke. "Do?" I managed between clenched teeth.

The Morrigan reached out with her staff and knocked the cup against the wall. The stone swallowed it without a sound. "That was the Cup of Power," she said. "If you had been tempted by it, I would have let the infection take you here and now. But you weren't." She shrugged, the crow-gown moving with her, and tapped the table with the staff. A new cup appeared, its contents pale and clear. "And so I will save you that you may serve me. Now drink. Morok is rising, and you have much work to do. Your pendant is not—"

"Lady Claire, you must drink," a faraway voice ordered.

"—others," the Morrigan finished. Her voice had gone hoarse, like that of one of the birds that made up her gown, and the edges of her form fluttered, like the flapping of wings.

"Lady Claire!"

I resisted the call. I'd missed the in-between part of what the Morrigan had said, and if a goddess spoke to me, I was pretty sure I needed to hear all of what she told me. "My pendant what?"

"Caawww!" she responded, her imperious black gaze fastened on me. Her entire gown moved now, a shifting mass of feathered bodies. She pointed at the cup with her staff and it rose to press against my lips. "Drink!" she commanded harshly. "You are not—"

"Drink!" the distant voice insisted. Hard fingers held my jaw, and liquid dribbled down my chin. I turned my head, but the cup followed.

"—others," the Morrigan finished again, and frustration clawed at me. I needed to know what she was telling me. Needed—

"Lady Claire, please!"

Across the cavern, the Morrigan dissolved into a cloud of crows that exploded outward from her, filling the space with a rush of feathers and discordant calls. The torch dropped to the floor and snuffed out, plunging me into darkness. My chair toppled backward, taking me with it.

The Morrigan was gone. And I—

Was drowning.

I gagged on the liquid pooling on the back of my tongue.

"Swallow," the voice insisted, no longer distant but right beside my ear, "or I will have the mutt sit on you while I pour it down your throat."

I tried to comply but choked and sputtered, coughing up most of it again.

"Shall I hold her?" Lucan asked, somewhere near my head.

Yes, please, I thought hazily, but the other voice—Keven, I recognized now—said it wasn't necessary. Spoilsport.

"She doesn't need much in her. As long as she's swallowed some of it, it will work. The Morrigan's magic is strong."

The Morrigan—she'd been here, too? Was she still? Or maybe Keven and Lucan had found me in the cavern. No. No, this was a bed under me, not a stone floor. And I needed to get up because...huh. The reasons were hazy, but I was sure they were important. Maybe. I struggled to sit, but the hard hand moved to my chest and held me down.

"Rest," Keven said. "Let the potion work."

"But the Morrigan," I mumbled. I pried open my eyes and the gargoyle swam into view. "She said I have work to do. I need to ask her—"

What? What did I need to ask her? She'd said something was coming, but I couldn't remember. She'd said something about my pendant, too, but I couldn't remember that, either.

The gargoyle looked at something behind me, and I tipped back my head to find Lucan standing on the other side of the bed. I scowled at him.

"You said gnomes weren't poisonous," I mumbled.

"I also said the bite did great damage," he reminded me. "The gargoyle's healing powers are less effective on a human. Your leg was infected."

I considered this. Then frowned again. "I can't feel it. My leg, I mean. Is it—did you—"

"Your leg is intact," Keven assured me.

Well, thank the goddess for that.

I blinked at the odd turn of phrase that popped into my head. Despite my brief dalliance with Wicca, I had never been able to embrace the idea of a goddess—too stuck, I supposed, in a lifetime of societal teachings. But the thought just now had been...organic. As natural as breathing.

Which made it weird.

It also reminded me again of the Morrigan. I tried to push aside Keven's hand, but it was like shoving aside a large boulder. As in not happening.

I scowled at the gargoyle. "I need to find her."

"And so you will," Keven assured me. "When she wants you to do so. Until then, you sleep." Unperturbed by my sputterings, she rolled me over, straightened out the sheet beneath me, rolled me back again, and tucked the covers around me. My eyelids drooped and the memory of the Morrigan started to fade. What had been in that potion of Keven's? Or had it been in the Morrigan's?

"Maybe just a short nap," I whispered. Then, with an effort, I opened one eye to find Lucan again. "You can, you know."

"Can what?"

"Hold me." I smiled, closed my eye again, and drifted off, humming *Love Potion Number 9* under my breath.

CHAPTER 21

MOROK.

The name returned to me the instant my eyes opened the next morning. And with it came a sense of foreboding unlike anything I'd ever felt before.

"Morok is rising, and you have much work to do."

I shivered within the fluffy warmth of the duvet at the memory of the Morrigan's words—and the dozens of questions ricocheting around the edges of my mind, each breeding more. Keven had pulled me away from her too soon. Far too soon.

So many questions. Would Keven and Lucan have answers?

I sat up in bed and examined my leg. The color and size were back to normal, the gnome bite had healed to an angry scar, and most of the pain was gone. The rest of my body, however, was another story, and getting dressed and down the stairs became an exercise in sheer determination.

I made it, however, and eased myself onto the bench opposite Lucan at the kitchen table just after seven, trying hard not to whimper as both he and Keven watched.

"You're still in pain?" Keven frowned.

"Not from the bite," I assured her. "Just some stiff muscles."

And ligaments. And joints. And was that a twinge I felt in my baby toenail? The gnome gauntlet had just about done me in, even without the bite. Apparently, I wasn't thirty anymore. Or forty or fifty, for that matter.

Lucan poured a cup of tea from the pot near him and pushed it across the table toward me. I winced as I reached for it. Goddess, even my fingers hurt. And there was that goddess thought again. Ever since my visit with the Morrigan—imagined or otherwise...

But no. I hadn't imagined it, because if Keven's healing didn't work well on humans, as Lucan had said, then my encounter with the goddess had been no dream. The Morrigan had healed me, and her warning had been real. *"Morok is coming."*

"The mutt told me about your friend." Keven set a plate of eggs and sausage in front of me. "I, too, have lost friends. I'm sorry."

"Thank you." I picked up a fork and pushed the eggs around, wondering idly how the gargoyle kept producing food when I had seen nothing but the herb garden as a source. Then wondering what kind of friends a gargoyle would have had. The sense of foreboding that had followed me downstairs prodded me into setting down my fork. No more wasting time. I looked across the table at Lucan. "Who—or what—is Morok?"

Lucan and Keven exchanged a long, entire-conversation-filled look, with questions asked and answered and me left out entirely. Again.

I growled under my breath, pushed my plate away, and snapped, "Enough already. Whatever you haven't been telling me, I need to know."

Their gazes turned to me. Keven poured more tea into my cup.

"Drink," she said. "You'll need the clarity."

And then she stomped out of the kitchen.

I stared after her, then raised an eyebrow at Lucan. "It's that bad?"

"She finds the memories difficult," he said. "And she's right. You'll need clarity."

I sipped from the cup. It tasted of rosemary and sage, with a hint of peppermint, and it reminded me of the tea Edie had given me when I fled to her house after Jeff told me he was leaving.

Edie.

I pushed away the ache and made myself listen to Lucan.

"When I told you Merlin wasn't the good guy," he said, "I meant it. He called himself a wizard, but he was nothing more than a court magician. A gifted entertainer, yes, and a master manipulator, but that was all. Until Morok came along."

A shadow passed across the window overlooking the garden and briefly cast a winged shape on the flagstone floor. I shivered and held the tea tighter.

"The name means darkness. He's a Slavic god of deceit, lies, and ignorance. No one had even heard of him until Merlin began serving him."

I'd never heard of him at all. "And you think he gave Merlin his powers?"

"I think he did more than that."

"What more could he do?"

"Gods and goddesses are the only beings capable of animating the inanimate, of giving life to objects like the gnomes or Keven. Or changing life like me."

"But I thought Merlin created—" I broke off. I hadn't told him about my conversation with Keven—or that I knew about his family. Between fires and gnomes and friends dying, there just hadn't seemed to be a good time to blurt out, *"By the way, I'm sorry about your wife and son,"* when he hadn't told me himself.

"Me?" Lucan nodded. "He did."

I hesitated, the words *I'm sorry* hovering on my lips, but the sentiment seemed inadequate under the circumstances. Naïve. And I didn't think Lucan would want it. I forged ahead. "Keven said Merlin changed the soldiers into wolves, and Morgana brought the gargoyles to life. She didn't say anything about the Morrigan or Morok being there."

"Gods cannot take physical form in this world. They need—"

"But they can," I interrupted. "I saw the Morrigan just last night. I talked to her."

"Not in this world."

"Where else would it have been? I was hardly in any shape to

—" I broke off with a gulp as his meaning sank in. Dear sweet Jesus.

I really had been destined to die in a cellar. Or at least a cavern.

Lucan poured more tea into my cup and nudged it toward me, but I didn't trust myself to lift it. I tucked my shaking hands into my lap beneath the table and curled them into fists.

Die.

I'd died and gone elsewhere and come back and—

"I see," I said, my voice the calmest part of me. "But if gods can't take shape here, and Merlin couldn't change you, then—" My jaw dropped. "Wait—you think Morok is Merlin? That he took over his body like some kind of demon possession?"

"That's as good a description as any, I suppose, so yes."

Thoughts zipped through my mind with lightning speed now, and I chased them around, trying to put them in order. "But if that's true, and what you said about the gnomes coming to life is true—"

The pieces came together in my head with a clunk that resonated all the way through my core. My entire being. A *god*? I had a *god* pursuing me? I pushed to my feet. My hamstrings whimpered in protest, but I had no attention left over to give them. It was all taken up by the ginormous, impossible, *oh hell no* that rattled up my spine and down again as I shook my head.

"You're wrong," I told Lucan, my voice giving up any pretense at calm. "You must be wrong. Mages—"

"Cannot animate the inanimate. Neither can Crones."

I paced to the counter and back, leg muscles protesting every step. "But what about Keven? Morgana brought the gargoyles to life. Wasn't she the first Crone? If Crones can't do that, then how —" Again I stopped. More ideas collided and fused in my brain. I put a hand out to the table to keep from toppling over. "Morgana—and the Morrigan?"

"Yes."

"Jesus Christ on a cracker," I said succinctly—and I missed my Edie-voice all over again.

❧

"So let me get this straight." I was on my fourth cup of clarity. I didn't think it was doing much other than making me desperately need to pee, but I was afraid that if I left the conversation now, I'd lose the fragile threads I was trying to weave together. Either that, or I'd run screaming out the door, gnomes and Mages be damned. I threaded my fingers into my hair, grasping a clump at its roots as I rested an elbow on my knee and scowled at Lucan.

Keven had come back into the kitchen a few minutes before, with my cat once again draped over her shoulders. She'd cleared away my uneaten breakfast and begun work on a stew. I didn't think my stomach would tolerate that, either, but I didn't have the courage to tell her. Not the way she was attacking the potatoes and carrots right now.

I took a breath and focused on my weaving, pulling up the threads from what Lucan had told me so far and ticking points off on my fingers as I went. "Morok didn't like sharing space in the Otherworld anymore, so he decided to help himself to Earth." One finger. "He needed a body to live in, however, and because Merlin craved power, they were a perfect match." A second finger. Then I frowned. "Does that mean they're both in Merlin's body? Or did Merlin die when Morok took over?"

"They would have shared initially, but now..." Lucan shook his head. "We don't know for sure."

Awesome. "And none of the other gods or goddesses besides the Morrigan cared enough to pursue him?"

Lucan nodded. "In a nutshell, no. Gods and goddesses are fickle at best. They intervene when it suits them to do so."

Cynically, I wondered what had motivated the Morrigan. But that thread wasn't part of the tapestry I needed to put together right now, so I dropped it and ticked a third finger. "Then the Morrigan joined with Morgana to try and separate them—Morok and Merlin, I mean—by splitting Camlann from the rest of the world."

My protector nodded again. "Intending to trap Morok and his creations—us—in the splinter."

"Why didn't it work?"

"Because the wolves—" A muscle in Lucan's jaw flexed, and his expression turned grim. "*We* attacked Morgana as she cast the spell. The division was incomplete. Instead of separating Morok and Merlin, it split only Morok's power, trapping half of it in the Camlann splinter."

My bladder nudged painfully at my focus, and I crossed my legs under the table.

"And Merlin—Morok—escaped."

"They did."

"Why didn't the Morrigan—Morgana—just go after him— them—herself? Themselves?" My brain hurt from trying to keep everything straight. I gave up on finger-ticking and reached for the clarity tea, mentally telling my bladder to deal with it. I took a slug of the now cold liquid.

"Power," Keven's voice supplied from the counter by the stove.

Mouth full, I peered at her over the rim of the cup. Her slicing and dicing had faded into the background, and I'd almost forgotten she was in the room. I swallowed the cold clarity. "Power?" I echoed.

"It corrupts," Keven said. "The Morrigan was afraid if she remained with Morgana, they would become like Morok."

Hence the nasty drink test in the cellar last night. The Cup of Power, she'd called it. I would never forget its stench. Perhaps that was what had stood between me and breakfast this morning.

A sudden light dawned. "That's why she made the pendants," I said. "To make sure the power stayed divided."

Keven looked over with a grunt of what sounded like approval, and I gave myself a mental pat on the back. Praise from Keven was hard to come by—at least in my experience. I would take what I could get.

"And giving the Crones the tools they needed to split the world again as needed," she agreed.

"Which happens when the pendants choose us, which happens because...?"

Lucan took over the explanation again. "Because even though Morok loses a little of himself with each split, he is still powerful. And he remains a god of darkness and deceit. His influence on your world is constant. It wears down humanity's consciousness and replaces it with delusion, illusion, confusion."

"Lies," I murmured, thinking of the state of world affairs splashed across my newspaper every morning. The politics. The rise of 'fake news' and disinformation. All because of—a god? I shifted in my seat. My bladder felt like it was a hiccup away from disaster. "He replaces it with lies."

"Yes. And each time the world reaches its peak of tolerance, the pendants choose new Crones, there is a new split, Morok's remaining power is cut by half again, and the world regains its balance—for a time, anyway."

I nodded, then shook my head. Something didn't add up. "But if he's losing power with each split, why isn't the world staying stable for longer? Why do we keep needing to—" I stopped mid-question, looked between Keven and Lucan as bells went off in my brain, and released a lungful of air in a rush of shock. A jolt of holy hell.

Because of course.

Morok wasn't the only one who lost a little of himself in each splinter.

The world did, too.

Crones were destroying the world a sliver at a time—and my bladder was out of patience.

I RETURNED TO THE TABLE READY FOR MORE TEA—AND with a solution so obvious that it dazzled. I couldn't for the life of me understand why no one had thought of it before.

"We should send him back," I announced, plonking onto my seat. "To where he came from—the Otherworld."

"An interesting suggestion," Lucan said, but the way he looked away as he spoke indicated otherwise.

Keven was more blunt. "Impossible. As long as he's attached to Merlin's body, he cannot cross into the Otherworld, and the body cannot be killed with him in it."

Good old Keven. It would have been nice to have had her approval for longer than two-point-five seconds before she shot me down.

I scrubbed both hands over my face and then wound my fingers into another fistful of hair like it was all that I had to hold onto. Which it was, in this world turned upside-down. I scowled at the gargoyle.

"So what do we do? Just keep dividing him until he runs out of steam and hope that happens before the world splinters one too many times?"

A stone shoulder lifted, along with the cat sitting atop it. "Or you trap him in one of the slivers."

"But for that," Lucan said, "you have to find him first, which no Crone has been able to do in fifteen centuries."

Not very efficient, were we?

"And in the meantime," Keven added, waving a meat-bloodied knife in the air—because, oh joy, there was more? "In the meantime, *he* has figured out how to find *you*, and now it's just a matter of time before—"

"Gargoyle."

Lucan's voice stopped Keven mid knife-wave. She glared at him.

"She needs to know."

"She needs her magick first."

"Perhaps this will be the impetus she needs to access the magick."

"And perhaps it will paralyze her even—"

"Perhaps," I interjected, "*she* should be included in the discussion."

Gargoyle and wolf-shifter stared at one another, both challenging, neither backing down. I cleared my throat.

"Let me rephrase that," I said. "She *will* be included."

Another second of staring slid by, then Lucan tore his gaze from Keven, sighed, and turned to me. "We're not sure," he said, "but we think Morok is trying to open a portal between here and the slivers. Specifically the Camlann sliver."

"For what purpose?"

"To reclaim the power he lost there. Which was half his initial power."

"Can he do it?" I looked between him and Keven, diligently chopping a slab of meat into chunks. "Is it possible?"

"Anything is possible. The question until now has been more about probability. Morok doesn't have enough power to open the portal on his own; he needs the pendants, too. There are two ways he might get them: either before a pendant chooses its new Crone, or if a Crone chooses to give it to him."

I snorted. Give a crazed god the power to finish off the world? Not likely.

"He would never risk exposing himself to come after them," Lucan continued, "but his Mages are—expendable."

I wondered if the Mages knew that.

"And while they were unsuccessful in getting to your pendant in time, they did manage to find it—for the first time in history. Which brings us to the question of how. What's changed? How did they know where to look?"

It was an excellent question, and one to which Gilbert, of all people, might have actually given me the answer.

"Technology," I said. "The internet. Gilbert, my neighbor, said he'd put a picture of the pendant on his website."

"Web-what?" Keven frowned over the chopping board of bloody chunks she carried to the stove.

"Website. It's like a..." I looked to Lucan for help.

"Like a magickal place of advertising goods and services," he said, looking like he'd just been stunned by one of the lightning bolts my own brain was experiencing. I double-checked my heat level to make sure I hadn't accidentally launched something at him, but everything seemed normal.

Normal being a relative term, of course.

Lucan rubbed a hand over his beard. "It never occurred to me, but I think you're right. Mer—" He shot a glance at Keven. "Morok has been here as long as I have. It makes sense that he'd have learned to tap into the internet, or at least his Mages would know how. He probably has a dozen or more web-crawlers working for him."

"Web-what?" I asked.

"Bots that can be programmed to crawl through websites searching for specific things—keywords, images, pretty much anything."

"Such as antique pendants that double as magnifiers." I put a hand over my pendant. "But how do we know he hasn't already found the others?"

"We don't, until you look for the other Crones. But, milady..."

Even as he trailed off, I knew what he didn't want to say. Because web-crawlers could find more than information and images and keywords. They could find people, too. And now that Morok had my name, he could find the people I cared about. He could find my family.

"No." Lucan rested a hand against the heavy oak door I tried to wrest open.

"Yes." I tugged at the door handle, but moving him was like trying to move a tree.

"The gnomes are gone, but their remains are still out there, along with goddess knows what else. The Mages themselves might be waiting for you, and I cannot protect you from them."

"I don't give a flying—" I broke off and inhaled deeply through my nostrils, counting to three in my head and skirting the *remains of gnomes* idea. "If Morok wants my pendant so badly, he won't hesitate to use my family to get it. I have to warn Paul. I'm *going* to warn him."

"And if they have something waiting for you out there in the woods again? You have no magick to fight them off, and—" He broke off and held up his free hand to ward off my anger. "And even if you did make it to town, they might well just follow you to your family. And then what? Do you really want to face choosing between them and the pendant?"

I didn't tell him that, in my mind, there would be no contest. I didn't have to tell him. His gaze raked my face and turned stonier than Keven's.

"Make no mistake, milady. I cannot allow that to happen. I *will* not."

"I thought you were my protector."

"I protect the Crone. The pendant *is* the Crone."

Not comforting. And not getting me anywhere.

I scowled at him. "I'm not an idiot, Lucan. I'll call them, not visit them in person. Now, *will* you please move?"

He glowered down at me. "Fine. I will take you as far as we need for you to get a cell signal. There's another clearing not far from here that isn't warded. If you promise to move fast and do exactly as I—"

"Natalie's phone died, and I don't have a charger for it. I need a payphone."

He closed his eyes. I suspected he, too, was counting in his head. But probably to more than three.

"Very well," he said through gritted teeth, "but on one condition. You learn to defend yourself first."

My hips groaned. I gaped at my protector. "Defend —myself?"

"We don't know what else we might run into, or if I will be able to keep it from you. Having no magick is bad enough. Having no way at all of fending off an enemy is unacceptable. You're not leaving the house until you can keep yourself alive long enough for me to get to you."

"You don't understand." I gestured at myself. "I'm spectacularly uncoordinated. Anything more complicated than walking takes me months to master. We don't have that kind of time. My family might not have that kind of time."

"Think of this as learning to walk softly while carrying a big stick," he retorted. "It's faster than learning magick. And it's non-negotiable." He took his hand from the door. "I'll be back in a minute. Please do not make me chase you down and carry you back to the house."

I opened my mouth to say something along the lines of *"you wouldn't dare!"* Then I shut it again, because we both knew he would. Without hesitation. I glared after his retreating form as he jogged up the stairs. When I got back from calling Paul, I would resume those lessons with Keven and learn my magick— if only to put a certain shifter in his place.

My shoulders slumped. Call Paul? Who was I kidding?

Because learn to defend myself? Me? At sixty years old?

I was never leaving this house again.

CHAPTER 22

KEVEN HAD BEEN A RUTHLESS TASKMASTER IN MY MAGICK lessons.

Lucan was worse.

I yelped as the long stick he wielded snaked past my attempt to block it and landed sharply against my hip. Again. At this rate, my entire body would be one big bruise before I landed a single hit of my own. Despair crept in. On top of my already sore joints and stiff muscles, it looked less and less likely that I'd be able to move at all, let alone walk into town.

Waving off my tormentor, I retreated to a corner of the great hall, bent over, and rested the staff I gripped across my knees. Sweat dripped from my chin, and my chest heaved with exertion. We'd been at it for more than an hour, and my hip throbbed where Lucan's multiple blows had landed.

So did both my shins, my left shoulder, and my ribcage—front, back, and both sides. Lucan, on the other hand, still had man-bun in place and hadn't broken a sweat.

Exhaustion and pain mixed with a healthy dose of frustration, and I blinked back tears as I lifted my head and glowered at him.

He shrugged. "You're not even trying."

I bit back the invitation to drop dead that hovered on the tip of my tongue. Resting my butt against the wall, I closed my eyes and focused on trying to pull myself together. To find an inner core of strength or stamina or *something*. But I was empty, and this was ridiculous. Piling this additional punishment onto my body made no sense whatsoever. All the attacks on me so far had happened at night, and it wasn't even noon yet. If we left now—while I could still walk—we could get into town, I could call

Paul, and we could be back in time for a late lunch—all in broad daylight.

I ignored the little voice trying to remind me that that had been my intention the day my house had burned down, too. Because this was different. And because if Lucan landed many more blows, it didn't matter how skilled I became, because I wouldn't be able to move at all, never mind defend myself.

I took a centering breath and assembled my argument. If I could just make him see—

A faint whistling sound approached. From the last hour's hard experience, I recognized the noise as Lucan's staff cutting through the air. Shock jolted through me—*he wouldn't*—but even as it registered, I instinctively swung my staff toward the sound. The impact numbed my arms and fingers, but I was already whirling away, opening my eyes, swinging the staff in a wide arc, and connecting with Lucan's unprotected ribs. He grunted and stepped back, his expression one of mixed surprise and satisfaction.

"I was wrong," he said. "You have been trying—but too hard. You have good instincts; you just need to stop over-thinking."

I crouched low, staff across my body at the ready, frozen in astonishment. I'd done it. I'd hit him. I'd actually hit him. But how? I hadn't even been looking—my eyes had been closed—

And Wednesday night it had been all but dark when I had wielded Merlin's carrier like a sledgehammer and battered my way through the gnomes blocking my path to safety. Without thinking. Relying on desperation, the drive to survive. Instinct.

Slowly, I stood upright again. I settled the end of the staff on the floor beside my left foot, pondering the magnitude of my realizations. Because I *had* survived. I, Claire Emerson, sixty-year-old grandmother, had slugged my way through dozens of creatures bent on my demise. Had stayed on my feet even after one of them had bitten me. Hell, I'd even ignored Lucan's orders and saved Merlin. The last thought made me snort-chuckle.

I'd saved the cat.

I'd survived the gnomes, saved the cat that had promptly abandoned me in favor of Keven, and now I'd hit Lucan, too.

A tiny spark ignited deep in my chest. Maybe I could do this after all. Maybe I could do this, warn Paul, and actually make it back to the house in one piece.

"Again," I said.

I avoided precious few of Lucan's blows over the next half-hour—and I landed even fewer of my own. But the spark in my chest persisted, and so did I. Of all the things I knew to be true about myself, it was that I had *grit*, as my grandmother had called it. I might not have done a lot with my life, or been particularly outspoken, or even stood up for myself all that well over the years, but neither had I turned tail and run from my life. I'd done what needed to be done.

Somehow, in the aftermath of the divorce, and the apathy and self-pity I'd allowed myself to sink into, I'd forgotten that. Forgotten my capacity. Forgotten my strength. Forgotten myself.

Remembering wasn't easy.

It was, in fact, downright painful—especially when Lucan's staff cracked across one of my shins for the fourth time in a row. How was he getting past me to that one spot so consistently? I was trying so hard to make my mind blank and to feel his movements rather than analyze them, but—

"Break?" Lucan suggested. "You're getting tired."

I gritted my teeth and shook my head, wiping the sweat from my forehead with the back of one hand. I was close to making a breakthrough. I was sure of it. I could *feel* it.

"Again," I growled.

Lucan hesitated, then shrugged and hefted his staff. He feinted left, danced right, and *crack!* Across my shoulder. Jaw clenched, I swung away, whirled, and brought my staff down in an arc. It connected with his and jarred through my arms. Damn it to hell and back, the harder I tried, the harder it became. What was I doing wrong? Maybe Lucan was right. Maybe I needed a break. Goddess knew my poor, battered body could use one. And maybe if I could think this through without worrying about the next whack—

My brain stuttered to a halt. Wait a second. Overthinking, Lucan had said. As in thinking too much. As in exactly what I kept doing with increasing desperation. I'd heard his words—I'd even agreed with them—and then I'd tried to think my way out of overthinking, and...and how in heaven's name did that make sense?

"You idiot," I muttered.

"What?" Lucan asked.

Frowning in concentration, I shook my head, still working through my dilemma. "Nothing."

Nothing at all, a little voice inside me agreed. It was that third voice again. Not mine, not Edie's. *Think nothing,* it said. *Anticipate nothing. Try nothing. Be still. Just...be.*

It's not that easy, my own voice disagreed. *I have to think. I have to be in control. What will happen if...*

"Hush," I whispered to it. Across the hall, Lucan raised an eyebrow, but I ignored him as my hands settled into a new grip on the staff and my body into a watchful pose of readiness. I fixed my gaze on my opponent, this time seeing him as a whole rather than watching for telltale signs that he might move in one direction or another. I settled my feet against the stone floor. Centered myself. Pulled ever more inward...

And then I exploded into motion.

Lucan blocked blow after attempted blow, parried thrust after thrust, met feint after feint with uncanny anticipation. But this time, I didn't care. I didn't get frustrated. I didn't think. My clarity increased. My attack became more measured. I landed a hit on Lucan's shoulder, another on his hip. He aimed one at my forearm. I blocked it, whirled away, dropped to a crouch and, with a sweeping arc of my staff, knocked both his feet out from under him.

He landed hard, flat on his back, and triumph shot through

me, electric in my veins. I'd done it! I'd brought him down. Defeated him. At last. *Hallelujah!*

Lucan didn't move.

My elation sputtered. Fizzled.

Why wasn't he moving?

My breath left me in a hiss. His head—the stone floor—had I knocked him out? Or—

Dear goddess, had I killed him? I flung the staff aside, and it clattered to the floor as I skidded onto my knees beside him, yelling for Keven. My fingers shaking, I lifted Lucan's long hair, loosened from its confines at last and pooled on the floor under his head. There was no sign of blood, and I could feel his breath on the back of my hand, but that didn't rule out injury—maybe serious injury. Goddess help me, what had I done?

I cupped his face in my hands and leaned over him, feeling the measured vibration of Keven's approach in the floor beneath me.

"Lucan? Lucan, can you hear me? Can you open your eyes? Are you okay? Oh, *please* be okay!" I patted his cheek with increasing sharpness. "Lucan! Open your damned eyes!"

Strong hands shot up and fastened on my wrists, and amber eyes opened to stare up at me, scowling. "You did it. You actually dropped me."

Only with great effort did I manage not to throw myself across his chest and hug him. "You're okay—I didn't kill you? Hurt you?"

"The mutt is harder to get rid of than you think," Keven's voice observed above me. "And he's too bloody hard-headed to be hurt by a bump on the skull. I imagine you've dented his pride, however. That might take him a while to recover from."

Lucan snarled something in reply that I didn't catch over the hammering of my heartbeat in my ears, and the gargoyle chuckled, a gravelly scrape of amusement. "Was that all you needed me for, milady?"

"I'm sorry," I whispered, my gaze fastened on Lucan's, still half-expecting him to pass out. Or worse. He'd hit so hard. "I thought..."

"No apologies necessary," the gargoyle said, appropriating my words. "I would have walked a hundred miles to see him like this." She stretched out a hand to haul Lucan to his feet, her sympathetic tutting noises losing something in her toothy grin. "Poor puppy."

"Kiss my ass, gargoyle."

Keven chuckled again, then pulled me up as well. She patted my shoulder, her hard hand landing squarely on a bruise and making me gasp. Not that she could have avoided it, because I was pretty sure my entire body was a single giant contusion at this point. The gargoyle grunted.

"I have something to put in a bath to ease your discomfort. Do you want it before or after lunch?"

What I wanted was to leave now and call my son, because the longer I delayed, the greater the risk to him and Natalie and Braden. But without the euphoria of defeating Lucan singing through my veins, exhaustion had set in and, oh goddess, but I hurt.

"How long do I have to soak?"

"Half an hour will do."

"Then during," I said. "I'll eat in the tub. And we'll go into town afterward." I met Lucan's gaze again, challenging him to disagree.

"There and back," he agreed. "As fast as we can move."

Keven's bath had better work a miracle.

BATH, TEA AND LUNCH MADE IT POSSIBLE TO STAND ERECT again without whimpering. Mostly. It did not, however, erase the ravages of the past two days. I dropped the damp towel on the bed and studied my naked reflection in the wardrobe mirror. I'd grown used to the sags and droops of my aging body, but seeing them—and everything in between—covered in varying shades of blue and purple? Talk about adding insult to injury.

Or in this case, injury to insult, I supposed.

No matter how I looked at it, the evidence of age was inescapable, and creeping self-doubt returned. I expelled a long breath from between pursed lips. Sixty years old and destined to go to war. Me, with my saggy boobs, stiff hips, and increasing dependence on the reading glasses now lost in a fire...

Along with the one person in my life who might have convinced me I was capable of any of this.

"Oh, Edie," I whispered. "I'm so, so sorry."

Silence responded, and my throat tightened. I hadn't heard my Edie-voice since before the fire, and what had once been annoying as hell was now desperately missed. I swallowed against the sting of tears, trying to shore up my own confidence. As much as I wanted to hide under the bed, Paul and Natalie and Braden depended on me.

Fat lot of good that will do them with a god after you, my Claire-voice mumbled.

An inspiring Edie, it was not.

I sighed and pulled open the wardrobe door. Balefully, I eyed the two garments hanging there: the white nightgown, and a long, dark robe. I took down the robe and closed the mirrored door. I felt ridiculous putting it on, but with my only set of clothes sweat-soaked, smelly, and crumpled on the bathroom floor, I had little choice.

It was a deep indigo, soft and silky to the touch. But it was still a robe, and I was still going to look damned odd parading into town to find a payphone. I laid the garment across the bed, then grimaced and went to get my bra and sensible panties from the bathroom. The thought of putting the undergarments back on made my skin crawl, but at least I'd be semi-decent *under* the damned odd robe.

With a shudder, I slipped into the clammy underwear. The robe followed, sliding over my head and settling around my body with a soft whisper of fabric against skin. I regarded my reflection again. It wasn't as bad as I'd expected. Long, yes, but it cleared the floor and wouldn't trip me up, and the fabric managed not to look entirely like a tent.

But it was still damned odd.

I picked up the pendant from the table and slipped it over my head. It nestled, glinting, in the dark fabric between my breasts. I was ready.

CHAPTER 23

LUCAN WAITED IN THE GREAT HALL, LOOKING UP AS I descended the stairs. His amber eyes glowed brighter for a moment, sending a tingle through my belly and making my step hitch. He swept another of his low bows as I reached the stone floor.

"Milady," he said. "The robe suits you."

I rearranged the folds of fabric and pretended I wasn't blushing. "Yes, well, it's not very practical. I'll use Natalie's credit card while we're in town so I can get some decent clothes."

"You want to go all the way into town?" He straightened again, and whatever I'd imagined I'd seen in his expression was gone, chased away by a frown. "I thought you could use the nearest phone."

"I'll be quick," I said. "We'll be there and back well before dark, and I need something to wear other than…" I waggled my fingers at the robe. "Plus, I need glasses if I'm to read the book."

"The dark isn't our only enemy," he reminded me. But he stood aside to let me pass.

I'd reached the door when Keven's voice stopped me. "Lady Claire, a moment. There's rain in the air. You'll need this." She held up a hooded cape of soft gray and, before I could object, draped it over my shoulders, fastened it under my chin with fingers that were surprisingly deft, given their size and composition, and stepped back with a nod of satisfaction. "Much better."

Oh joy. My transformation to medieval lady was complete. Shopping was going to be…interesting.

I smiled my thanks, promised to be careful, and turned again to the door. This time, the appearance of the staff in front of my nose stopped me. I stared at it, then at Lucan.

"You don't seriously want me to take that into town with me."

"You are seriously not leaving this house without it," he countered.

I scowled. "I already look like I'm going to a costume party. *That* will get me arrested."

Lucan shrugged. The staff stayed. "Call it a walking stick."

"Oh, for—" I snatched the staff from him. "Happy now?"

"No. But somewhat more content." He pulled open the door and waited for me to precede him.

"It's not like I can fight in these clothes anyway," I muttered, stomping past him onto the stone step and tugging in annoyance at the robe and cape swirling around my legs. "It'll be a wonder if I don't fall flat on my face just walking."

Unperturbed, Lucan closed the door and joined me on the path. "I'm sure you'll manage."

Keven was right about rain. It started when we reached the trees, a steady downpour as if someone had turned on a shower. I paused to pull the hood of the cloak up over my head, then scurried to catch up with Lucan, who had rounded the corner of the house. He pushed into the trees and set a punishing pace down a narrow path that ran in the opposite direction of the one we normally used. It was crisscrossed by roots and strewn with twigs and branches, and grew slick underfoot as the rain fell. I stumbled more than once, but he never slowed and never looked back, and I grew breathless from trying to match his step and dodge the sopping branches that swung behind him toward my face.

I rubbed at the wet sting of a missed one across my cheek and stuck my tongue out at his back. He was annoyed to be here and making his feelings abundantly clear.

Silence hung around us, except for the sound of our footsteps and the patter of raindrops on leaves. I frowned. Something to be concerned about? I heard no birds, but this deep in the trees at this time of year, that was no surprise. No crickets, but again, there wouldn't be here. I slowed, focusing my entire awareness on listening. No distant shrieks. No tramp of approaching footsteps.

A black squirrel bounded gracefully across the path and disappeared with a soft rustle. My ears picked out other, similar sounds, and I relaxed.

"Milady?" Lucan had stopped a dozen feet away to look back over his shoulder.

"Coming," I said. I stumbled as I stepped forward, then glanced down and froze.

A hand the size of a child's had clamped itself around my toe. A hand that emerged from a blue sleeve. A sleeve that ended at the elbow in... nothing but mud.

Horror snaked down my neck to the base of my spine, setting my body aquiver in one, giant *hell no*. Bracing myself with the staff, I lifted my foot and shook it. Hard, then harder. The hand stayed attached to my running shoe. I teetered on one leg and tried to keep the mounting panic from my voice.

"Um, Lucan?" I held my foot out toward him. Scowling, he retraced his steps, stooped, and pried the hand from my toe. Then he straightened again, crushed the little appendage in his fist, and tossed the remains into the bush.

"Are you all right?"

Apart from his *I told you so* tone and the creepy crawlies making their way across my skin?

I pressed my lips together and nodded. "They didn't die when I..." *Shattered their itty-bitty skulls?* my Claire-voice suggested, but I couldn't bring myself to say it aloud.

"They were never alive to begin with. Only driven by magick."

"So the pieces just...keep moving? How far? And for how long?"

"As far and as long as it takes them to achieve their purpose."

I gaped at him. "You're kidding."

"Sadly not."

I held his gaze for a long moment of utter appall, then peered past the edges of my hood into the trees. The soft rustlings I'd thought normal turned sinister. That sound there— was that a squirrel rummaging in the fallen leaves? Or another Gnome-hand coming for me? I tightened my grip on the staff and tried to keep the squeak from my voice.

"How many pieces are there?" I had no idea how many I'd shattered with the cat carrier.

"I don't know. But we should assume a great many," Lucan said. "The faster we move, the harder it will be for them to find you."

Shit.

I closed my eyes. Swallowed. Took a deep breath. Looked up at him again. "I'm ready."

The undergrowth became denser as the tree canopy thinned overhead, and the trail narrowed accordingly. I used the staff to block the branches swinging toward my face, unreasonably irritated with Lucan for being right—yet again—for insisting I carry it. Was the man never wrong?

Although, seeing as he was my protector, I supposed I should be grateful for the fact he wasn't.

My toe caught on something. I looked down, sidestepped a chunk of blue ceramic that flopped there, re-focused on Lucan's back, and pressed on through the rain.

The cape proved surprisingly water resistant, and I made a mental note to thank Keven for it when we got home. The robe beneath it was less so. As the trail turned to thick, black goo, the line of mud clinging to my hem climbed until it was halfway up my shins and weighed down my every step. Doggedly, I swung my feet forward as best I could, thinking about the sensible pants and shirts I would buy in town.

The mud squelched over the tops of my running shoes.

I'd buy boots, too.

Stray gnome bits found their way to me twice more. The first was another arm that crawled out from under a bush and raised itself up on its elbow like a cobra, blocking my way. I swallowed my disgust and sent it back into the woods with a flick of my staff and not so much as a misstep. The second, however, stopped me in my tracks.

A head. Or most of one, severed from its body, apple-cheeked, white-bearded, topped with the trademark pointy red cap, missing a chunk where its left eye should have been...and baring a mouthful of needle-sharp teeth.

I stared at it, equal parts horror, disgust, and quiet terror crawling over me. I tried to call out to Lucan, but only a whisper emerged, not enough to reach him as he continued walking, unaware of my predicament.

Some protector.

Get a grip, Claire. Just think of it as a spider.

A really big spider, but I actually didn't mind spiders that much. I could do this.

I took a deep breath and brought the staff down like an ax on the snarling head. Ceramic shattered, the pointy red hat fell away, apple cheeks disintegrated, and the mouthful of teeth broke in two—with both pieces snapping at me. Revulsion gained the upper hand, and I struck again. And again and again, until tiny shards of ceramic were scattered everywhere, all too small to be any kind of threat.

Panting, I stared down at the littered path and slowly lowered the staff to rest again on the ground. Then I wiped my palms against my robe, twitched its folds into place, and crunched across the remaining bits of my downed enemy. Lucan waited for me just before a bend in the trail.

"All good?" he asked.

I lifted my chin. "All good."

"Excellent. Because we're here"—he pointed through the trees to a quiet street—"and this is where I change."

CHAPTER 24

I STRODE THROUGH TOWN IN MY MUDDIED ROBE AND CAPE, staff in one hand, leash attached to Lucan the wolf in my other, and toes squishing inside my soaking shoes, trying my level best to pretend nothing was out of the ordinary.

The stares directed our way and the near-accidents narrowly avoided at three separate intersections as we waited for crossing signals didn't make it easy. Astonishment, amusement, and outright gawking dogged our every step, making the walk to find a payphone seem interminable. Going into a clothing store might be more than just interesting.

Lucan's reasons for taking his wolf form before entering the town had been valid—if anything happened, it would be a lot harder to explain his shift than it would be to explain him just as a wolf—but it wasn't easy, having him alongside me like this.

My agitation grew as we tried three payphones in a row, none of which would accept either the change Lucan had brought with him or Natalie's credit card. We were almost in the center of town by now, with the house in the woods—and the safe haven it offered—becoming more distant with every step. The concerned looks directed our way were becoming more frequent. If they hadn't already, someone was going to call the cops on us soon: the dotty old woman in a robe with a wolf at her side.

Falling back on old habits, I mumbled under my breath, "Cheesy rice on a cracker!" No Edie-voice corrected me, and I blinked back a sudden welling in my eyes. Goddess, I missed her.

Another payphone swam into view, and I used my leash hand to dash away my tears. I eyed the phone booth. It was half a block down the one-way street we traveled, sitting on a corner outside a service station. We'd come farther than I would have liked, but it was still daylight and no woods here. Which meant, theoretically, that we would be safe from shades and gnomes.

Emphasis on theoretically.

I tightened my grip on Lucan's leash. Maybe he'd been right about this little venture. Maybe—

A police cruiser pulled up to the curb beside me, its lights flashing.

"Oh, heck," I muttered under my breath. And then, given the seriousness of the situation, added, "*Bloody* heck."

I considered walking by as if I hadn't noticed, but the opening of the driver-side door across my path quashed the idea. A familiar police officer exited the vehicle into a puddle, and settled her hat on her head. I recognized her as the one who had come to the house the night of the shade attack. A good thing, I hoped.

I stepped into the shelter of a store awning and slipped off my hood. "Constable"—my gaze dropped to her nametag— "Abraham. It's nice to see you again."

K. Abraham stepped out of the puddle onto the cobblestone sidewalk. Her gaze on the wolf at my side was narrow.

"Mrs. Emerson, isn't it?" She looked me over from head to muddy toes and back again.

"Ms., actually. I'm divorced."

"Where are you heading, Ms. Emerson?"

"To call my son. I was going to use the phone booth there." I nodded toward the service station.

"No cell phone?"

"It died."

She pointed at the staff. "That's an unusual walking stick."

"Um," I said.

She turned her attention back to Lucan. "Ms. Emerson, you know it's not legal to keep a wild animal in captivity."

"He's only half wolf," I said. Another not-quite-lie.

"Some of my colleagues might think otherwise."

Her colleagues...but not her? I wasn't quite sure how to respond.

"It was your house that burned down the other day." She took off her hat and tucked it under one arm, then leaned back against her vehicle beside the open door, oblivious to the rain. "You've had a lot going on in your corner of the world lately."

I really didn't know how to respond to that.

She didn't wait for me to figure it out. "I'm sorry about Edie."

Edie. Not *Mrs. James*, or *your friend*, or even *your neighbor*. Edie.

K. Abraham was full of surprises. Since turning sixty, I didn't much like surprises.

"You knew her?" I asked, shifting my grip on the staff and loosening my grip on Lucan's leash. Just in case he sensed an imminent threat here and wanted to attack on my behalf or something.

But a quick glance down at the wolf beside me found him stretched out on the cobblestones, tongue lolling as he watched the traffic roll by. Seriously?

"I did," K. Abraham said. "Rather well, actually. She and I..." She trailed off and regarded me, her expression undecided.

"You and she what?"

The cop took a breath and squared her shoulders, as if bracing herself. "We were in the same coven."

Coven.

She and Edie.

Together.

I looked at her properly for the first time. At the woman behind the uniform she wore. Behind the bold yellow POLICE emblazoned across her protective vest, the crest stuck to the hat tucked under her arm, the heavy equipment belt at her waist, the gun at her hip. K. Abraham wasn't that much younger than I was, I realized with a start. Her short-cropped hair was salt-and-pepper, her face was lined by experience and life, and her brown gaze behind gold wire-framed glasses was steady. Knowing. Watching. Waiting.

I might have stood gaping at her forever if a cold nose hadn't nudged my ankle beneath the robe, making me jump. I stared down into Lucan's amber eyes. Reassurance stared back at me, then looked at K. Abraham. *I trust her*, his expression said.

And I trusted Lucan.

"Coven," I echoed. Edie—my Edie—had been part of a *coven*? "So you're—"

"A midwitch," she replied. "Like Edie. There are six of us in town. Well, five now."

"Five witches." I didn't mean to sound so obtuse, but I couldn't quite come to grips with a coven idea, which sounded like it was straight out of a book. Or a horror movie.

"Five midwitches. There are a lot more witches in the area than just us." She frowned. "But you must know at least some of this, Ms. Emerson, because you're one of us yourself, right? A solitary?"

"Claire," I said faintly. "Please. And uh...not exactly."

"Kate," she responded. "So then what? Exactly."

Was that the cop or the midwitch asking? Lucan's nose nudged into my hand. He'd stood up again, and now his warmth pressed against my leg. I took a deep breath. He'd better be right about this.

"Crone," I said. The word rolled off my tongue with an ease that surprised me. It was the first time I'd said it to anyone other than Lucan or Keven, I realized with a jolt. The first time I'd laid claim to it aloud. It felt...right. I lifted my chin and repeated it, this time with more certainty. "I'm Crone," I said, "and I serve the Morrigan."

Kate Abraham stared at me. Her lips formed a silent 'o' and her gaze flicked over my outfit again, then settled on the pendant I wore around my neck. There was no denying that my words meant something to her, but I couldn't gauge what. I braced myself for questions. Or worse, laughter.

Because even if Kate knew about Crones, I was pretty sure an eccentric old lady wearing medieval robes and carrying a stick wouldn't fit her picture of what one looked like.

But the police officer neither laughed nor interrogated. Instead, she straightened up from leaning against her car, closed the driver's door, and joined me under the awning.

"Edie was right, then. Those were Mages hanging around your street. That will be who attacked your house and set fire to it, and I'm guessing they're still in town." She reached for her cell phone.

"Wait." I stuck out a hand, forgetting I held the staff. It waved under her nose, and she drew back a little. I retracted it but shook my head. "You know about Mages?"

"Of course I know about Mages. I just told you I'm a midwitch."

I opened my mouth to tell her I didn't have the faintest what that really meant, but decided it was best to skip that part for the moment. I shook my head. "You can't call it in. You—the police—"

"I'm not calling it in," she said, seeming equal parts surprised and annoyed by the suggestion. "This isn't a police matter. But the other midwitches need to know. We can call wards and set them around town. They'll be spread too thin to deflect much magick, but they might give us some warning if the Mages try anything else."

A thrill leapt through my veins. My staff waved under her nose again. "You can call wards?"

She used the hand holding her hat to push aside the stick. "Of course—" She stopped and regarded me, her brow furrowed. "Wait. Why haven't *you* set them around town?"

"It's a long story. A very long story. But we don't have time right now. The Mages—my family—" Lucan's nose nudged my leash-holding hand, and I made myself stop and take a breath. Put my thoughts in order. Separate terror from hope. For the first time since my birthday, I had a magickal ally in Kate

Abraham—one who wasn't bound to me personally. I potentially had several, if the other midwitches would help, too.

If they could protect my family, maybe I could keep the pendant from the Mages long enough to get a grip on my magick and find the other Crones and—

La, la, la, la, la! sang my Claire-voice, refusing to go any further down that path. I didn't blame it. One thing at a time.

"I don't know how much you know about Crones," I said, "but the Mages are after my pendant, and I think they'll try using my son and his family to get it. Will you—will the midwitches—can you help? Please?"

She rested her hands on the equipment belt wrapped around her hips, one still clutching the brim of her hat. "Given that you think you need to ask, I seem to know a great deal more about Crones than you do," she retorted. "Just how long is this story of yours, anyway?" Then she waved the hat at me. "Never mind. Suffice it to say it's our job to help you. What's your son's address?"

I gave it to her, and she jotted it down in her notebook.

"Anyone else we should know about?"

Jeanne, perhaps? And Jeff and his new family? Guilt stabbed through me. None of them had even occurred to me until Kate asked, and now that they had, I wondered how much of a threat any of them would be to the safety of my pendant. Would I be tempted to trade it for one of them?

I didn't like what it said about me that I even wondered. I gave their names and addresses to Kate.

"Right," she said briskly, tucking the notebook back into a vest pocket. "Consider it done. We'll set wards around all three and keep watch over your son and his family. And you?"

"Me?"

"What's your plan? How are you going to deal with the Mages?"

There were several things I'd been spectacularly unprepared for in life: childbirth, motherhood, discovering my husband was having an affair with someone half my age, divorce and starting over at age fifty-nine. But this eclipsed them all.

"Me?" I wanted to squeak.

I also (not for the first time) wanted to turn tail and run.

Instead, I looked down the street of the town I called home, and thought of the family I loved more than life itself. The friend I'd lost and the ones I still had. The world beyond Confluence that was being led further astray every day by a god who thrived on lies and deceit. And the other women out there—the Crones—who suddenly found themselves thrust into a war they were completely unprepared for. Like me.

Okay, maybe they weren't quite as unprepared as I was, but still.

Still.

"Ms. Emer—Claire?" Kate's voice nudged. "You do have a plan, right?"

I closed my eyes, shushed the Claire-voice babbling about bad ideas in my head, and took a deep, steadying breath. Then I looked at Kate.

"I'm working on it," I told her. Because I would, just as soon as I got back to the house with those reading glasses and settled in to some serious studying.

Midwitches, I thought as Kate's police car disappeared down the street. Five of them. A whole coven watching over Paul and Natalie and Braden. That was a good thing, right? So why didn't I feel better? Why did I still feel the nagging unease that had followed me into town?

A young couple sidled by on the sidewalk, wary gazes under their umbrellas alternating between me and Lucan, as if undecided as to who was the bigger threat.

Not me, I thought at them as they hurried away. *Definitely not me.*

Lucan tugged at the leash, pulling in the direction of the phone booth. I hesitated. Even with Kate's assurances they'd look after my family, I still yearned to talk to Paul myself. To hear my son's voice. To warn him to be vigilant. I pivoted, scanning behind us. Rain dripped from the awning overhead, and puddles on the street reflected back the old stone and new glass storefronts lining both sides. A delivery van drove past, tires swishing against the pavement. Overhead, dark gray clouds hung low in the sky.

Nothing was out of place. But everything felt wrong.

Lucan tugged again on the leash. I hesitated another second, then hustled to join him. "All right," I said, "but we need to make it fast, and if this one doesn't work, we're giving up."

THE PHONE WORKED, BUT AS PAUL'S TIRADE CONTINUED IN my ear, I would have almost preferred it hadn't. After a half-dozen attempts to break into his words, I gave up and let the flow continue, waiting for him to wind down. I watch the street, *mmm-hmming* in what I hoped were the right places.

"Mr. Arthur seems like a nice guy and all, but—"

Mr. Arthur? Who was—I looked down at Lucan, sitting outside the booth and watching me. Oh.

"—worried sick about you—"

Lucan Arthur. Cute.

"—haven't been answering Natalie's cell phone—"

Distant black specks circled beneath the clouds at the far end of town. Were those crows?

"—haven't called—"

The specks swirled closer. Definitely crows, and the flock looked even bigger than the one that had visited my house on my birthday. Just before my life became so complicated—and, as Edie had said, weird.

"—insurance and police reports—"

I'd forgotten about those. Should have probably asked Kate about them.

"Braden...Natalie..."

Murder, I thought. A flock of crows was called a murder. And why were so many of them flying in the rain like that? The unease that had dogged my steps into town returned and flared into something more.

"Mom!"

I jumped. "What?"

"I said, are you still there? Are you even listening?"

"Of course I am." But I wasn't. I couldn't.

Something—

"Something's coming," I whispered.

"What?" Paul's voice turned angry. "For chrissake, Mom, what the *hell* is going on?"

A crow dropped away from the murder swirling overhead and swooped toward the phone booth. Wings flapping and claws scrabbling for a hold, it landed on the roof above my head and cawed. The very air around me thrummed with warning.

I banged on the phone booth door to get Lucan's attention. Why was he just sitting there? Couldn't he feel it? Hadn't he heard the crow?

Amber eyes met mine for a fleeting instant, and then the wolf stood, the ruff around his neck and shoulders raised as he lifted his muzzle to sniff at the air.

"Damn it, Mom—"

Paul. I cut across his angry concern. "I have to go," I said, my words tumbling out in a rush, "but Paul, you need to be careful. You might be in danger—Natalie and Braden—just be careful. Please."

First Edie.

I gripped the receiver tight in fingers gone numb.

Now my family.

My heart caved beneath the weight of a loss that hadn't even happened. Yet.

"I have to go," I said, abandoning all thought of new wardrobe and reading glasses. "I have to stop it."

The crows followed me and Lucan all the way home, their

incessant cawing the only sound between us. Lucan had shifted back to human form when we reached where he'd hidden his clothes. I'd turned my back while he dressed, and we'd started back down the trail without a word.

There had been no more parts of gnomes. Only the crows and a growing sense of urgency that demanded I get back to the house in the woods. Lucan looked askance at me once, when I followed so close behind him that I stepped on his heels, but I tightened my lips and shook my head. I had no answers. I just knew we needed to be *there*.

His gaze narrowed on me, then he turned and pressed forward, increasing his pace until I was half-jogging to keep up. The crows followed, their raucous cries ringing from the tree-tops. Lucan didn't seem to notice. I tried to ignore them.

I didn't know what I expected to find, but when we broke through the trees into the clearing, the house stood as it had when we'd left. Solid, safe, undisturbed. As we walked toward it, I examined every inch of its façade to be sure. Then I exhaled a shaky breath.

Paranoia, I thought. It had been nothing but paranoia. The crows were just crows. They hadn't been harbingers of anything except me losing it. The house was still here, I'd freaked out poor Paul in a way that would likely make Kate's job harder because he'd demand a search for me, and—

The murder of crows descended onto the rooftop of the house, turning it black. Cold spiked through my core like shards of ice. My limbs turned to lead. In unbearably slow motion, I turned toward Lucan, my knees sagging beneath the weight pressing me into the ground. My protector's gaze met mine, and alarm flared in it. From a long way away, I watched him reach for me, saw but couldn't feel his arms go around me.

His lips moved, but the wind rushing through my ears drowned out his words. Worry creased his brow. As well it might, because something...

"Something is coming," I whispered.

CHAPTER 25

"TELL ME WHAT HAPPENED," KEVEN ORDERED, SHOVING A mug at me with one hand and dropping a blanket over my head with the other. "Exactly."

Safe inside the house, the oppressive sense of impending doom had eased, and I peeled the blanket away and tried to arrange it around my shoulders without spilling the tea. The muddy robe clung to my ankles under the table. I shook one foot, then the other, but it made no difference.

"I don't know," I said. "Something is just...off."

Keven frowned, the ever-present Mergan wrapped around her shoulders. "Off what?"

"It's an expression," Lucan said. "It means something isn't right."

Keven glared at me. "But *what* isn't right?"

"I don't know." I shrugged, and the ill-placed blanket slid off my shoulders. Lucan stooped to retrieve it, tucking it around me properly. "I feel like something is coming. It started when I was talking to Paul and watching the crows."

"Crows?" Keven's voice turned sharp. She shot a look at Lucan, who shook his head. "What crows?"

"The ones circling over us in town." I frowned at Lucan. "One landed on the phone booth, and the entire flock followed us home and landed on the roof. There were at least a hundred —you must have noticed them."

"These crows—have you seen them before?"

"A few times," I replied. "On my birthday, when I saw the Mage outside my house, when I found this house..." I trailed off as my words registered in my own head. "Oh. They're not real, are they? That's why no one else notices them."

"They're real enough for you," Keven said grimly. "They're messengers from the Morrigan."

I remembered, then—the cavern, the goddess, the robe made of crows—and the connection in my brain completed itself. Remembered and felt supremely dense. Talk about a *duh* moment. And wait—messengers?

I shivered under the blanket. "What kind of message?"

"Premonition," the gargoyle said.

Lucan squatted in front of me. "I'm going to go and see if I can find out what you felt," he said, "and how far away it is. Stay in the house until I return. Don't even go out to the garden, understand? The wards are strongest around the house itself."

Which explained why the sense of doom had lightened a little when I came inside. But it was returning in spades, now. Especially at the thought of Lucan leaving.

"But—"

"Your word, milady. Windows and doors closed."

I curled cold fingers around the hot tea. "You have my word," I said. "But where—"

Before I could finish my question, Lucan's empty clothes had settled to the floor beside the open back door and his wolf had slipped outside.

I stared at the crumpled shirt. Keven scooped Mergan off her shoulder and set him down on the bench beside me. The orange cat nudged my elbow, demanding to be picked up again. I set my tea on the table and scooped him onto my lap, holding his warm body tight against my chest and burying my chin in the soft fur. The rumble of his purr reached inside me and found an answering vibration. I took a slow, deep breath.

Keven lumbered across the kitchen to close the door. She dropped a heavy wooden plank into place across it, snugging it into supports on either side.

"Precautions," she said, pausing to meet my gaze before she closed and bolted the wooden shutters over the window above the sink. "It's unlikely anything will break through the wards, but with the mutt away—"

"How long will he be gone?"

Keven strode past me and out of the kitchen and, still holding the cat, I followed. I found her in the parlor, closing another set of shutters.

"Until he finds the source of your discomfort," she said over her shoulder. "It might be Mages nearby, or it might be something else that's been..." She shrugged. "The Morrigan will guide him. He will follow the ley lines. It will take as long as it takes."

She closed the second set of parlor shutters. "And you will be ready when he returns. Now, come. We'll close the rest of the shutters and then continue your training."

And because that idea seemed far preferable to contemplating what the *something else* she spoke of might be, I set Mergan on the back of a couch and went to help her with the upstairs windows.

"TELL ME ABOUT THE LEY LINES. I'VE HEARD OF THEM, BUT I don't know much. You said Lucan would follow them." I sagged onto the stone floor of the cellar with my back against the wall. The uneven surface dug into my right shoulder blade, and both floor and wall were cold, but I was too tired to care. It was almost midnight, Lucan remained absent, and despite my best efforts, I hadn't been able to recreate so much as a hint of a connection to the earth.

Keven had wanted me to practice spell work because she thought it might ease my way into my magick, but I still had no reading glasses, and she, it turned out, knew neither spells nor how to read.

"At all?" I'd asked, staring down at the *Crone Wars* book that served as both history and grimoire.

"I've never had reason to learn," she'd said without rancor.

And I'd fallen silent at the tacit reminder that it was I and not she who fell short of expectations.

We'd abandoned the grimoire and turned again to trying to connect me to an element—any element—but again without success. Now I braced an elbow on my knee and rested my forehead in my upraised hand, regarding her through the hair that had long ago escaped the string she'd given me to tie it back. I was too weary to do anything about that, too. But I did manage to make a mental note to buy hair elastics if I ever made it back to town to go shopping.

Keven lowered herself into a crouch on her haunches, the light from the torches along the walls dully highlighting her granite face. Did gargoyles get tired? Or just tired of trying to teach the unteachable?

"The ley are lines of energy that crisscross the Earth," she said. "Magick is at its strongest where they intersect. Mages are adept at tapping into them and using the lines as paths to direct their creatures to their targets."

"Creatures like the shades and the gnomes."

The great stone head dipped in agreement.

"So Morok didn't need to be here to send the gnomes." That would explain the sheer number of the things. Despite Jeanne and Gilbert's propensity for buying and gifting them, I didn't think the entire town of Confluence had that many.

"He could be anywhere. As Lucan said, he is adept at remaining hidden."

Awesome.

"Are Mages the only ones who can tap into the intersections?"

"No. Crones can do so as well. Midwitches, too, but to a lesser extent."

A tiny hope sparked in my chest, and my pulse quickened. "What if I was at one of them?" I asked. "An intersection, I mean. Could I use it to help me connect? To learn?"

Keven's shoulders hunched. She traced a granite finger over

the floor with a sound like nails on a chalkboard multiplied by a thousand. I cringed and gritted my teeth.

"Well?" I prodded, raising my voice over the noise. "Would it not work?"

Keven stopped scraping rock against rock and looked up to meet my gaze. "Milady," she said heavily, "we're already sitting at an intersection. That's how this house exists. How it moves to where it is needed for the next Crone."

Oh, I thought.

"Hell," I said.

"Indeed," Keven replied.

I groaned, folded both my arms over my raised knees, and buried my head in my forearms. "I'm sorry."

"For what?"

"For being..." Wearily, face still buried, I waved a hand. "Thick. Difficult. Useless."

"Milady, you are none of those things," the gargoyle replied, but her tone and her words didn't quite mesh. She rose from her haunches, towering over me and holding out a stone paw when I looked up at her. "You are tired. Sleep, and we will continue in the morning."

Too bone-weary to argue, I allowed myself to be hauled to my feet and pushed toward the stairs. "What about Lucan?"

"He will return when he has news."

I lifted a foot onto the first step. I thought about the dark night outside and the wards that protected the house but relied on me to keep them strong. About how I didn't know how to do that. About how there would be no wolf outside my door to protect me if they failed. I shivered and wrapped my arms around my belly.

"Sleep," Keven had told me. But would I?

Could I?

Halfway up the cellar stairs, I turned. "Keven?"

"I will be in the corridor outside your room," the gargoyle

said. "You should leave the door open, however. My hearing is not as acute as the mutt's."

My cheeks flushed. Was I so transparent? So obviously helpless? Shame crept over me. Some wise woman of power I was.

I nodded into the shadows. "Thank you."

CHAPTER 26

DESPITE MY MISGIVINGS, THE NIGHT PASSED WITHOUT event. I fell asleep faster than I expected, secure in having Keven's solid, looming form in the corridor just outside the door. And I slept well and deeply, without the dreams—or nightmares—I probably should have had. The gargoyle was gone when I woke to gray light creeping around the window edges.

I lay staring up at the ceiling for a long while, reluctant to push back the warm duvet or face the day ahead. Something about the house's stillness told me Lucan hadn't returned yet, which I supposed was both good and bad. I'd grown used to having my protector around, and my reliance on his presence was more than a little unsettling after such a short time. It had taken me months to learn how to be alone when Jeff left, and a part of me resented losing that sense of independence.

Plus, Lucan's return would mean he'd found the source of my unease. A source I would likely have to go up against in some kind of battle for which I was nowhere near prepared.

Magick.

I groaned and pulled the duvet over my head. Oh, I wasn't denying that I had it anymore. I'd thrown a table at Keven and rooted my own feet to a stone floor, which pretty much proved I had it in spades.

But in not pursuing witchcraft all those years ago, I'd missed out on the training I was supposed to have had, and to call my powers sporadic would be putting it mildly. Despite Keven's best efforts, I was no nearer to controlling them now than I had been the day I found the house. And I was no closer to accessing them when I intended to. Edie had already died because of me, and now my family was in danger, and...

And whatever Lucan found in his ley line travels, I had no illusions about my ability to deal with it.

My complete *lack* of ability.

A muffled *thunk* reached me through the duvet, and I pushed the cover down enough to peer over it. Keven regarded me implacably from the bedside.

"Tea." She pointed at a mug on the night table. "And breakfast is ready in the kitchen when you are."

My stomach growled at the offer. Impending doom or not, a Crone had to eat. I levered myself upright against the pillows stacked against the headboard. "Thank you. I'll be down soon."

Keven nodded. She crossed the room to open the curtains, then lumbered away, leaving the door wide open behind her.

The better to hear my screams if something came through the window after all?

I reached for the mug Keven had left and wrinkled my nose at the pale, mushroom-colored liquid it contained. Not only was it not the coffee I craved, it wasn't even real tea. I sniffed the mug. Woodsy. Humus-y. Not unlike my compost pile at home when it neared completion.

My old home.

The one that had burned to the ground and taken my best friend with it. My throat tightened. Would I ever stop missing her? Or her unsinkable faith in me? Goddess, what I wouldn't give to hear her voice again.

I focused fiercely on the tea, swallowing a mouthful of it along with my threatening tears. It curled over my tongue, tasting tasted pretty much the same as it smelled, but it wasn't unpleasant, either. I sipped again, and the heaviness of the morning receded a little as I returned to pondering my situation. I had lost my friend, yes, but I still had my family...at least for now.

I took another gulp of tea, swallowing past the ache in my chest at the memory of my grandson's arms wrapped around my neck and his soap-and-mud-and-grass scent. Putting it away from me as I reminded myself that, while I likely had a host of enemies waiting for me, I also had Lucan and Keven on my side. And a wolf-shifter and a stone gargoyle were no small forces to be reckoned with.

Another sip. A spark of optimism flared in me. And then there was the magick. Because I, Claire Emerson, could do *magick*. Admittedly not well, and sometimes—most times—not at all, but Keven was right. I could learn. I just needed to focus, to become Crone. To—

I drew back and stared suspiciously at the mug in my hand, remembering how Keven's previous concoction had been so good at calming me after my battle with the gnomes. I sniffed again at the tea, hesitated, and then downed the remainder in one long drag. Whatever she'd put in there, it gave new meaning to the phrase *liquid courage*, and heaven knew I could use all of *that*—real or imagined—that I could get my hands on.

I half-set, half-slammed the mug onto the night table again, tightened my lips, and swung my legs over the bed's edge. Time to get this magick show on the road.

THE TEA'S PROPERTIES CARRIED ME THROUGH THE OATMEAL breakfast Keven had prepared and down the stairs to my next lesson. The bravado it supplied, however, did nothing to help with ability. Or patience. And all too soon, it wore off altogether.

"Oh, for Pete's sake," I growled, throwing the stick Keven had given me across the cellar. A wand, she'd called it, claiming it would help direct my intent. But in my hands it was no more than a twig, inert and entirely devoid of anything resembling magick. I glowered at the gargoyle.

"It's hopeless," I declared. "This is never going to work."

"The Morrigan—" Keven began.

My pity party was only just starting, however, and I cut her off. "What if Lucan was right? What if the Morrigan made a mistake? You said yourself I was supposed to have had a whole lifetime of training before this. And that I'm *not* supposed to be able to throw fire *and* call on the Earth."

"I agree there are anomalies, but—"

"Maybe I'm not even Crone at all." I paced back and forth along the wall, flailing my arms wide. I was well and truly on a roll, now—or more specifically, a downward spiral into a frustration that surprised even me with its intensity. "Or at least, I'm not the Crone you're looking for"—*Really, Claire? Really?*—"and you're just wasting your time on me. Maybe we're both wasting our time here, with all of this."

Another wave of my arms encompassed the cellar, myself, my frustration and—

And a swirling gray mass taking shape between me and the gargoyle?

My hands stopped moving, and I stared as the mass grew larger and darker. Streaks of light flickered within it, and a low rumble echoed through the stone chamber. My jaw dropped. Was that a storm cloud? The skin along the back of my neck and shoulders prickled, and I cast a quick glance around the cellar. Had I done that? But how? And why was Keven watching it with such bemusement?

No, not bemusement. Outright dismay, coupled with alarm.

"Um...Keven?"

"It's not possible," the gargoyle murmured, hands on haunches as she stared at the cloud.

A jagged fork of lightning darted from the cloud and zapped my shoulder, and I yelped and retreated behind the shelter of Keven's body. Thunder growled in the lightning's wake. Yup. That was a storm cloud, all right. I reached up and shook—or tried to shake—a granite shoulder. "What's going on, Keven?"

Keven's head swiveled all the way around, like an owl's, and she regarded me with the same dismay she had the cloud. "I didn't think it was possible."

Irritation surged in me, and the cloud emitted another fork of lightning. This one struck the table, leaving a black, smoldering char mark in its center. The thunder that followed shook the floor.

"Milady." Keven's tone was urgent, and a heavy hand closed around my arm and shook me. My teeth all but rattled in my head. "Milady, remember how you were rooted to the floor?"

How on earth could I forget? "Of course—but I'm not now." I lifted a foot to prove it.

"No, because this isn't Earth magick. It's Air magick."

"It's what? But I thought you said—"

A bolt of lightning zapped one of the gargoyle's ears, knocking a chip from it, and Keven's expression turned stern. "Forget what I said. What do you feel?"

Petrified, of course! But I bit back the obvious answer, knowing it wasn't what Keven meant. Wasn't what she asked. Thunder shook the cellar floor again, and I tried to suppress the panic blooming in my chest. The storm was getting stronger by the second, and if I really was causing it, I had to figure out how.

Still in the shelter of the gargoyle, I lifted one foot again, then the other one. Definitely no roots. I examined my hands. No blue fire, and no heat coursing through my body, either. So what the hell...?

Prickles.

My head snapped up, and I stared past Keven at the storm. A tingle had begun on the back of my neck, spreading like quicksilver along my shoulders to my arms. At first, it seemed like a reaction to a cool rush of air over my body. But it wasn't that. It was the other way around. The air wasn't causing the sensation, the sensation was stirring the—

A gust of wind tore through the room, flinging open the storage cabinet and scattering papers and dried herbs across the floor. I squeezed my eyes shut against the onslaught. Braced to stand against it. And without Keven's steadying hand, I would have toppled when it dissipated as suddenly as it had sprung up.

The cellar went silent. I took a deep, shaky breath and opened my eyes.

The cloud was gone.

"Prickles," I said.

"I beg pardon?"

"Across my skin. Prickles, like goosebumps. I thought it was because of the wind, but..."

"But instead, it caused the wind," Keven finished. She studied me for a long moment, her stony gaze watchful. Wary.

I scowled at her in return. "First you tell me I have Fire magick, then you say it's Earth, and now it's Air? How is that even possible? You said the Morrigan divided the elements. Each Crone has only one. You said so."

"Because it has been that way since Camlann. This—" Keven walked around me, examining me from every angle. "I don't know what this is."

I knew exactly what it was: a mistake. A ginormous, terrifying, impossible mistake.

I opened my mouth to tell Keven so, but a loud trill cut me off. I froze, staring at her. She frowned and stared back. Was that...a *cell phone*? But it couldn't be. There was no signal here. And the one Natalie had given me had died anyway, and I had no charger for it, and it was upstairs in my bedroom, and I wouldn't be able to hear it from here even if—

The trill came again.

That was definitely a cell phone.

I took the cellar stairs two at a time, pulled open the door to the back staircase beside the kitchen, and raced up those stairs, too. Arriving breathless in my room, I stared at the uncharged cell phone on my nightstand. It rang again.

I let go of the door frame and slowly walked over to the device. Another ring. I picked it up. The display lit up. *Paul*, it said. I thumbed the answer icon and put the phone to my ear.

My daughter-in-law's voice came through before I drew breath to say hello, and her panic landed like a fist in my gut.

"Claire? Oh, God, Claire, he's gone! There was an awful noise—I thought it was an earthquake but it wasn't and his window—the wall—and then Paul—and he's gone!"

I folded under the weight of her words as they piled up on one another.

"Natalie, slow down." I groped for the bed and collapsed on its edge. "Who's gone? Paul? Did you have a fight?"

"No! Not Paul, Braden! Something took Braden!"

Keven arrived in my doorway, scowling. "Lady Claire—"

I flapped a hand to silence her. My heart alternated racing and stuttering and I tried to calm it enough to let myself think. *Information. I need more information.* And then what? *Questions first, Claire.*

"Something—what? What did you see, Natalie? Was it flying?"

"What? No! I don't know. I didn't see it. I just heard—we heard—we were watching TV and then the house shook and there was so much noise, like the whole building was collapsing. We ran upstairs—" Natalie stopped to inhale a wrenching breath, and my heart twisted in an echo of her pain. "Braden was asleep in his room. We went to get him, and his wall was gone. The whole wall, Claire. Like something ripped it away. And Braden—his bed—"

Sleeping? Why had he been sleeping in the middle of the—

I looked over my shoulder at the night that had fallen outside my window. I'd been down in the cellar for the whole day, and I was still no closer to controlling—

I tamped down my rising alarm. I didn't have time for another pity party.

Something's coming.

"Paul," I said. "Where is Paul?"

"He went after Braden. He told me to call 911 but someone already did and the police are everywhere and—"

"Natalie," I cut across the terror rising again in her voice and threatening to trigger my own. "Breathe."

Another harsh gulp for air. Another ragged exhale.

On both ends of the connection.

My mind raced. Seized on an idea. Clung to it like a lifesaver.

"Natalie, listen carefully. You need to find a police officer by the name of Kate Abraham. Constable Kate Abraham. No one else, do you understand? Only Kate. Tell her to bring you to the house on Morgan's Way." Dear goddess, please let Keven have been right about the house being found if I willed it. I'd never willed for anything so hard in my life.

"There's a path at the end of the road," I continued. "It leads straight to the house. Have you got that?"

"But what about—"

"I'll find Braden," I said. "And Paul. I promise. Just get to Constable Abraham and tell her Morgan's Way. Remember that."

"Morgan's Way," she repeated. "I'll remember, but—"

Downstairs in the great hall, the front door crashed open, and Keven lunged for me even as Lucan's distant bellow echoed up the stairs.

"Gargoyle! Protect the Crone!"

And then, from beneath my closed window, came a child's thin, high-pitched scream.

Braden.

CHAPTER 27

BRADEN.

I fought the arm wrapped around me and pounded with both fists on the granite back over which I was draped. "Put me down!" I yelled. "Damn it, Keven, put me down! That's Braden! That's my grandson!"

I might as well have pounded on the stone walls of the house, for all the good it did. My head bounced up and down and my teeth slammed together as Keven jogged down first the back stairs, then the ones to the cellar. I fought on.

Braden.

Paul.

"Let me go!"

With her free hand—the one not effortlessly holding me captive over her shoulder—the gargoyle smashed the shelves from the cellar cabinet. She shoved me into the wooden shell, snarled, "*Stay*," and slammed the door in my face.

Blackness closed around me. I pushed against the door and bellowed again. Continued pushing even after the padlock snapped into place on the outside and I heard the pounding of stone against stone—the hard, granite footfalls of Keven running to Lucan's aid.

I pushed some more as a part of my brain tracked the gargoyle up the stairs and down the hall toward the front of the house, her footsteps growing fainter. Then came the distant noises of wood splintering. Deep, guttural bellows. A roar of pain. Fury. A high-pitched shriek.

Braden.

My hands fell to my sides. My breath rasped in my ears. I tried to sort through the sounds, to determine what belonged to whom. To convince myself that my grandson's high-pitched shriek had been one of fear and not pain.

Terror became a rising, bitter bile in my chest and throat. What had brought him here? And how in *hell* could I stop whatever it was?

The muffled battle noises raged on. I pulled my focus away from them and turned it inward. What would work best? Fire? Air? *Think, Claire, think!*

In turn, I tried to summon each of the ones I had called on before. The heat of Fire magick, the prickle of Air magick, the roots of Earth magick. I focused. I strained. I held my breath and released it, curled my hands into fists and flexed them wide, pressed my feet as hard as I could into the cabinet's floor. I did everything I could think of, including reminding myself *not* to think, and still I got nothing. Not so much as a hint of power or a glimmer of—

The cabinet rocked under my feet, throwing me off balance. No, not the cabinet. The house. The entire house shuddered, trembled, and then shook as a mighty *crack* that boomed through the cellar. My heart swooped down to reside in my toes. Goddess, now what?

The shaking subsided, and through the door came the muffled scrape of something moving—or being dragged—across the floor, faint at first, then growing louder as it drew closer.

My thoughts turned slow. Heavy. This was it. The time for choosing had come. My grandson's life, or the pendant that would set a god on the path to destroying the world. My hands went to the chain around my neck. They closed over it, one on each side.

Lift it over your head, Claire, I urged myself. *Take it off and give it to the Mages. It's only one—it doesn't mean Morok will get the others. There are still three Crones, and—*

"CLAIRE!"

The voice was loud and unexpected and—

"Edie?" I croaked. I'd jumped backwards into a corner of my

prison, and something sharp poked into one shoulder blade. I shifted to one side and blinked into the darkness. Dear goddess, I'd well and truly lost it now.

But no, I hadn't imagined it, because the voice spoke again.

"You can hear me? Finally! Fuck it all, woman, I've been trying to reach you for days. You really need to start listening to your elders."

My what? I thought.

"But how?" I asked.

"Never mind that. You have no time. You have to get out of here, my friend. The Mages are outside with—whatever that thing is. It has Braden, and they want you."

"No," I said. "They want the pendant."

"No," Edie replied grimly. *"They want you."*

"But—"

"You know they'll never let you go. Even without the pendant, you're too powerful."

Another time, I might have laughed. But right now, somewhere outside, a monster held my grandson, and a wolf and gargoyle fought to protect the Crone I never wanted to be—and my inability to save any of us was anything but funny. "I'm not," I growled at my friend's voice. "I can't—"

"You must."

"It's not as easy as—"

"You might want to stand back."

Something scraped against the cupboard exterior, and a faint rectangle of light filtered around the door's edges. I ducked back further. Edie? Or—

With a screech of iron pulling from wood, the door and its hinges parted way with the cabinet, and a tree branch filled the opening, its leaves dancing as if in a breeze.

A tree branch attached to a larger limb, attached to—my gaze trace it backward. A tree trunk. Growing where no tree could or should grow, right through the stone floor in the corner of the cellar, where I'd thrown the wand Keven had given me.

A linden wand, she'd said. Because linden would protect me as its wielder and bring balancing energy to me, and—

"They've almost breached the wards, my friend," Edie's voice said quietly. *"It's time."*

Time to what? I wanted to ask. *What is it you think I can do?* But I didn't, because regardless of what Edie thought, I knew what I *had* to do. And I had to do it now, before it was too late for my grandson.

I grasped the cabinet frame around the door opening, one hand on each side, and pulled myself to the front of the cramped space. The tree branch gave way before me, leaves rustling. It retracted again when I stepped down onto the stone floor, then again when I moved forward, staying just ahead of me. When I reached the stairs, it extended itself to accompany me, growing extra branches and leaves as it did. Earth magick, I knew. If only I had more time to figure out how.

I paused at the top to get my bearings. More precisely, hoping to get a bearing on either of my would-be champions. But the battle sounds had subsided, and the house stood silent and empty except for me and my tree companion.

And that.

A faint, low chant drifted down the corridor from the front hall. My core went cold. The Mages. Which meant the wards had fallen.

I homed in on the sound. More than one voice—at least two men and a woman.

Underpinned by the wail of a child.

My heart split in two. I lunged forward, but the tree blocked my way, sprouting multiple branches that wove together into a lattice.

"Move," I hissed, shoving at it. The lattice stayed. My voice dropped to a growl. "I said move, or I swear I will break every branch in your body."

The linden hesitated, then slowly unwound itself, retracted

the extra branches, and withdrew to one side. I took a few steps forward, then stopped.

That the tree had sprung from my Earth magick, I had no doubt. But I hadn't intended it to manifest, and that worried me. Nor could I be certain of how to control it now that it was here. With my luck, I'd barge in on those voices in the great hall, tap into the wrong element altogether, and bring down fire or a hurricane by accident.

Or both.

Or nothing.

The chanters' voices grew louder, and I caught snatches of words. "...our will...darkness rise...fire burn..."

Freaking hell, that didn't sound good. I strained to listen for the child's voice, but there was nothing. Goddess, Braden would have nightmares for the rest of his life after this. Assuming he survived. Assuming I saved him. Somehow.

Damn, but I could use a gargoyle and a wolf-shifter right about now. There was only me and my tree, however, and—

And then I heard the first whisper.

It wasn't a human whisper. It was more like the soft rustle made by the rub of fabric against itself, coming from overhead.

I looked up in time to see a gossamer-fine black filament drop from the ceiling to the floor near my feet. It ignited the instant it touched the stone, flaring bright white before fizzling out when it found no fuel. Others followed.

They drifted like fine spider silk caught in a gentle breeze, each one bursting into flame when it touched a surface. The ones that landed on the floor flared as harmlessly as the first had done. The ones that brushed against the wall, not so much. More and more of them formed, a rain of fire falling so fast that by the time I fully registered the threat, realized that they seemed to be moving ever closer to me, it was too late.

Beside me, the tree drew back as flames engulfed the corridor's wood-paneled walls, cutting off any chance of escape. The crackle of fire drowned out the chanting from the front hall. A filament landed on one of my shoulders and sparked white. I beat at the flames with my other hand, but instead of dying out, they spread and clung to my hand, too, searing my skin. I scrubbed palm against hip. The flames spread down my leg, to the back of my hand, to my wrist.

Pain lanced through me and surprise spiked into fear, then panic. Another filament drifted toward my head, and I had the impression for a second of tiny, malevolent black eyes. They were *alive?*

I ducked, staggering against the tree branch beside me. As if galvanized by my touch, it lunged upward and wove a tight canopy of leaves between me and the threads raining down. Leaves blazed and branches burned. More took their place. More met the same fate.

Dimly, I recognized three things. First, the tree couldn't hold off the filaments forever. Second, my arm and leg were still on fire. And third, somehow the tree's agony had joined my own, twisting inside me as if it were a part of me, like another limb. Its otherwise silent shrieks filled my brain and made coherent thought impossible. Acrid smoke filled my lungs and made my eyes water. The flames devouring my charred arm licked along my shoulder.

Then, through the chaos raging inside me, a voice spoke. My third voice. Calm. Quiet. Certain.

Water, it urged. *Summon water.*

So I did.

CHAPTER 28

CEILING, PANELED WALLS, FLOORS, LIGHT SCONCES. THINGS that should have held next to no moisture at all suddenly contained oceans of it, and it gushed from everywhere, rising up from the cellar, flowing out from under doors, filling the corridor. In seconds, it swirled around my knees, then my thighs. The filaments hissed and spat as it swallowed them, drowning them out of existence. The water reached my waist. I thrust my burning arm into it and splashed it across my shoulders. The fire consuming me sizzled and died; the pain lived on.

Overhead, the charred tree sagged beneath the water raining down on it. I reached up with my good hand to support it. The water had reached my shoulders, and my feet lifted from the floor. I was floating now, and a new panic stirred in me. It was echoed in the voices from the great hall that no longer chanted but shouted instead. The water must have reached them, too.

Abruptly, the filaments dropping from the ceiling vanished, but water continued to gush from ceiling and walls. My head bumped against the branches sheltering me. They parted and slipped under my arms to hold me above the flood—but not above the fear threatening to drown me just as surely as the water would.

I had no Keven to talk me through releasing the magick I'd called. No Lucan to reassure me. There was only me. Me and the chanters and—

Braden.

The thought of my grandson brought a sudden clarity with it. The monster still held him, and if I didn't save him, he would die.

Because of me.

What do you feel? Keven's voice whispered through my memory.

Petrified, of course. And sad, and guilty, and—

But not rooted.

Not hot.

Not prickly.

Fluid. I felt fluid. Like I was made of water. Like I could feel it in each and every one of my cells, and in every molecule of the world surrounding me, every atom. Like—

My feet bumped against the floor. The tree withdrew its branches from beneath my arms and drooped beside me. I'd done it. I'd let go of water, just as I'd released air and earth, and—

A roar came from the front of the house. It was unlike any animal I had ever heard, either in person or on film. And as exhausted, soaked, and burnt to a crisp as I was, it spurred me into motion. I staggered through the kitchen toward the garden door, clutching at the fire-scorched, sodden wall. If I could avoid the Mages chanting in the entry, maybe I could get to Braden without giving up the pendant after all. The roar became a rending and tearing of wood, and still following at my side, the tree branch trembled. Fear and pain rolled off it, mingling again with my own.

Even if I did avoid the Mages, this wouldn't be easy.

The door between kitchen and garden stood wide, and together the tree branch and I slipped through it. I stopped dead in my tracks. Beneath the full moon, the forest beyond the garden had been destroyed, trees broken and uprooted and tossed about like sticks, great swaths of it flattened as far as the moonlight could illuminate. Ruin didn't begin to describe it.

My linden tree's pain became an agonized grief that almost brought me to my knees. I took a great, sobbing breath and fought through it. Pushed it away.

No time.

"Stay," I rasped at the tree. Not waiting to see if it obeyed, I staggered to the edge of the garden, which had turned to a sea of mud. My calling of water, it seemed, had gone beyond the walls of the—I flinched mid-thought as lighting split the night sky. Thunder snarled on its heels.

Or maybe I'd done something else.

I slogged and slid my way past Keven's ruined herb beds, through the gate, and around the corner toward the front of the house. I needed to be quick. Needed to find the monster and—

I stumbled to a halt and gazed up in horror at the mountain towering over me. It was at least ten feet tall and built like— well, a mountain. With granite contours not unlike Keven's carved, bunched muscles, it had hands the size of giant boulders, patches covered in sparse fur, an elongated face with a dog-like muzzle and beady eyes, and—

And oh hell, were those bloodstains on its teeth?

I wanted to cry.

My charred arm and leg throbbed with pain, I was exhausted beyond anything I had ever thought possible, my muscles were seized with cold from the water, and I wanted nothing more than to collapse on the spot, curl into a ball, and howl like a baby.

Lightning flared again, backlighting the mountain.

I stared at it. Beady eyes stared back at me. Then it threw back its head and screamed, a hoarse, raw sound that seemed to go on forever, rolling across the remains of the forest and mingling with the thunder.

The cry ended at last, and the mountain's eyes fixed on me again—just as my own gaze found the straggly group at the edge of the lawn where the entrance to the path had once been. Paul, Natalie, Braden, Kate Abraham, Keven. My heart leapt and plunged almost in the same instant.

All here, yes.

And all vulnerable, all in imminent danger, all wholly my responsibility. I wondered for an instant where Lucan was, but decided it was best that he wasn't here. If I was going to hand over the pendant, I didn't want him to see it—or to interfere as I thought he might. Whether he liked it or not, the decision was mine and mine alone. It had to be.

And if Edie were right and the Mages didn't stop with just taking the pendant—well, that would have to be, too.

Movement at the corner of my eye snagged my attention, and I looked toward the house, then gaped. Three figures stood on the stone porch, and behind them—behind them, the entire front entry had collapsed into stone rubble and splintered wood. Light spilling from the sitting room to the side shone across fallen beams and the debris-littered staircase, where the suits of armor stood guard no more. No wonder they'd been able to get past the wards, I thought. And now I needed to get down to business.

There are only three, my third voice whispered. *You are stronger.*

I ignored it.

"Mages!" I called, keeping one eye on the mountain in front of me. "Call off your dog so we can talk."

The mountain snarled, its hot breath rushing over me in a feculent gust that smelled like rotted meat and death. I gagged and held my hand over my nose. One of the figures on the porch barked an order, and the mountain shambled two steps away. The stench of its breath remained.

One of the figures stepped away from the others. A man. The same one, I thought, who had stood at the end of Gilbert's driveway and stared across the street at my house. He limped as he walked, his feet squelching in the wet grass, and swayed a little when he stopped again after a few steps. Brief satisfaction flared in me. Good. I wasn't the only one.

"Crone," he said. "You know why we're here. Give me the pendant, and the boy lives. Call on your powers again, and he dies."

Call on my powers? I held back a snort. If he only knew. Oh, I had power, all right, and plenty of it. I'd proven it each time I managed to connect to one of the elements, tonight included, and I was sure it was more than enough to stand up to three Mages. But it was also enough to lay waste to the people I was trying to save, and to wreak who knew what other havoc if it got away from me. Which, given my track record, wasn't just possible, but probable.

No. I could not, would not take the risk.

"You'll get no fight from me," I said. "But the boy and the others leave first." If I were about to die, I needed to know it was for a purpose.

"Lady Claire, no!" Keven growled. The mountain rumbled back at her.

I ignored her as I had the voice, even as disquiet churned in my core.

"Purpose." Edie didn't hold back her own snort. "Death has no purpose here, Claire, and you know it."

I shushed her impatiently. How many voices did a woman have to ignore, anyway?

"Do we have a deal?" I asked, slipping the pendant from my neck and holding it out at arm's length in my charred fingers. The Mage turned his back on me and faced the others for a whispered consultation I couldn't hear. He turned back again.

"We have your word?" he asked.

"If you want it," I agreed. Was a Crone's word binding somehow? Not that I planned on going back on it, because I truly believed this was best. Safest. "Then yes, you have my word that I won't—"

"Too many fucks, Claire Emerson," Edie grated. "That's always been your problem. Too many goddamn fucks."

Her last word hadn't even faded when a brilliant light flared from the direction of the scraggly little group that was my family, aimed directly at the mountain, which threw up its arms with a snarl of surprise and pain. In the brief afterglow, I saw Keven launch herself at the creature, and at the same time, a four-legged shadow slipped around the corner of the house and attacked the Mages still on the porch. Chaos ensued.

It took me a split-second to realize that without Keven, my family was no longer protected. Another second to realize that yes, it was, as Kate Abraham's fingers danced in the air and a sparse few glowy bits of light—wards, like the fireflies Lucan had said they resembled—rose from the remains of the forest floor and gathered to form a netted dome over Paul, Natalie, and Braden.

Then Kate was at my side, grabbing the pendant from my still outstretched hand and dropping the chain over my head. "Keven and I will handle whatever that thing is," she shouted. "You need to take out the Mages."

I opened my mouth to object, to tell her I couldn't, but she placed a hand against my back and shoved me toward the nearest Mage, then raced to join Keven, who had lost her element of surprise and had been thrown to the ground. The mountain roared. Braden screamed. I wavered, helpless.

"Don't just stand there!" the Mage shrieked at the creature towering over Keven. "Finish it!" Not waiting to see if his order would be followed, he ran toward me and grabbed for the pendant. The fingers of both his hands closed over it, and his face turned triumphant. Gloating. He pulled. And pulled. And pulled again. Gloating turned to fury, and he pulled harder.

I seesawed back and forth under his attack, my head flopping. The chain bit into the back of my neck but refused to give way.

"Wait," I cried, but my voice was lost in another scream, this one of agony—and from Lucan. My heart staggered to a halt, then thudded back to life. Lucan. Bound to me as my protector, fighting once again for me, this time alongside Keven and a woman who was essentially a stranger—all sworn to serve me as Crone while I—what? Chose saving my own family over the fate of the world? Played it safe? Took no risks...again?

"Too many fucks for too many years, Claire," Edie's voice

echoed in my head, this time from that fateful night of my birthday party. *"It's time to divest yourself of them."*

Had she been right? Was she right now?

The ground rose up to grab my feet.

Panic rose in my belly.

Too much! my Claire-voice warned. *You can't control it. It's too big—too dangerous!*

A tree root snaked up from the earth between me and the Mage. It encircled the Mage's wrists, tightening until he cried out and released his hold on the pendant. Then it withdrew into the wet ground, pulling him with it. Down, down...

His hands disappeared into the soil, and horror snaked through me. "Stop," I begged the root. "Please stop."

But it didn't, and the Mage's arms sank beneath the surface. He struggled now, wildly, panic flaring in his eyes as he looked up at me. He opened his mouth, but soil filled it before he could scream, and still the tree root pulled. Belatedly, I jolted into action, dropping to my knees to scrabble at the mud around his sinking body, but to no avail.

Desperately, I looked around for help. My gaze fell on Lucan, half man and half wolf, down on all fours before the remaining Mages. They stood over him, grim-faced and exultant, bombarding him with bolt after bolt of blue fire mixed with orange and purple, each one manifesting in an outstretched palm. Each making Lucan's body convulse. Making him writhe. Wringing a mangled half-howl from his throat.

And there, to the left, the mountain of a monster, raining blow upon blow on the motionless lump of granite that had been my gargoyle.

With Kate crumpled in the grass beside them.

And the light-net of wards coming apart under a shade's attack. The creature shrieked as the booted feet of the mage I'd tried to save disappeared beneath the earth with a wet, sucking sound. Nothing but the mud beneath my nails remained to mark his passing.

No help was coming. Not for me, and not for my family or friends. We were alone. *I* was alone.

I pushed upright. Stumbled. Caught my balance. I looked from one unfolding scenario to another, despair clawing at the edges of my psyche. I clenched my fists, and pain from my charred fingers ricocheted up my arm. *Fuck,* I thought. *Fuck, fuck, fuck.* I couldn't just stand here, but what could I do? I had never felt so helpless.

Divest yourself, Edie whispered.

Prickles slid across my neck and down my shoulders.

You can't, my Claire-voice whispered.

Heat pooled in my chest.

You'll lose control, the voice warned.

The earth thrummed against the soles of my feet.

It will be too much! my Claire-voice shouted.

She was right. I knew she was right. Already, I felt my edges unraveling, and the build-up of something inside that terrified me. But it also exhilarated me. Spread through my veins like a liquid promise. Dared me to unleash it.

"Divest," Edie whispered.

Beneath the wards, Braden wailed again. The something inside me snapped, and the last of my restraint vanished.

"Fuck!" I roared, and then I let go.

I chose fire because I wanted the Mages to feel the same pain they inflicted on my protector—the same agony that I heard in his voice, first in his wolf's screams, and now a man's grunts as he absorbed the punishment inflicted upon him. It rose in me, hot and white before it even left my body. I knew because I could see it in my mind's eye.

I watched it gather at my core and travel down my arm. Felt it sear my palm and my already burnt fingers. Absorbed its heat, held it, and then released it. The seething white ball flew straight and true, smashing into the Mages standing over Lucan before they ever saw it coming. Before it fully disconnected from me. Through it, I felt their shock, their sudden flare of fear—and then, as their eyes exploded with the fire devouring them alive, their all-consuming agony.

It was more than I'd intended it to be. More than I was prepared for. It felled me to my knees again as their mindless cries washed over me. But it didn't last long, extinguishing along with their life sparks in the breath of an instant. There...

And then gone.

With their demise, the shade gave up its attack on the wards protecting my family and flapped away, out over the forest that was no more. The monster's battering of Keven slowed and then ceased, and it looked around in dull puzzlement. Its gaze met mine and it stared at me. I climbed to my feet and stood swaying and exhausted and empty, trying to brace for a final attack and wondering how I would summon any more magick —any more anything.

But the mountain looked down at its victim and then tilted its head back and howled. A single, unbearably mournful cry that wrapped around my soul and made my throat go tight.

Pain, I thought in dull surprise. *It's in pain.*

Then it rose to its feet, trudged to the corner of the lawn near the former woods, and disappeared into two lines of bright green light that flared, briefly intersected, and evaporated again.

I stared at the destruction I'd wrought.

From beneath the wards, my son's voice called hoarsely, "Mom? For God's sake, Mom, what the *hell* just happened?"

CHAPTER 29

I HAD KILLED.

Not once, not twice, but three times.

I gripped the edges of the blanket Lucan had placed around my shoulders and stared past my protector's shoulder into the blaze he stoked in the sitting room fireplace. Blue and yellow-red flames danced and swirled and crackled, shooting up into the chimney, but they held no heat.

At least, none that reached me.

Everything I had feared about magick had been true. I hadn't been able to control it. Hadn't been able to close the door on it once I had allowed it to open.

I had killed.

Lucan straightened and turned toward me. The dancing light at his back threw his face into shadow, but I could still feel his eyes on me. Feel the worry behind them.

"Another blanket, milady?" he asked.

I shook my head. Then, for lack of a better topic and because I couldn't bear my own thoughts anymore, I said, "That —thing. That was what took Braden from his house?"

"The goliath? Yes."

"The—" I blinked. This might be a better distraction than I'd hoped for. It certainly beat counting the drips of water falling from the entry roof onto a ruined suit of armor. "As in David and Goliath?"

"Not Goliath the myth. Goliath the creature. An unfortunate merging of Merlin and Morgana's magick. Not quite wolf, not quite gargoyle. And damned near impervious to both me and Keven put together. If you hadn't—"

I flinched. "Don't," I said, my voice husky. "Just—please don't."

Lucan fell silent. My thoughts crowded back. I returned to staring into the flames.

The sound of rock sliding against rock heralded Keven's limping approach. She came into the sitting room slowly, carefully, dragging one leg behind her through the devastation I'd wrought in the front entry, a cloth slung over her shoulder. In the hand that had three claws because of another time I hadn't been able to control my magick, she carried a bowl. In the other, newly cracked across the wrist, a mug. A large chunk was missing from one cheek, giving her face a lopsided, misshapen appearance. Her expression held the same worry as Lucan's.

She set bowl and mug on the low table before me and, in silence, lifted my charred hand and arm from beneath the blanket. One at a time, she lifted strips of bandage from the bowl and wrapped them, dripping with pale green goop, around my blackened arm and hand.

Mergan, who had followed her into the room and jumped up onto the sofa beside me, rumbled approval as he watched the proceedings. Lucan moved to lean against the still shuttered and barred window. At least that part of the house's facade was still standing.

I cleared my throat. "How are they?"

Outside, Paul had torn Braden from my arms when I had gone to them, hurling accusation after bitter accusation at me, screaming about how I had almost killed them all, and snarling that he never wanted me near them again. Any of them. Especially Braden.

I knew his words were born of fear, and I doubted he'd even meant them. But as I watched Keven lead the shell-shocked little group into the house, through the rubble of the ruined entry, my heart shredded into a thousand bloody ribbons because my son was right.

I should never have brought them here. Never opened the house to them finding it. Never involved them in any of it. If I had listened to my Claire-voice and handed over the pendant to the Mages at the very beginning, none of this would have happened. Edie wouldn't have died in the fire that consumed my house. Braden wouldn't have been taken by a monster and traumatized for life.

I wouldn't have killed.

Not once, not twice, but three times.

"You had no choice, my friend," Edie whispered.

I turned away from the reassurance I didn't want. Didn't deserve. I looked up to Keven for her answer.

"They're in the kitchen, milady," she said, her voice as soft as granite could be. "I have given them tea, and they're sleeping. The midwitch is with them."

Right. I'd forgotten about Kate. I was responsible for bringing her here, too.

Lucan stopped pacing and came to crouch at my knee. His long hair was matted with dried blood and dirt. I cringed from the sight of his wounds. One eye was swollen shut, the other almost as bad. Blue and purple merged together in more shades than I'd known existed, highlighted by an angry black lump at his temple and a raw, red scrape across one cheekbone. Keven would heal him, of course, but...

I tried to turn my face away, but he caught my chin in strong fingers and refused to let me.

"None of this is your fault," he said, his voice rough. "The Mages—"

I pushed his hand away. "The house was supposed to be safe," I interrupted. "My family—Kate—they should have been protected here. They should have been able to get inside. I wanted them to. Why did the wards fail?"

Lucan's mouth tightened and his gaze slid away. My chest clenched and my stomach rolled. That was my fault, too?

"What did I do?" I asked.

"I don't—"

Keven put a hand on his shoulder, stopping him. He rose and went to stand by the fire, staring into the flames, one hand braced against the oak beam mantle, the other resting on his hip.

Keven took over. "When you were in the cellar, milady, what happened? How did you get out of the cabinet?"

"I..." I frowned, trying to think back to what felt like a lifetime ago. Everything after Natalie's panicked phone call to me was a muddled mess in my head. "I kept trying to call on my magick—the heat, the tingling, the roots—but nothing worked. I couldn't connect to anything. And then everything shook—the whole house, including the stone floor. It felt like an earthquake. When it stopped—"

When it stopped, I could hear Edie again—and look where that got me.

"When it stopped?" Keven prompted.

"When it stopped, a tree tore the door off the cabinet. A linden tree. I think it was the wand you gave me. It grew in the same corner where I threw it, and its roots cracked open the floor. I'm pretty sure that was what caused the shaking."

Gargoyle and battered wolf-shifter exchanged a glance, then without speaking, Keven carefully wound a length of dry bandage around the herb-soaked ones she'd applied to my arm. She mopped up the drips from the table, then gathered her bowl and cloth. Only then did she meet my gaze, and the concern etched in the stone visage made my heart skip a beat.

No, not concern. Wariness.

Wariness that was reflected in Lucan's expression.

"What?" I asked, my breath turning shallow as I looked between them.

"Milady, the Mages didn't destroy the forest." Keven's voice was quiet. "Nor did the goliath. When the Earth shook, there was—" She paused. "I'm not sure how to describe it."

"A wave of energy," Lucan said grimly. "Like a blast that radiated out from the house. It flattened almost everything, and it destroyed the wards."

"You mean, it broke them apart."

"No, milady. I mean destroyed."

Bile rose into my throat. Killing the Mages had been bad enough, but the wards, too?

I thought about the tiny creatures that had woven themselves together to protect my house. To protect me. Tiny creatures as old as the Earth itself, willing to band together to deflect almost any magickal attack in exchange for a bit of dandelion fluff and the rainwater harvested from roses Keven grew outside the kitchen door. They'd held the shade at bay, kept out the gnomes, protected countless Crones before me, and I'd destroyed them?

It was beyond unforgiveable.

"All of them?" I asked. My voice was a thread of sound, barely audible to my own ears.

"Most," Lucan said, and I knew he was being kind. "The others fled. That's when the Mages were able to get into the house and turn the fire pixies on you. You were lucky you were able to access water."

I gave a short, bitter laugh. "Lucky?" I echoed. "How in hell can you call any of this lucky? I'm supposed to have one magick, Lucan. *One*. Instead, I have four, none of which I can control, and now I've killed three Mages and—"

"You're her," Kate's voice broke into my tirade, and all three of us turned to her. She stood in the sitting room doorway, cradling my grandson in her arms. Her uniform was torn and filthy, her face was scraped on both cheeks and across the forehead, and Braden was sound asleep against her chest.

I caught my breath, aching to get up and take him from her, but Paul's words held me in place. *Stay away from him, do you hear me?*

Three dead Mages helped.

"Who?" Lucan asked Kate.

"Claire. She's the fifth Crone."

"There is no fifth Crone," he said. "There have always been only four, one for each of the elements."

Kate shifted Braden's weight and widened her stance. She ignored both Lucan and the gargoyle and frowned at me. "You haven't read the book, have you? *The Crone Wars.*"

"Since when do midwitches know about the book?" Lucan demanded.

"We've always known about it. It's as much a part of our history as it is hers." Kate nodded at me, then raised an eyebrow. "Well?"

"I haven't had the time." And I still didn't have the reading glasses.

"You might want to make time because if I'm right..." she trailed off, regarded me thoughtfully, then nodded. "I am right. You're her. The fifth Crone. You're here to end the war."

"I—" My mouth flapped a couple of times. "I'm what?"

"It's in the book. We midwitches know of it only by word of mouth, of course, but it's in there somewhere. A fifth Crone, one who can draw on all the elements, will bring the others together to end Morok."

Doubtless seeing the skepticism in all our faces, she rolled her eyes. "It was always intended to be five—like the five points of the pentagram. One for each of the elements: earth, air, fire, and water"—she held her fist out from Braden's sleeping body and opened her hand one finger at time as she recited them— "and the last for spirit. You are spirit. Mind over matter. The one above the others."

A memory tickled in the back of my mind. The Morrigan. Was this what she'd tried to tell me?

"Your pendant is not—others... You are not—others."

I wasn't *like* them. That's what she'd been trying to say. I wasn't like them, and my pendant wasn't like theirs and—and holy hell. A whole new level of panic clawed at my belly. Being Crone had been bad enough, but at least I'd had the comfort of knowing there were others like me. The illusion of belonging.

But this? The one above?

Why now? I wanted to demand. *Why me?*

Instead, I scowled at Keven and Lucan, who both looked like they'd been caught in the headlights of an oncoming truck. "For fuck's sake," I gritted. "A fifth Crone? How did you not know about this?"

"I—" Keven said.

"I—" Lucan said.

"Don't blame them," Kate said. "Their job has been to serve and protect the Crones. The Crones' job was to protect their knowledge. If Morok had known a fifth pendant would come, he would have tried a lot harder to get at the other four."

"And will he know now?"

Kate sent a wry glance over her shoulder at the wrecked entry. "I suspect he'll have guessed," she said. Then she sighed. "Look, this kid weighs a ton, and if I'm going to get everyone home before Keven's concoction wears off, I'm going to need you two"—she inclined her chin toward Keven and Lucan—"to help me get them loaded into my car."

"Concoction?" I asked, my mind reeling under her revelations—and implications therein. "What concoction?"

"It's best if no one remembers what happened tonight," Keven said. "The tea I gave them has made them sleep, and it will erase the details. The midwitch will fill in new ones when they arrive home and wake."

"What new details will you give them?" I asked Kate.

"We wanted to keep it simple," she said. "We have a...friend with access to meteorological records who placed a microburst on the radar in your son's neighborhood. Our story is that it tore off the front of their house, Braden got scared and ran away, and he ended up hiding in someone's shed a few blocks away. I'll radio in as having found him once we're back in the area so they can call off the search, and we'll take care of any damage control."

Simple. Because creating a microburst on radar was simple. And midwitches had the power to do that plus damage control. And *fifth Crone?*

"I knew you were special," Edie said.

Kate shifted Braden again, moving him higher onto her shoulder. "I really need to go. Did you want to say goodbye before we leave?"

I stared at the child in her arms. Ached for the feel of his little body nestled against my own. For the sound of his laughter and the smell of grass and soap and happiness all mingled together.

Ached for...and mourned the loss of, because I wouldn't—couldn't—didn't dare—

"They'll remember none of this, Claire," Kate assured me. "Everything will be like it was."

I laugh-snorted, a sharp sound that was half angry, half bitter, and not at all amused. "Nothing will be like it was, Kate. It can't be. Thanks to this"—the blanket slid off my shoulders as I threw my arms wide to encompass the room, the house, my entire world—"Morok knows about me *and* them. You don't think he'll try to get at them again? To force me—"

"I don't, actually." She shifted Braden to the other shoulder. He stirred briefly, stretching out an arm, but settled back to sleep. "He's smart enough to know he can't take you on in his current state. You wouldn't be able to kill him, but neither could he kill you or take the pendant, which makes you a waste of time and energy. I think he'll do everything he can to get at the other Crones and their pendants before you find them. If the stories I heard from the book are right, the five of you together will be able to separate him from his Merlin body and force him back into the Otherworld—sight unseen. If he's going to survive, he needs to open that portal."

I stared at her. "So I..."

"You should come and say good night to your grandson," she said, "And then get some sleep. Tomorrow, read the damned book."

"She's right, milady." Lucan held out a hand to pull me up

from the sofa. "We've done all we can for now. We all need some rest. Your family will be safe. The midwitches will see to it."

"Of course," Kate agreed. "I'm really not expecting any more trouble, but we'll set wards just the same."

"You mean I didn't destroy them all?" I hadn't thought I'd been able to feel the presence of the wards before, but the acuteness of their absence now told me otherwise. My not-so-little house in the woods felt barren. Vulnerable. Bereft.

"Goddess, no. You inflicted damage on them here," she said, sadness flitting over her face, "but wards are born of the very energy of life itself. As long as Earth survives, they will replenish themselves—although you might need to work at getting them to trust you again. But one thing at a time. For now, come say goodnight so I can get your family home before my coworkers turn the entire town upside down looking for them *and* me, if they haven't already."

While Keven and Lucan went to get Paul and Natalie, I took Braden from Kate and hugged him close, breathing in his scent and smoothing back the blond hair from the soft skin of his forehead. When I thought of his tiny little frame in the grip of the goliath and what might have happened—

I shuddered and tightened my arms around my grandson. He squirmed and mumbled in his sleep, and I loosened my hold. A little. With great effort.

I met Kate's calm brown gaze over his head. "Thank you," I said. "For everything."

She smiled as she took my grandson back from me. "Serve and protect," she said, "that's what I'm here for. What *we're* here for."

Her words held a double meaning, and I didn't pretend not to understand.

Keven and Lucan returned with Paul and Natalie, the former draped over Keven's shoulder and the latter carried by Lucan. I kissed both their foreheads—Paul and Natalie's, not Keven and

Lucan's—lingering a little over each because I wasn't sure when I'd see them again. Or if.

There was a lot riding on how well Keven's concoction would work to lessen my son's animosity toward me.

There was a lot more riding on me.

Lucan was last out of the house. He paused on the porch, all that remained of the front entry, and looked back at me, bloody, bedraggled, lucky to be alive—and still concerned with my wellbeing.

"Will you be okay?" he asked, his voice rough. Beyond him, Keven and Kate trudged across the clearing with their loads, heading for the path to the road and Kate's vehicle.

Not *are you okay*, but *will you be*. I appreciated the nuance that meant I didn't have to lie. I nodded. *Serve and protect.* Kate's words had reached into me and taken root in a quiet corner of my heart—one that was wasn't bleeding in the aftermath of what I had done. What my son had said.

Because deep down, I recognized Paul's wasn't the only truth. Knew that I would recover. Already girded my loins—proverbial and otherwise—for the next phase.

"I will," I said in answer to Lucan's question.

"You know you had no choice."

"He's right," Edie whispered.

"I know," I told them both, even though I still shrank a little from the words because uttering them aloud made them real. Made my acceptance of them real. I'd killed. Not once, not twice, but three times.

Because I'd had no choice.

Serve. Protect.

The Morrigan. The world.

"And going forward?" Lucan asked. "There may be no choice again, milady."

I hugged myself, rubbing my hands over my upper arms. The night air was cold when there were no walls between you and it. And when you faced a future that would almost certainly give you no choice again.

"I know," I said.

"Atta girl," said Edie.

My protector nodded his own brisk approval. "Go back to the fire," he said, "and stay warm. The gargoyle and I will be back as soon as we get your family into Kate's car."

Said gargoyle's voice bellowed across the clearing, "Damn it, mutt, get moving! We don't have all night."

"Keep your pebbles together, gargoyle, I'm coming!" Lucan snarled back. He pointed a finger of the hand under Natalie's shoulders toward the sitting room. "Fire," he ordered, then he followed in the wake of the others.

A flashlight beam came on at the edge of the clearing, and I watched until it faded into the night and silence closed around me. Then I turned to the empty house and picked my way toward the sitting room, stepping over fallen beams, shattered wood, and bits of metal armor.

The fifth Crone. Wielder of all four elements, here to end a war I hadn't even known about a week ago. A week ago, before I'd wrecked two houses, lost my best friend (but sort of found her again) and possibly my family, killed three mages, and—

And then I remembered.

I stopped beside a dented helmet and looked over one shoulder at the gaping hole in the house front, over the other at the stone staircase leading up to the impossible second floor, and then down at the pendant laying against my grubby, still-damp robe. A snort burst from me. It turned to a chuckle. Then to the kind of belly laugh that made things funnier the longer it went on.

I laughed until I hurt. Until the tears ran down my face and the memories of Mages faded and my heart began to heal. And then I laughed some more.

"What's so funny?" Edie asked.

I wiped my eyes and gasped for air, still giggling.

"Purpose," I told her between wheezes. "For my birthday. That's what I wanted. Purpose. And now I have magick to learn, four Crones to find, a god to defeat, and a war to end. You know what, Edie?"

"What, Claire?"

"I really need to be careful what I wish for in future," I said.

We were still cackling when Keven and Lucan returned.

ALSO BY

The Crone Wars

Becoming Crones

A Gathering of Crones

Other Books by Lydia M. Hawke

Sins of the Angels (Grigori Legacy book 1)

Sins of the Son (Grigori Legacy book 2)

Sins of the Lost (Grigori Legacy book 3)

Sins of the Warrior (Grigori Legacy book 4)

Other Books by Linda Poitevin

Gwynneth Ever After

Forever After

Forever Grace

Always and Forever

Abigail Always

Shadow of Doubt

ABOUT THE AUTHOR

Lydia M. Hawke is a pseudonym used by me, Linda Poitevin, for my urban fantasy books. Together, we are the author of eleven books that range from supernatural suspense thrillers to contemporary romances and romantic suspense.

Originally from beautiful British Columbia, I moved to Canada's capital region of Ottawa-Gatineau more than thirty years ago with the love of my life. Which means I've been married most of my life now, and I've spent most of it here. Wow. Anyway, when I'm not plotting the world's downfall or next great love story, I'm also a wife, mom, grandma, friend, walker of a Giant Dog, keeper of many cats, and an avid gardener and food preserver. My next great ambition in life (other than writing the next book, of course) is to have an urban chicken coop. Yes, seriously…because chickens.

If you'd like to learn more or connect with me, I can be reached through my website at www.LydiaHawkeBooks.com.